LINKED BY DECEPTION

A PSY-IV Team Novel

JAMI GRAY

HUMAN
AUTHORED

Sign up for free reads from Jami!

Join Jami's newsletter to be the first to hear about new releases, free books, special prices and other nifty events.

Sign up at: https://www.subscribepage.com/jami-gray-books

What Readers Say...

About Arcane Transporter:

"Taking a refreshing approach to fantasy magic, this fast-paced, economical thriller is told from a highly likable perspective." —Red Adept Editing

About PSY-IV Teams:

"This story is an emotional roller coaster, from betrayal, anger, fear, love…" —InD'tale Magazine

About the Kyn Kronicles:

"…a fantastic paranormal action novel is quite possibly the best book I've read this year. I could not put it down, and had to exercise serious self-control to keep from staying up all night to finish it." —The Romance Reviews

About Fate's Vultures:

"…if you like your characters with a bit more bite, with secrets, with hidden agendas, and all those sorts of things, and your worlds are a far more deadlier place, then this is for you." —Archaeolibrarian

ARCANE WONDERLAND

Last Call

Bitter Spirits

Rune & Tonic

ARCANE TRANSPORTER

Ignition Point (*Prequel Novella*)

Grave Cargo

Risky Goods

Lethal Contents

Collision Course

Blind Spot

Terminal Drift

THE KYN KRONICLES

Shadow's Edge

Shadow's Soul

Shadow's Moon

Shadow's Curse

Shadow's Dream

Shadow's Fall

Tangled in Shadows (*Short Story Collection*)

FATE'S VULTURES

Lying in Ruins

Beg for Mercy

Caught in the Aftermath

Fear the Reaper

PSY-IV TEAMS

Hunted by the Past

Touched by Fate

Marked by Obsession

Fractured by Deceit

Linked by Deception

BOX SETS

PSY-IV Teams Box Set I (Books 1-3)

The Collapse: Fate's Vultures (Books 1-4)

The Kyn Kronicles Box Set (Books 1-6)

Arcane Transporter Box Set I (Books 1-3)

Arcane Transporter Box Set II (Books 4-6)

This one wouldn't have been possible without Chris Roberts, who came up with the brilliant baddie hacker name, Gatekeeper!
Thank you, Chris!

Acknowledgments

For every book I write, there is an entire silent support team that keeps me going. They have infinite patience as they listen to me find my way through each book. So as always, they have my undying gratitude. So thank you to my writing crew - DeAnna, Camille and Dave - my reading troupe - Monica, Jo and Nana - and my fearless editor, Sarah. As always, my love and thanks to my boys who manage to keep me stable every time I do this writing thing.

Contents

Prologue

RABBIT

Holy shit, I'm in! After spending nearly a week of solid eighteen-hour days dodging nasty virus-filled traps and triggers that were swimming in a deeply masked server, I stared at a neat list of incriminating files. If the original owner, Major General Garrett Hawes, hadn't already been six feet under, this information would have locked his ass away faster than the bodies he'd left in his wake.

I clicked through the files, scanning the contents. Names, dates, and mind-boggling monetary amounts were attached to a variety of illegal vices—everything from weapons running to human trafficking. The one that had tripped him up was treasonous trading of classified information. Hawes was a greedy but prolific bastard—that was for sure. And if it hadn't been for one very brave young woman, he would have kept rolling in the green even as he sold out my team and his country, staining his uniform with innocent blood.

"You found something." The husky feminine voice coiled around my heart and squeezed hard. A cup of coffee hit the table next to my laptop, jerking my attention away from the screen and toward my personal frustration-temptation, Jinx.

"That I did." As she leaned in to read the screen, the hint of spiced vanilla teased me.

I nabbed the coffee, a safer option than wrapping my arm around her hips and dragging her into my lap to further explore that tantalizing scent and how far it went. As much as I enjoyed flirting with the fairer sex, taking such liberties with my teammate was highly inadvisable. Not that my libido cared. Hell no. It was more than happy to live dangerously. I, on the other hand, enjoyed both my job and my ability to keep breathing.

"Hawes was a busy bee, wasn't he?" Jinx snagged my mouse and clicked through the recently deciphered batch of encrypted files, starting with the most recent. "Did you see this?" She turned to look at me. Caught in the gold-streaked depths of her dark eyes, I needed a second to break free and pay attention.

I sucked back some coffee, set my cup next to her hand —which was braced against the table—and focused on the screen. Reclaiming the mouse, I scrolled through a series of messages. Jinx snagged her chair and dragged it next to mine until the armrests clashed.

I read through the exchange and clued in to the trail of breadcrumbs she identified. "He was working with a hacker."

"Makes sense."

"Since the information he was passing along is highly encrypted, yeah, it does."

No way had Hawes possessed the know-how to mine the

information he'd gathered and sold. No, that skill belonged to someone else, and based on these conversations, that same hacker had managed to make a pretty sum for the jobs.

"Do you recognize their handle?" Jinx was so close that if I turned to look at her, I wouldn't be able to resist kissing her. It was best to keep my eyes on my screen.

Dammit, man, mind on the job, not on your dick.

Years of military discipline kicked in, and I focused on the task at hand. *What was her question? The hacker's handle, right.* I stared at the string of characters—*G8K33pr*—and tried to place it.

"No, but I can do some discreet asking around." After years of skulking through the darkest corners of cyberspace at the behest of my government, I'd collected a wealth of contacts. If anyone knew of a black hat going by the unremarkable handle of Gatekeeper, it would be those people.

"You think that's safe?" Jinx's question was valid, considering the fact that the files I was combing through belonged to a high-ranking military officer, albeit a dead one. Plus, we were trying not to raise any flags with our investigation.

"Probably not, but it's a starting point."

Hawes's death and the true circumstances surrounding his sudden life-status change were known only by a select few, all of whom were personally vetted by our fearless leader, retired Colonel Charlene Delacourt. Her decision to keep his death on a need-to-know basis bought us breathing room—enough so that we could crawl through Hawes's electronic life quietly. But time was running out, and I could feel the air disappearing.

At my nonchalant answer, Jinx looked at me with a gimlet eye. "And if your legion of fellow cyberheads can't help, then what?"

"Well, then, we'll just go to Plan B."

"Does Plan B require utilizing your less-than-legal skills?"

Since there was only one obvious response, I didn't bother to answer. The lackluster information on hand left us with a blurry picture of Hawes's motives, but based on what we'd pieced together, it was safe to assume that Hawes had been working with Falcon, the mercenary group of bad-guy psychics who were the yang to the PSY-IV team's good-guy yin. To get that picture into sharp focus, we needed solid confirmation of that connection. Tying this hacker to Falcon would be a great start, but if my contacts came up empty, it would be time to pull a rabbit out of my proverbial cyber hat. Thanks to a genetic quirk that made technology and me best buds, manipulating electronics was one magic trick I could do.

Jinx narrowed her eyes when I didn't say anything. "You'll be careful." Her voice held a demanding bite.

I didn't dare release a grin of satisfaction. Instead, I leaned back in my chair and drawled, "Always, *cher*."

My reassurance didn't ease her frown. She turned to the screen and went back to reading the string of messages. Stifling a sigh, I sipped my coffee and let her read over my shoulder. I scrolled at a snail's pace so we could both follow along. After nearly a year of working alongside Jinx, I'd become good at ignoring the urge to hoard every fascinating part of herself she reluctantly revealed. For each piece I patiently managed to uncover, a plethora of others remained hidden deep, like an endlessly fascinating puzzle. An added challenge to my quest was the metaphysical hand she kept raised in her determination to lock me inside her neat box marked Friend. My patience and I were all but done with that situation. But I would have to deal with it later.

I needed her to step back from the ledge of worry she was pacing. Imagine my surprise when I first discovered that the frighteningly capable Jinx was, in fact, a closet worry-wart. Anyway, she could relax, because the upside to this investigative clusterfuck was the fact that we belonged to one of the PSY-IV teams—an off-the-books ex-military shadow team of psychics—so the rules could be bent. Hell, even if we broke one or two, it wouldn't earn us more than a hand slap and a frown from Delacourt.

Jinx leaned forward, focusing on the screen. "Rabbit, check this out."

I stopped scrolling and zeroed in on the section she indicated. Hawes's messages had lost their vague, detached professionalism and now carried a blunt desperation.

"Scroll back up to the first message for me," Jinx said.

Following her directions, I took us back to the top so we could determine where the tone shifted.

"Look!" She pointed to the date on the very first message. "Do you recognize that date?"

Hell yeah. I set my coffee aside and leaned in, fingers flying over the keyboard as I pulled up a file on Megan Rouser, Delacourt's administrative assistant. Sure enough, the date of Hawes's initial message to his contact was just after our team pulled Megan out of the warehouse where she was being held and tortured.

"Someone was trying to cover his ass."

"Big-time," Jinx muttered. "And whoever is on the other end of this is not happy with his excuses."

We both fell silent as we continued to read. "Here." I stopped scrolling so Jinx could follow.

She sucked in a sharp breath. "Tell me I'm not seeing things."

"If you are, then we're both seeing the same damn thing."

"Looks like he's trying to curry favor by offering them something they need." She kept reading the vaguely worded correspondence.

"Yeah, but there's something…" My mind picked up speed as I brought up another screen and flicked through Hawes's previous messages, looking for his initial approach to Gatekeeper. "This, here." I stopped the dizzying scroll so Jinx could read the side-by-side screens. "Look how the dates fall."

Jinx was no slouch and put the pieces together quickly. "He wasn't offering a thing—he was offering a who."

"He sure was." With the two messages grouped side by side, there was no doubt that Hawes was trying to offer his big boss the services of our mysterious hacker. And it looked like the hacker was seriously considering taking the job. The more we read, the more certain I became that the big boss was none other than Falcon.

Jinx turned away from the screen, her eyes bright with anticipation. "Hawes was playing broker."

"Yeah, he was."

We continued to read through Hawes's exchanges with his hacker partner. The farther I got, the clearer the plan morphing in my brain became, but I held off voicing it. There was no sense in saying anything until we talked to Delacourt.

We came to the last message, and Jinx sat back, dragging her hands through the sunlit strands of her honey hair. "We have an in."

I stifled a wince, though I wasn't surprised by the news

or by how fast Jinx mirrored my thoughts. There was a reason we worked well as partners. "We *might* have an in," I corrected.

She dropped her hands and folded her arms. "Might? According to that last message, his boss is waiting for him to supply a date and time for the initial meet with the hacker. That sounds like an in to me."

Lack of sleep wore the edge of my temper thin, leaving a quick fuse on my frustration. "It's not that easy."

Instead of pushing, she did the sneaky, twisty thing she always did, turning the conversation around. "Don't tell me you're not up to this. You, king of all things electronic."

Okay, that just wasn't nice at all. Even knowing what she was doing, I couldn't help saying, "I'm up for it."

The flash of triumph in her eyes was quickly veiled by her long lashes. "Okay, then, I say we give Delacourt a sitrep and get this show on the road."

"*Mais* you're so *tête dure,*" I muttered under my breath because the woman was more stubborn than a jackass.

She shot me a look. "I heard that."

I sighed. Of course she'd heard me, because she had ears like a damn bat. "Fine, you call Delacourt." I went back to my keyboard, opening up a window.

She pulled out her phone. "Who are you contacting?"

"My fellow…" I paused. "What did you call them? Cyberheads? Delacourt's going to want information on our mysterious Gatekeeper." *Plus, I'd rather know just how black a hat I'll be wearing.*

Chapter One

JINX

THREE WEEKS LATER

Sitting blindfolded in the back of a new-smelling sedan was not how I thought I'd be spending my Friday night —although for the last three weeks, thanks to an unexpected development, my normal routine had been turned on its ear. Rabbit's Q and A with his Ethernet friends had unearthed a treasure trove of information on our mysterious black-hat hacker, Gatekeeper. In fact, the amount of information Rabbit's friends had shared left me certain that one or two of them worked with the NSA, the FBI, or the CIA—dealer's choice. Considering how quickly Delacourt disappeared into a hush-hush meeting and came back with a green light on the plan Rabbit and I suggested, I was betting on the NSA.

From the start, things moved faster than normal, which meant we weren't the only ones hoping to shut down the cesspool that Major General Hawes's dirty deeds had managed to stir up. When Delacourt returned from her meeting, she informed us that prior to Hawes's death, Gatekeeper had been picked up on an unrelated case and had since become a permanent unacknowledged guest of the US government. Before Rabbit could get too excited about having a clear shot at stepping into Gatekeeper's shoes, Delacourt added a double twist. Not only was Gatekeeper a *she*, but there was also a high chance that she was only one half of a two-person team. The problem was, while no one could confirm that the mysterious second person really existed, they also couldn't rule it out—which left Rabbit sidelined and me up to bat.

With the Colonel's additional information, Rabbit and I adjusted our plan, factoring in the expectation that further contact with Gatekeeper would be made at some point—it was just a question of when. Whatever murky transaction Hawes had set in motion required a high level of hacking skill, and the best person for the job was Gatekeeper. Utilizing the past pattern of communication and behavior between Hawes and his mysterious boss, which the investigation pieced together, we had little doubt that Hawes's boss wouldn't pass up a chance to employ Gatekeeper's services. We just needed to be the ones who answered that call.

When we first set this operation into motion, anxiety was my constant companion. Every incoming call or text left me jittery. But as the days passed and things stayed quiet, my hypervigilance downgraded to just vigilance. Now that they'd finally made the first move—kidnapping me— my nervousness was mitigated by a keen eagerness.

Rabbit's low voice sounded in my ear, thanks to the skin tag that doubled as a personal tracking device and comm system. "You're heading into Carmel Valley."

Since the device was hidden behind my ear, my escorts hadn't detected it during their frisk. There was no sign of

Rabbit's sexy accent, but that was always the case when we were working. It was one of my partner's many curious facets that I refused to dwell on—that way lay dragons, and I'd given up chasing mythical creatures long ago. Though I enjoyed indulging in the flirty byplay he did so well, I knew better than to take him seriously.

I shifted in my seat, crossing my legs in an effort to ease the ache in the balls of my feet. Initially, I'd held high hopes of being able to wear jeans, T-shirts, and hoodies during this operation—stereotypical hacker wear. Instead, I ended up with a wardrobe of posh, expensive labels and ridiculously high heels that hurt like hell despite costing a small fortune—all part and parcel of the unlikely face of Gatekeeper's real-life persona, Elena Drake, an in-demand, highly paid corporate consultant. While the exact details of what she consulted on were a little blurry, she had a successful legit business that catered exclusively to high-end clientele.

You would think that would be more than enough to keep her busy, but nope. Her polished mask hid a brilliant yet ruthless opportunist. After spending hours poring over her file and watching the taped interviews that were couriered to Delacourt, I was equally fascinated and appalled by what I'd read and heard. Much like the nightmare megalodon shark, she hunted in the darkest depths of data, targeting rising underworld market demands in some seriously nasty shit and leaving only microscopic clues in her wake before surfacing as the dominant predator. Self-possessed to an arrogant degree, she truly believed she was untouchable. And she was. Well, until she wasn't. That arrogance became my key to unlocking her persona.

Between posh liquid luncheons and neatly penned-in consulting appointments, she managed an even more lucrative illegal business by providing a set of skills that ran the gamut from hacking highly classified databases to breaching critical infrastructures and industrial control systems. It was appalling how many companies quietly paid mind-boggling ransoms to get their technology out of mercenary hands. What left me even more stunned was that the first response of these companies wasn't to regain control of their systems and data. Nope, it was to pay the money. Talk about skewed values. That behavior would make it scarily easy to blackmail big-money organizations, crash critical infrastructures, or—worse-case scenario—collapse a faltering economy.

As much as I enjoyed my job with the PSY-IV teams, discovering the dirty truth of what really happened behind the scenes sometimes scared the crap out of me. In this age of everything tech, there was something to be said for going off the grid. Unfortunately, I enjoyed life's little electronic luxuries too much to take that step.

The smooth ride of the car slowed, and I braced myself as we took a soft curve.

"You're pulling into Cedar Creek Winery. You won't see them, but Ghost and Bishop are on your six." Rabbit's voice in my ear acted like a touchstone, and my last bit of nerves disappeared.

Anticipation slipped like an electrical current under my skin, flipping my senses to high-def levels. Sounds were amplified, like the rasp of cloth against leather as one of my escort-kidnappers shifted in his seat next to me. The change in position stirred the air, releasing the faint scent of stale tobacco. It wasn't overwhelming, so my abductor was not a heavy smoker but was probably indulging while waiting to "acquire" me. There weren't many ways to fight off boredom while waiting for a target to appear. The dance of shadows across my blindfold meant we were passing under trees. The car slowed, and we rolled to a stop.

A firm hand grasped my elbow. "This way, please."

Such a courteous kidnapper.

Even his initial approach couldn't be faulted. In dire need of caffeine, I'd left Elena's high-rise condo, where I'd taken over her life for the last few weeks, to make a run to a nearby coffee shop. Before I could place my order, I was stopped by a nonthreatening "Ms. Drake?"

A head turn and a nod later, I was politely but firmly being directed into the back of a sedan and offered a blindfold—an unorthodox approach, sure, but an effective one for someone whose business dealings were on par with devil's bargains.

Allowing him to maintain his hand on my arm, I slid as gracefully as possible across the soft leather. Fortunately, I'd forgone nylons, which would inevitably snag, and made do with tanned bare legs, a Southern California staple. I set my needle-thin heels delicately on the ground. The shift and roll of stone underfoot meant continued dependency on my kidnapper's support unless I wanted to risk a sprained ankle. The gravel didn't last long before it smoothed out. Based on the sound of my heels, we were on a stone walkway.

The sun was warm against my face, and the soft breeze carried the scent of wet earth and green growing things. Even if Rabbit hadn't clued me in, I'd have known we were removed from the city. There were none of the low-level sounds normally associated with urban sprawl. Instead, it was quiet with the occasional interruption of some unidentifiable noise. The weight of the sun disappeared, and the air changed as we moved into an enclosed space. The stone underfoot was replaced by something less dense that changed the muted tap of my heels to a sharp click.

"Ms. Drake, thank you for coming." The greeting was given in a pleasant male voice with no betraying accent and nothing to set it apart from a myriad of other voices. It took skill to be that bland. My curiosity was piqued.

"I'd say it was my pleasure, but…" I indicated the blindfold.

"I apologize for the inconvenience, but I find it safer to be discreet." His response held no true remorse—just cool politeness. "If you could bear the eccentricities for a moment longer…"

Recognizing that it wasn't a question, I slipped deeper into Elena's personality and managed a slight sigh that carried an air of impatience. "Of course."

The grip at my elbow disappeared, and a hand took mine. "This way, then."

With no choice, I followed my mysterious host. A few steps in, I heeded his murmured "Watch your step." The air shifted to artificially cool, and the temperature changed enough to raise the hair on my arms.

After a few more steps, my hand was freed, and he gave me permission to remove the blindfold. Blinking my vision clear, I offered the blindfold to the man standing in front of me. He matched his voice. He was not much taller than my heels-enhanced five foot ten. Despite his well-worn jeans and linen shirt, I was almost certain his outfit had cost more than my shoes. Add in the sun-streaked brown hair, clean-shaven jaw, and brown eyes, and he was the epitome of a wealthy young owner of a thriving winery. I gave him credit for a job well done, because as someone who routinely changed my face and appearance, depending on the job, I recognized a successful mask when I saw it. His was good, but I was betting mine was even better.

I did a deliberate scan of the foyer we stood in. Thick

wooden beams crossed the high ceilings. Impeccable furnishings were meticulously arranged to encourage intimate conversations in front of massive windows overlooking the endless rows of vines spinning from the house. All in all, it was a stunning house and a perfect stage for my host.

When my gaze returned to him, a faint sense of familiarity niggled at the back of my mind. While I mentally sorted through the possibilities, I offered him a cool smile. "Lovely place."

"Thank you." He turned and gestured toward a hall leading away from the expansive living space and farther into the house. "Shall we go to my office? I can offer you a drink."

I followed him down the hallway, noting the gorgeous artwork on the walls that gave no insight into their owner. They struck me as pieces a professional design company would use in a corporate retreat—pretty but flat. I wondered how deep Rabbit would have to dig to find the real owner of this place. Maybe he'd bump into a shell company instead. I knew which one I was betting on.

Inside the office, plush furniture and lush carpets over stone floors continued the overall theme of quiet elegance. I settled into one of two leather club chairs situated next to a table that was a repurposed tree stump, light bouncing off its high-gloss top. When my host didn't follow, I turned to find him moving toward a wet bar neatly tucked into the corner of the room.

"I understand we interrupted your morning coffee run. I'd be happy to rectify that." His subtle message of *We're watching you* was skillfully done.

I did him one better. "I'd prefer an old-fashioned, if you don't mind."

Amusement flashed, there and gone, in his eyes. "Of course."

He moved around the bar and began the process of putting my drink together. Not bothering to be subtle, I watched him, ensuring that only whiskey, citrus, and bitters went into my glass. Before long, he was handing me the heavy cut glass and carrying one of his own. I took a sip as he claimed the chair on the other side of the small table and leaned back, getting comfortable.

"Once again, I'd like to apologize about the clandestine nature of this get-together, but…"

"Apology accepted." Resting my glass on the padded armrest, I tapped a faultlessly polished nail twice against the crystal. It was a nervous tell I'd noted when observing Elena during one of her interview tapes. With my free hand, I tucked my newly dyed chin-length ash-blond hair behind my ear, careful to avoid the small electronic tag that allowed Rabbit to listen in. "I understand the need for caution, although I'm a tad confused as to why I'm here."

That last bit earned me a sharp look. "It was my understanding that you were recently approached about a possible partnership."

"I was." Staying true to the savvy, deceitful entrepreneur that Elena was, I let only mild curiosity show in my face. "But after recent tragic events, I believed that partnership was no longer on the table."

Once Rabbit and I had taken what we found to Delacourt, a simple but well-crafted narrative surrounding Hawes's death began to circulate, which proved that the US government could be efficient when necessary. The accepted story involved an unfortunate car accident while Hawes was en route to his office. Within a week of the tragic news, an impressive funeral followed, dutifully attended by many notables.

My host gave a somber nod, his mouth turning down with what appeared to be sincere sorrow. "It's a huge loss. One that will be felt deeply."

I wanted to applaud. He even had the remorseful tone down pat. Unfortunately, my sixth sense—honed by years of subterfuge—whispered, *Bullshit.* Not that his sincerity mattered. This was simply business after all. I made the appropriate noises so he could continue.

"We'd like to continue the initial conversation." He cocked his head, the glass pausing halfway to his lips. "That is, if you're still interested?"

I held his gaze as I swirled my drink with a deliberate absent-mindedness as if deciding whether to see this through or not. "Perhaps." I lifted my drink, sipped, and set it back down, watching closely to see if he fell for the uninterested play.

I knew he was hooked when I caught the barely perceptible widening of his eyes and the tightening of his lips in disapproval, as if he were wondering, *How dare this woman, a mere cog in the wheel, not jump at this opportunity?*

Before he could get into a snit, I added, "Our mutual friend was rather light on the specifics."

Not surprisingly, his gaze darkened with suspicion, and for a second, the predator lurking underneath was revealed. "I was under the impression he'd already explained the parameters of our proposition."

A person would have to be deaf to miss the underlying threat, and my hearing was damn good. Maintaining my air of unconcern, I sat back, recrossing my legs. "I'm not sure what he told you, but he simply offered to connect me to an interested party who would be willing to pay my fee plus ten percent." I accompanied my sharp yet polite smile with a one-two tap of a nail against the armrest, letting him see that I had a predator of my own lurking about. "I expressed an interest but required more details. He explained he would reach out with my request and get back to me once further disclosure was approved. I heard nothing more, and when I read about his accident a week and half later…" I pulled off a casual yet delicate shrug. "I assumed that was the end of that."

"Understandable." The ruthlessness slipped back into the shadows as my host relaxed into his chair. He tipped his drink back and forth, his gaze on the mesmerizing movement inside the beveled glass. "Well, we'd like to reopen negotiations."

He brought the glass up to his mouth, his eyes meeting mine. I caught a familiar disdain, which was easily recognizable after my years of working in a male-dominated industry. My host was one of those men who thought beauty and brains were mutually exclusive.

Poor deluded bastard. It was going to be fun to prove him wrong. I held his gaze, channeling all of Elena's arrogance, as I let the hint of curiosity slip through my air of minor annoyance. "Negotiations are always welcome."

"Wonderful." His satisfied smile rode the edge of smugness. "First, I should disclose that I'm simply acting as a representative of the interested party. However, they are willing to give you double your normal job fee plus five percent of profits in exchange for exclusivity."

His disclaimer, an obvious attempt to establish distance between him and his puppet master in case things hit the fan, took a back seat to his offer. I wasn't sure if I should laugh or be offended at the ridiculously low terms. Either reaction might take this conversation somewhere I did not want to go—not if we were going to draw out our target.

Deciding to play it safe, I kept my voice and face noncommittal. "Define their idea of *exclusive*."

"You would work solely for them, no side projects, no independent contracts." His attention didn't waver as he lifted his drink to his mouth.

This insulting offer had to be an opening gambit to see what it would take to get me to listen. There was no way his bosses would be this openly contemptuous of an individual who was the acknowledged best of her ilk. Testing my theory, I said, "And the anticipated length of this… arrangement?" I sneered the last word, making it clear which way I was leaning.

Something flashed in his eyes before his eyelids drifted down to hide it. He leaned forward and set his glass on the table. "Open-ended."

There was no stifling my disbelieving snort, so I didn't even try. "Give up freelancing?" Before he could answer, I was shaking my head. "You're wasting my time. Why would I consider severely limiting my opportunities?"

"They'll make it worthwhile." He straightened, watching me with a disconcerting intensity.

Ignoring it, I let the ruthless businesswoman take control, my voice hardening as I slapped him down. "I haven't heard anything remotely worthwhile yet. If you or your employer did your research, you'd recognize that first and foremost, I'm a businesswoman. A very successful businesswoman. Scaling down to one client for an indefinable amount of time is not in my best interest, nor is it remotely profitable, considering the long-term impact." I reclaimed my drink, taking a healthy swallow without wincing. Still holding the glass, I wagged my finger at him. "As flattered as

I am by your offer"—I made sure my voice sounded distinctly unimpressed—"it would be unwise of me to accept. My neutrality and ability to move between parties is crucial to my continued success. I'm not willing to risk that."

My tirade barely dented his arrogance—not that I'd expected it to. He raised a brow in that snotty way some people managed and slipped through the crack of possibility that my lack of a hard no gave him. "Does this mean exclusivity is off the table?"

Pretentious, tricky bastard. Lifting my glass in silent acknowledgement of his neat trap, I decided to see how far I could reel him in. "I'm not sure your interested party can afford the price of my exclusivity."

"Would you like to present a counter?"

That was not the response I'd expected. The seriousness underlying his question made me pause. I tapped a nail twice against the crystal, my mind spinning for a realistic figure.

Like the devil himself, Rabbit's low tone came through. "Limited run."

Considering his expertise in this particular area, I lifted my chin, narrowed my eyes, and said, "I propose a trial run."

Like a hunter catching the scent of his prey, my host came on point. "To ensure clarity, perhaps you should define what you consider a trial run would entail."

As Rabbit provided the logistics in succinct shorthand, I laid it out. "I'll agree to one month of exclusivity at triple my fee, half up front, half when complete, and ten percent of profits on each completed job during the thirty days. If I find my margins are unsatisfactory, we'll part ways—cleanly."

Unsurprisingly, he took the bait. "And if the partnership proves beneficial?"

"Then we can renegotiate the terms."

The quiet settled between us, heavy with tension. I waited, knowing I couldn't be the one to break first or it would undermine the ground I'd gained. Eventually, my host heaved a put-upon sigh as he pushed to his feet. "I'll convey the parameters of your counter." He moved to leave the room then paused. "Fair warning—if they do accept, they may request that you work on-site at a location of their choice."

In my ear, Rabbit added one last caveat, and I fought not to grit my teeth because it could be the spark that would blow this arrangement into unrecognizable smithereens. Unfortunately, it was a necessary risk if I intended to get through this assignment still breathing. "If that's the case, you'll want to inform your party that my services come with an assistant and their accompanying salary."

Caught off guard, my host asked sharply, "Assistant? We were unaware you had an assistant."

Maybe because until a few seconds ago, I didn't. But being able to adjust a story on the fly was crucial to a successful con. Thanks to my untraditional childhood and chosen career path, running cons was my specialty. In this case, being isolated while pulling off the kind of hack expected in an assignment like this could be a big problem. Hence, my need for backup and for an introduction of Elena's possible partner to this fast-changing game.

Affecting a casualness I was far from feeling, I shrugged. "Should this deal move forward, I'm sure your party would rather the public believe they're employing my services as a corporate consultant. Such an in-depth job would be both complex and multifaceted and would require more than one pair of hands. Hence, my assistant."

I could feel him staring, and it wasn't a comfortable feeling. "I'll pass along your request, so long as you understand that she will be fully investigated," he said.

"He."

"Excuse me?"

Considering the note of confusion in his voice, my correction was unexpected and confirmed my suspicion that my host might be a tad biased. *Seriously, a male assistant shouldn't be such a shock.* I shifted in my seat until I could see him then aimed a sharp smile in his direction. "My assistant is a him, not a her."

For all his skills at giving a good poker face, he failed to hide his flash of contempt as he reassessed my request through the lens of his misguided opinions about women. "Are you sure that's wise? This offer isn't to be taken lightly."

It wasn't hard for me to stay in character, because his false assumption pissed me off. "How is my bringing an extra set of hands an indicator of unprofessionalism?"

"A male assistant?" The sneer went from implied to a straight-up lip curl.

Since I didn't think a male assistant was out of the norm, I didn't bother responding. Not that it would have changed his inappropriate assumption. Staying silent meant he could keep doing an outstanding job at digging his ass into a deep pit of male chauvinism.

Sure enough, he just kept shoveling. "Couldn't you be more original?"

Channeling the hard-ass, take-no-shit demeanor exemplified by my boss, Delacourt, I stood up and smoothed my skirt before I met his gaze. Ensuring that he couldn't escape the contempt in my eyes or the frigid tone guaranteed to start the next polar ice cap, I said, "If recognizing the value of utilizing skilled individuals in their areas of expertise is considered original, then perhaps you should reevaluate your hiring criteria." Not about to let him off that easily, I cocked a hip, lifted my chin, and made sure he couldn't mistake my unspoken sentiment. "Of course, if you and your employer are satisfied with subpar performances, perhaps we should reconsider this negotiation, as I wouldn't want to jeopardize my preeminent reputation, nor am I inclined to work with those who accept less than the best."

My implications hit their mark. His face darkened, and a muscle jumped in his jaw. Whether it was anger or injured pride, I really didn't care. Instead of firing back, he gave me a stiff nod and disappeared through the door.

Chapter Two

JINX

The discussion between my host and whoever was on the other end of his phone stretched a nerve-wracking fifteen minutes. Instead of giving in to the urge to poke around the office on the slim possibility of finding something good, I spent my time cradling my drink and ostensibly enjoying the view of the rolling vineyards, occasionally taking an appreciative sip. If the room was being monitored, it was better to be safe than sorry.

Behind my casual facade, my mind spun through possible scenarios with stomach-churning speed. This was our best investigative lead into Hawes's motives for targeting the PSY-IV teams. Despite my verbal taunt, I knew my host would come back with an offer. Considering that his employers needed the Gatekeeper's skills enough to risk allowing him to conduct a kidnapping in broad daylight, chances were good that my terms would be matched. Besides, his actions up to this point said more about their desperation level than our conversation laced with threats and counterthreats did.

My demand to include my assistant was a dangerous curveball to throw, but it was necessary. Whether or not Gatekeeper was really a two-person team, we could play it that way if we kept our potential employer in the dark about our true purpose. If they accepted my offer and required that the work be done at an off-site location, we would have a chance to finally infiltrate the core group behind this mess. To do that, I would need Rabbit. Without him and his technical expertise, there was no way I could pull it off, not to mention that any secrets tied to an electrical signal would crawl right out from under their computerized security blanket into Rabbit's arms, willingly offering him whatever he wanted. The man was a damn menace to anything with an electronic signature.

Or anything female. That barbed reminder belonged to a part of me I tried very hard to ignore. Unfortunately, the more I partnered with Rabbit, the louder that voice demanded my attention. When we first started working together, him being a card-carrying flirt didn't bother me—much. But once I'd gotten to know the Cajun charmer's depth of character, it became irritating. I could have lived with mere irritation, but my feelings kept growing more intense for reasons that I was reluctant to identify. Something threatened to nudge our friendship toward an irreversible change, one that didn't bode well for our future working relationship. I didn't want to give the feeling a name, because doing so would make it real. Stupid me was holding on by my fingertips to the faint hope that if I didn't think about it, it would go away. So far, that wasn't working.

"Background is set." Rabbit's voice dragged me out of my ill-timed thoughts and shoved me back on track. "Mercer Somers, thirty, ex-SEAL, USC Berkeley business graduate, single, and employed by Elena Drake for the last five years."

Being limited to a one-sided conversation could be frustrating, but at the moment, Rabbit's voice was my security blanket. In pure Rabbit style, he wasted no time creating our backstory. I recognized the name as one of the assumed aliases of Elena's possible partner who'd been discovered by the investigative team—the same name that had finally tripped Elena up. With a few magical keystrokes, Rabbit had made the rumored partner a virtual truth. The edge of tension riding my spine eased.

Mercer's background made inherent sense. It was a Russian nesting doll of covers. As an ex-SEAL and USC Berkeley grad, Mercer would meet Elena's requirement for a top-notch employee. Not only would his education make him an accomplished assistant, but his service record would also add weight to his secondary role of bodyguard. And his past military career would explain why he wouldn't want his face out on the dark web.

I'd worked with enough SEALs to understand why Rabbit had chosen that unit for Mercer's resume. SEALs tended to be adrenaline junkies, which made them highly effective. That wasn't a bad thing, but to make the cut, they needed ruthless self-control as well. The two attributes made them excel at being unobtrusive and lethal, a profile that was a far cry from the attention-seeking drop-dead gorgeousness portrayed in many action flicks. Not that I minded. I still indulged in watching those kinds of movies whenever I got the chance, although—thanks to my job—I tended to side with the bad-boy types more than with the military heroes. That might explain why Rabbit, who could easily go either way, fascinated me more than was healthy.

Course correct, Corporal. I hid a sigh by raising my glass and taking a sip. I hated waiting. Lowering my drink, I tapped a nail against the heavy cut glass then stilled when I heard footsteps. I turned from the window and made my way back to the sitting area to set my drink down. Behind me, the footsteps grew louder, a clear indication of my host's return.

When he stopped just inside the room, I kept my back to him and said, "Not to be rude, but I do have other appointments today." I turned from my unfinished drink to find my host watching me. Or more specifically, watching my ass. *Figures.*

His earlier emotions were tucked behind a mask of politeness and an empty smile. "I appreciate your patience, Ms. Drake." He said that as if I had a choice in the matter. "You'll be pleased to hear that your conditions have been found agreeable. However, as I warned, your assistant"—he managed the word without a sneer this time—"will be subjected to an in-depth background check." He paused, which made me wonder if he expected an argument. I was happy to disappoint him. I lifted an eyebrow. His lips thinned. "Once that's complete, travel arrangements will be sent to your business email."

That was no surprise, but I had a more important issue to address. "And my down payment?"

"As a good-faith gesture, half will be in your account tonight. The other half will follow once you safely arrive at your worksite and complete your assignment. You have the next two days to make the necessary arrangements in regard to your other clients." His tone indicated that there was no room for debate.

Two and a half days would be more than enough time for us to prep. "That's tight but doable."

"I take it that you agree to these terms?" There was an avid light in the muddy depths of his eyes.

I took my time answering, just as any self-respecting criminal-minded businesswoman would, weighing the pros and cons of the deal. Finally, as he began to lose his amicable facade, I relented. "For now, yes." I held out my hand.

He wrapped cold fingers around mine in a cruel vise. "I'm sure it's unnecessary, but I must remind you that discretion is key to a successful partnership. My client would be highly displeased should our confidentiality be breached."

Refusing to react to the ache in my fingers or the not-so-subtle threat, I offered a sharklike smile of my own. "I choose my clients carefully and ensure that their experiences are exemplary. I've yet to have any complaints. I don't plan on that changing anytime soon."

Chapter Three

RABBIT

I watched Jinx emerge from the back of an unremarkable sedan, and the band around my chest relented enough that I could take a breath for the first time in two hours and —I checked my watch—forty-two minutes. On video feeds borrowed from various storefronts near the coffee shop, I followed that sexy sway of hips as she headed inside, probably to get an overdue caffeine fix. The amount of coffee that woman downed was astonishing. Sure enough, ten minutes later, she was back on screen, an indecently large cup in hand.

I monitored her progress to the condo. It wasn't a hardship. Despite the recent changes she'd undertaken to become Elena Drake, Jinx still fascinated me—I was as obsessed with the illusion she'd created as I was with Jinx herself. Her normally tawny mix of sable and gold was now heavy on the blond side, the ends brushing just below her jaw. Her chocolate-brown eyes were hidden behind green contacts and the oversized lenses of her sunglasses. Then there was the skirt and silk top that clung to her curves in a way her typical cargos and T-shirts never did. The cherry on top was a pair of sexy-as-shit heels that made her legs hard to resist. Yeah, keeping an eye on Jinx was a favorite pastime of mine.

As she moved inside to the condo's lobby, I switched to the interior security cameras, happy to note that the strect appeared clear of any trailing shadows. She swept through the entry and called the elevator. She sipped her coffee and, over the edge of her sunglasses, sent me a wink that left me shaking my head and fighting a grin. The woman got off on this covert business.

A soft ping snagged my attention. I clicked on the facial-recognition program running in the background to find that the still shot of one of Jinx's kidnappers had gotten a hit. Information scrolled down the screen—a pricey gun for hire, choosy about his jobs, who tended to stick to playing bodyguard. His employment history read like a who's who of white-collar criminals, making him a perfect fit for a polite snatch and grab.

It was a good start, but I needed more. I added key indicators into another program that was already working on uncovering the owner of the vineyard Jinx had visited. When I heard the front door unlock, I stood up and left the counter where my laptop hummed along.

I detected four sharp clicks of heels on tile and then a soft groan. Leaning a shoulder against the archway to the kitchen, I watched Jinx kick off her remaining heel. She left the shoes behind in a carnage of fashion and tossed her sunglasses on the table along the entry wall. After few more steps in, she stopped and lifted a foot to rub it along her calf.

"Feet hurtin', sugar?"

Her nod was accompanied by a grimace. "Why did Elena have to be a glutton for punishment?"

"Not sure she considers fashion a punishment."

"She should." Jinx came closer, her feet bare, hips swaying, and hair mussed.

She made it damn hard to focus on the task at hand. But after working with her as long as I had, I was an old hand at ignoring my unprofessional imagination and the never-ending curl of hunger that prowled under my skin. *Practice makes perfect.*

That didn't stop my mouth from going on automatic. "Want a foot rub?"

She stopped as if seriously considering my offer, taking another sip of her coffee. Something in the way she studied me made my pulse thud in anticipation. If I didn't know better, I'd have sworn her thoughts were swimming in the gutter with mine.

Then she lowered her cup. "Tempting, but I'll pass."

My half-formed bad ideas went back to pouting in the corner. Managing a shrug, I waded in and brought us both back to shore. "Your performance was award-winnin'."

She gave a big genuine smile—a rare occurrence—as she sketched a half-hearted curtsy. "Thank you." The smile dimmed as she headed into the kitchen.

I turned, keeping her in sight, my gaze arrowing in on her ass. *C'est ça, couillon!* I jerked my attention back to safer waters before she could notice, and I became an even bigger fool.

Oblivious to my mental struggle, she kept talking. "I thought bringing in Mercer was going to kill the deal."

For a moment, I'd been worried about that as well. In a rare stroke of luck, it turned out that the possibility of Elena having a partner was going to help us, and we needed to take advantage of that. Plus, there was no way in hell I was letting my partner go off to some undisclosed location with no backup. Something about this whole situation wasn't sitting right. The fact that I couldn't pinpoint it was beyond irritating.

"It's a good thing they're desperate." She set her cup on the granite counter and turned, her gaze going to the oversized clock on the wall behind me. "As a concerned assistant whose boss may have missed a morning appointment, shouldn't Mercer be knocking on my door shortly?" Her attention came back to me. "You know, in case they're watching."

We both knew they were. "He'll be along shortly." Still worrying about the itch in my gut, I rubbed my chin as my mind spun with various scenarios, none of which could be ruled out with the minimal information available.

Jinx was no fool and could read people better than anyone I knew. She folded her arms and nailed me with a look. "What?"

Her irritated question yanked me out of my head. "I'm not likin' this."

"You're not the only one," she admitted quietly. "But we needed an in. This is it, Rabbit. Our choice is to walk away and try to work with what little information we have or to suck it up and play it out." She got close and curled her hand around my forearm. "I know which way I want to go, and I'm not keen on doing it solo."

Staring into her face, I fought not to give in to the emotions rumbling through me and cup her face, knowing the gesture wouldn't be welcome at the moment. With my luck, it would never be welcome. That didn't mean I wasn't anticipating a chance to find out.

But no matter what happened, there was one solid truth she could count on. "I've got your six, sugar."

"Good." Jinx squeezed my arm then let me go. She

backed up until she could lean against the end of the counter. "You know it's part and parcel of our job, Cajun man."

Still simmering in my misgivings, I missed her change of direction. "What's that?"

"Wading into a cesspool of corruption. Not to mention facing off with our evil counterparts."

Obviously, I was not alone in the worrying department, and she might have a point. Maybe the depth of the swamp we were considering diving into was what was tripping all my alarms. "We've swum in worse."

"True, but still, if it is Falcon…"

It wasn't hard to follow her thoughts, but we both knew better. "No ifs about it, yeah? We might be short on hard evidence, but the breadcrumbs all lead back to those bastards." Calling the psychic mercenaries who worked for Falcon *bastards* was an understatement.

"I'll give you that," she said, her gaze steady. "Agreeing it's Falcon, does that change our plan?"

It drove me nuts when she used that reasonable voice, no matter how warranted. Regardless of who was pulling the strings, they had to be stopped. I ran a hand through my hair, wishing I could shove my misgivings back. "No, just wish we had better intel on their abilities." Falcon's psychic crew held to a murky moral code, and trying to infiltrate them without a solid assessment of what we faced was enough to turn my bowels to water.

She heaved a sigh and dragged her cup along the counter until she could perch her butt on one of the barstools at the counter. "What do we know as fact about Falcon's team?"

I took the seat next to her, snagging my laptop to bring it closer. A quick check confirmed that my program was still sorting through possible matches for the vineyard owner. I set it aside and hooked a foot on Jinx's stool. "Cyn and Ghost took out their Syphon."

"Nasty piece of work," Jinx muttered, shifting her stool closer to mine.

"Dangerous piece of work," I countered, happy with my new footrest. Syphons were psychics who absorbed the power of other psychics. The worst part was that they didn't just take in the psychic ability but also tended to take in their victims' memories, and the end result tended to fracture the Syphon's mind, leaving a monster in its wake. "*Motier foux*, too."

"Yeah, that kind of crazy comes with the territory." She propped her chin in her hand. "So no more Syphon, and Tag and Risia shot down the man behind the plan to eavesdrop on covert missions."

"And Tag topped that off by taking out their bioweapon supplier after he took Risia." The team's touch empath had not taken kindly to having his woman threatened.

Jinx ticked off our team's next accomplishment. "Wolf and Meli intercepted the unmarked gold stolen from that clusterfuck of a tribal negotiation."

I was even happier about the fact that Meli's stalker had been permanently neutralized, considering the nightmare she'd endured at his hands. "Not sure Falcon even felt that, *cher*."

She lifted a finger and wagged it in my face. "Money is money."

Okay, I'd give her that. Losing that gold might not have crippled Falcon, but it surely messed up whatever plan the group had for it. And although our team had managed its wins by the thinnest of margins, each one still counted in the overall picture. "Okay, but even you have to admit that losing that gold was a minor hiccup in the scheme of things."

She shrugged. "Maybe, but this last op with Major General Hawes was far from minor."

"True, and given that Hawes was a sociopathic telepath, I'm sure he was key to Falcon's plans."

Vicious and utterly ruthless, Hawes had kidnapped Megan, Delacourt's administrative assistant, and kept her for months while he invaded her mind, trying to turn her into a sleeper agent. Luckily, Megan's dormant dream-walking abilities saved her from serious mental damage. Unfortunately, the experience had left her with a bad case of PTSD, something our teammate Bishop was keen on helping her work through.

"Thank God Megan didn't break, or we'd be in a world of serious hurt," I said.

"Too damn bad Bishop's shot took out Hawes." Jinx winced and rubbed her forehead before sending me an apologetic grimace. "Not that I'm complaining."

"I don't think anyone is complainin' about that." I ran my hands over my face then flattened them against the counter. "At least we managed to eliminate their biggest threat—the Syphon. Hell, he managed to go through… what, six victims before we dropped him? Damn glad he's no longer on the board." Unfortunately, one of those six was Cyn's sister, and while her death had brought Cyn to the teams, it had been hard to witness.

"I think Hawes is right up there with him," Jinx said, her voice dark.

I had to agree, especially after witnessing the fallout of Hawes's behavior. When Bishop first brought Megan out of that hellish warehouse she'd been held in, I wasn't sure she'd survive. Not only did she survive, but she was also the one to turn the tables on Hawes and throw open the door to all his ugly secrets. And there were many. The deeper I dug into Hawes's life, the darker it got. I couldn't prove it, but I wondered how big a hand he'd had in his son's supposed lethal overdose and the murder of his wife in a bungled burglary attempt. Considering the estate he'd inherited, my guess was it was pretty damn big.

Jinx sighed and added in a tone of grim cynicism, "We still have no idea just how deep or how far his reach went."

There was no way to disagree with her assessment. For every sticky string I untangled, I hit more knots. It would take time we didn't really have to unravel the twisted mess Hawes had left behind.

"I'm not sure we'll ever find out," I said. "At this point, Delacourt is focused on shutting down Falcon once and for all. If we do that, maybe we can leave the rest of the cleanup to someone else."

"Really?"

"Really what?"

She leveled her gaze on me, disbelief lightening her eyes. "You don't want to see this to the end?"

"The end of Falcon, yeah, but the rest of Hawes's mess?" I shrugged, unable to articulate the uneasiness that plagued me every time I considered what facing down Falcon would entail. "I think if we dive into that, we're just askin' fate to come along and kick our ass. So far, our team's been lucky. We're all still breathing."

I didn't have time to react before her warm palm was covering my mouth. "Don't jinx us, Rabbit."

Instinct blew right past logic, and I took advantage, pressing a heated wet kiss to her palm.

She jerked her hand away so fast I swore my hair moved in the wake she left behind. "What are you? Three?"

Proving her point, I shot back, "You started it."

Color rode under her skin, and she curled her fingers instead of wiping her palm on her skirt. "Focus," she chided. "What else do we know about their crew?"

Going back through the few face-to-face interactions and pieces I had on Falcon, I said, "One of them is a pyro-kinetic."

A frown marred Jinx's forehead then cleared. "From the Vegas op, when Risia was infected with a viral nanotrap."

"Right." I rubbed my chest as the memories surged. I'd crashed into the smoking Vegas penthouse behind Wolf and Tag, only to find the smoldering remains of what used to be a human being. Then there was a split second of bone-chilling fear that the pile of ash was Risia—and an even faster spurt of relief that Jinx had been downstairs and safely out of the line of fire. Yeah, that was not a scenario I was keen on repeating. "Y'know, we can sit and speculate all damn day long, but it won't do us a bit of good. Our best bet is to keep our eyes open and our guard up."

"SOP," she murmured.

"Yeah, standard operating procedure is right." My laptop gave a soft chime, indicating that the program had found something.

She drummed her fingers on the counter. "What about Delacourt's mole?"

"What about them?" I brought my computer closer and began scrolling through the results.

"They're in deep."

"Maybe too deep." I paused at a fuzzed-out image. Something about it held my attention. A few keystrokes brought up another program. I dumped the image in and began sharpening it. "They might not be able to help."

"Do we know what their ability is?"

I turned from my screen and thought back through all the bits and pieces Delacourt had shared about her inside plant, including a few I had *stumbled on* for curiosity's sake. "Considerin' how long they've been embedded, I think it's safe to say it's similar to yours."

She blinked with a slow sweep of long, thick lashes. "You think they're a hallucikinetic."

"You don't?"

She gave a half-hearted shrug.

"You told me once that your ability to create realistic illusions was based on a unique mix of mental and visual manipulation."

"Right. So long as the illusion matches their expectations, it works and becomes truth. My host expected Elena Drake, so that's who he saw. The trickiest moment is the initial meet. If I can't match their expectation, the illusion won't hold." She looked away and picked up her coffee. "It's an obscure offshoot of telepathy and psychokinesis."

"All of which means you're basically a human chameleon."

"That's one way to think about it." She paused with her cup halfway to her mouth, and her nose wrinkled. I was damned if I didn't find that cute.

"So who better to be a deep cover operative?"

She slid me a look from the corner of her eye, and I knew she was conceding my point. Another ping from my computer drew her attention. She leaned over, trying to see the screen. "What are you running?"

I shifted the computer around so we could both see the screen. Satisfaction coursed through my veins as my program provided a name. "Might have an ID on your prospective headhunter." I brought up the cleaned-up image. *Well, I'll be damned.* I knew that face. I sat back, giving her a clear view of the screen. "Recognize him?"

Her eyes widened as she pulled the computer closer. "I've seen him before. Alexander Spires." Her gaze rose to mine. "He lightened his hair, changed his eye color, and ditched the English-professor look for an upper-class Southern California one. He was at the auction in Vegas with a…" Her eyes narrowed. "A blonde, if I remember correctly."

"You remember right." I shifted the keyboard, hit a couple of keys, and turned it back to her. "But Alexander Spires is not the name he's going by now."

"Zane Seward." She scanned the information on the screen, a collection of tagged social media posts complete with pictures. There weren't many, but it was enough for my program to work with. She frowned. "There's not much here."

"True, but we found these because it's nearly impossible to avoid getting caught in people's selfies nowadays." The limited amount I'd managed to dig up did more to confirm my suspicions than to alleviate them. No one's social media footprint was that small unless the person was actively avoiding leaving one.

As if hearing my thoughts, she said, "That kind of avoidance means either he's Delacourt's plant or he's an operative for Falcon."

Studying the image on screen, I saw an edge of something around the eyes that I couldn't pinpoint but that convinced me he wasn't our mole. "I'm leaning toward operative."

She looked at the image. "Me too. Which means he's probably our pyro." She suddenly shivered.

I couldn't blame her. Hell, I was shuddering just

thinking about how badly things could have gone this morning if our guess was right. "Yep, which means we need to be extra careful if he's the one we'll be working against. One wrong move…" I flicked my fingers up and made a whoosh sound.

Proving that her mind was right there with mine, she offered me a wan smile. "Guess it was good he didn't fry my ass for pushing things."

Unable to resist the urge to wipe some of her worry away, I teased. "Not sure he'd last in Falcon if he went around turning those who pissed him off into pillars of ash."

"No, that'd be bad for business." She sucked in a deep breath and pushed the laptop away. Quiet settled between us. Then she cautiously broke it. "So we're getting in bed with Falcon."

"Yeah."

A grimace washed over her face as she traced the base of her cup with a polished nail.

I bumped her shoulder. "You feelin' the need for a shower yet?"

My dark humor earned me a laugh, and her expression lightened. She pushed away from the counter and stood up, doing a feminine stretch that left my mouth watering and my mind switching gears. "Guess it's a good thing Elena's got herself an ex-SEAL as a body-guarding assistant."

"Damn straight." Checking the clock, I tucked away our digital finds and powered down my laptop. "Speaking of which, it's time Mercer brought his boss her coffee so they can strategize before their afternoon consultations." After rinsing my cup and setting it aside to dry, I took the laptop and walked to the table, where I tucked it into the leather messenger bag.

"Rabbit."

The almost hesitant way she said my name had me bracing myself, my hands flattening against my bag. Without turning around, I prompted, "Yeah?"

"About Mercer."

Oh, this ought to be interestin'. I turned slowly, leaned back against the table's edge, and folded my arms. Then I waited and watched the color deepen under her cheeks. Seeing that expressly feminine reaction brought a flare of satisfaction I didn't even try to ignore. *Oh yeah.* This wasn't one-sided. It was nice to know I wasn't the only one pondering the possibilities about our roles.

She tried for casual and failed. "How are we playing this?"

There was an answer I wanted to give her, but I didn't. "Carefully, *cher*. Very, very carefully."

Frustration edged out her obvious embarrassment as she waved a hand between us. "No shit, Sherlock, but you know that's not what I'm talking about."

Okay. I'd been very good, considering how hard and how often she denied the attraction between us. "You askin' as Elena or as Jinx?"

A flash of confusion tinged with panic was there and gone. "I'm one and the same."

I pushed away from the table. As I closed in, she took a tiny step back and went still. Undeterred, I kept advancing until she had to tip her head back just a bit to hold my gaze. "You sure you want an answer?"

Her chin lifted in silent challenge, and feminine need flared before she managed to douse it. Seeing that shifted my low burn up a notch. When she answered, her voice did nothing to cool the effect. "I'm not asking for the hell of it. We're partners, and we need to be on the same page."

Her challenge nudged me that little bit over the edge. This time, I didn't try to stop my fall. "Well, then, brace, sugar, because I'm going to make sure we're reading from the same book." With a single finger, I drew a soft, slow line along her jaw, under her chin, and down her long neck, stopping at the base of her throat, where her pulse visibly beat. Then I ripped away the last of my shredded denial, exposing the brutal truth. "I want you, Jinx. No matter what face you wear, I want you."

Her face paled, and she jerked back. "Don't do this."

Curling my hand into a fist, I absorbed the pinch of pain because I understood the fear that lay behind her words. But that understanding wasn't going to stop me from seeing this through. I'd been patient long enough. "Do what? Admit what we've been circling around for months?"

"We're partners, and it's good. You take us there, it'll ruin it." Equal parts anger and desperation wove through her voice.

If we continued dancing around it, one of us—probably me—was going to trip and hurt us both. It was better to fall on my face now than in the middle of a damn mission. "How?"

"You're a gold-card-carrying flirt, Rabbit." Her husky accusation would have held more weight if a hint of hunger hadn't lit her eyes.

"Yeah, I'm a flirt." There was no sense in denying it. "That doesn't make what I feel any less real."

She shook her head. "We can't do this."

"We are doing this, sugar." She went to take another step back, but I caught her wrist, holding her in place. "Because we don't have a choice. Ignoring it won't work." I fought the urge to shake her as her lips thinned in a mutinous line. "You're the one who told me the best con is the one based on truth."

She jerked in my hold. "So what? You want to have a relationship to bolster a cover story?"

I thought I caught a hint of hurt in her voice. Not keen on that possibility, I pushed forward, laying it out. "No, I want a relationship, regardless of mission status." Her eyes widened, but I didn't let her interrupt. "But while we're on this one, there is no way in hell I'm letting you out of my sight, so it's a good thing Zane thinks you and Mercer are lovers."

By the time I finished, bad temper had wiped away her astonishment. "Don't be an idiot! We can't be lovers for real. Emotions will get us killed."

"No." My denial was stark, slicing through her objections. "Emotions will keep us sharp. And we will be lovers, so there's no 'can't' involved. If you'd stop denying it, you'd know just how good it could be."

She jerked her wrist free, not that I was fighting her. "Oh my God, could you be any more arrogant?"

Fighting back my frustrated anger, I bit out, "Tell me you don't feel this attraction. Convince me that there isn't a part of you dyin' to find out what would happen if you took a chance." *On me.* The last bit was unsaid but fell between us with a resonating impact.

Color flamed in her cheeks, and her breath quickened even as she kept fighting from her corner. "Not during a job! God, Rabbit! That's a rookie mistake. Relationships have no place in covert operations. This is the worst time to do this." She dragged her hands through her hair, and despite our heated exchange, I didn't miss how her movement pulled the silk tight across her breasts.

Thanks to a mix of lust and anger, my voice came out

rough. "Maybe the timing sucks, but it doesn't make it any less true, Jinx. I'm not going into this snake-infested pit playing games with you."

"I'm not playing games." Her voice rose. "I'm not playing hard to get. I'm not a challenge you have to win."

She was right and wrong. Whether she admitted or not, she was playing games. I might be a flirt, but I spent enough time with women to recognize the signs when someone was considering moving things to a deeper level. I caught those same tells with Jinx more and more frequently. It might not be a conscious decision to play hard to get, but there was no missing the fact that she had great big gigantic emotional walls armed with howitzers around her heart. So yeah, she was a challenge. Getting through those defenses would be a hell of a task, but it wasn't enough to discourage me. Hell, if a man was any kind of man, he got off on challenges. No one wanted a doormat.

To prove my point, I said, "Convince me it's one-sided, and I'll back so far off we can pretend this conversation never happened."

Jinx proved she was exactly the woman I thought she was—one who didn't bullshit anyone, including herself, when it counted. She dragged in a deep breath, lifted her chin, and fisted her hands at her sides, her eyes flashing with a mix of temper and fear. What came out of her mouth was not a denial but a reluctant concession. "Why are you pushing this now?"

"Because you asked." Before she could respond, I kept going with brutal honesty. "Because this job could go sideways in a blink." *Simple enough, considering the layers to this masquerade.* "Because one or both of us may not walk away from this. And most importantly, because I want you."

Unable to keep my distance, I stepped toward her,

wrapped one arm around her waist, and pulled her close. Her hands went to my chest, but they didn't push me away. Instead, they slid to my shoulders and around my neck until we were pressed against each other. The feel of her lit my neurons on fire. I brushed the top of her head with a soft kiss. Her head fell forward in silent concession, the strands of her hair moving like silk under my lips while the hint of vanilla teased my nose.

Her breasts rose and fell against my chest. "This isn't smart." Her breath was warm against my throat.

Tucking a finger under her chin, I tilted her head back, needing her to see me—to see just how real this was to me. Need, wariness, and desire were all there in her eyes. She wasn't saying no.

"Smart is overrated," I said. Then as she rose on tiptoe, I breached the slight distance between us and took her mouth in a gentle but hungry kiss.

Chapter Four

JINX

R abbit's taste hit me, shattering the crumbling barriers I'd tried so hard to maintain. This was no simple kiss, no cautious wading in to test the depths. Nope, this was a full-on storm surge of hunger, wild and gentle and so damn dangerous that all I could do was hold tight to him and hope we both managed to break the surface.

His mouth moved over mine, swallowing my quiet gasp as his tongue teased and tempted, even as he added an occasional taunting nip that sent fire streaking through my veins. It wasn't long—a breath, maybe two—before I was meeting him move for move and making a few demands of my own. It was hard to lie to myself when I was going up in flames. I'd needed this—Rabbit's lips on mine, his taste in my mouth, his body against mine—far longer than I wanted to admit. Part of me was curious about whether he was really as good as he seemed. But the other part was nothing but need and dangerous want.

His tongue tangled with mine as his fingers left my chin to brush down my throat and trace along the edge of my silk blouse. At his barely there touch, my thoughts slipped into a haze of sensation. My breath caught and stuttered as I waited to see how far he'd go and how far I'd let him go. He kept sliding his finger along the blouse's edge as his mouth lifted just enough to let him lay a tormenting trail of soft kisses along the side of my neck. Chills broke along my skin as his tongue swept out to up the sensation level. I dug my nails into his shoulders as I mapped my own trail along his jaw, giving him more access. The heat curled through me, leaving me craving more and crowding everything else out for a blissful mindless moment. I set my open mouth against his neck and indulged, thrilled when he jerked against me.

"*Mon Dieu*, Jinx." Rabbit's muffled groan was broken against my ear as he moved down my neck to where it met my shoulder. Interspersed with his debilitating open-mouth kisses was the sensation of his teeth grazing along the sensitive line of my neck. A vicious hunger rose like flames meeting gasoline, sweeping everything else under.

When he brought his mouth back to mine, I was drowning in touch and taste and need, lost in his kiss. I would have happily stayed lost if Rabbit hadn't finally let me up for air. I was trying to pull in much-needed oxygen when sanity broke through and reality began to reform. Rabbit had me pinned against a wall, his hand wrapped in my hair. His hold didn't hurt, but it kept me where he wanted me. The dominance of his move was so unexpected that it triggered a staggering sense of vulnerability. That, more than the explosive need, snapped me back into focus.

My hands were buried in his hair, and I was sucking in air as if I'd run a marathon. I blinked, and the red mark that now marred his neck came into focus. My internal alarms, which had been drowning under Rabbit's kiss, surfaced in a surge of painful clarity. *What the hell am I doing?* Unable to hurt him, I gently tugged my fingers free of his hair. Hands to his shoulders, I stepped back. Or I tried to. Thanks to Rabbit's arm around my waist and the wall at my back, I didn't get far.

"Stop, Rabbit. We have to stop."

My voice lacked any real conviction, but fortunately, he heeded my words. He untangled his fingers from my hair and dropped his head to rest against my sternum, his breath falling down my shirt and over my sensitized skin, leaving behind a painful ache. I wasn't sure this position was any better, but my brain was kicking into gear, and eventually, my body would follow.

He was muttering something I couldn't quite make out, but I made no attempt to decipher it. I was more concerned with ensuring that when I let go of his shoulders, I wouldn't collapse into a boneless puddle on the floor. When I finally put space between us, he lifted his head. Unmistakable hunger left his gaze dark and hot, while a ruddy flush rode along his cheeks.

His hands went to my waist, and he put another reluctant inch between us. I couldn't stop my slight sway forward before I forced my body to still. Not missing the movement, his fingers tightened, his touch searing and deep, as his gaze roamed my face. "That's not one-sided, *cher.*"

I swallowed, trying to find enough moisture to make my voice work. What I managed was a rough rasp. "Still doesn't make it smart."

His lips curled into that cocky grin that left damp panties in its wake. Irritated that mine were no exception and frustrated by my chaotic emotions, I let go of his shoulders, flattened my palms against his chest, and pushed. "Move, Rabbit."

It came out sharp, but that was better than desperate, which was how I felt. That kiss was everything I feared it would be. Rabbit wasn't just my partner—he had become my best friend, the one person who seemed to have no problem accepting me and my hang-ups. Taking us out of the friendship zone into something more intimate, no matter how tempting, was dangerous as hell. It could ruin the one relationship that I had come to depend on. If I wanted to get through this mission without screwing it up— without screwing us up—I had to control whatever this was between us. I squashed the little voice whispering that there was no controlling Rabbit.

He let me go and held up his hands. "Ease down, Jinx. I'm not tryin' to start a fight here."

"Could have fooled me," I muttered as I turned to stalk away.

I didn't get far. His hand locked around my arm, holding me in place. "Jinx."

There was an intensity to the way he said my name. I looked back over my shoulder, forcing myself to meet his eyes. "What?"

His gaze drifted over my face before a muscle jumped in his jaw. "This isn't finished."

Ignoring the spurt of fear caused by his comment, I focused instead on my resentment at being dictated to. No, he didn't get to call the shots. I had too much to lose. "For now, it has to be."

Revealing the temper that swam under all that lazy charm, his eyes flashed with masculine determination, and he shook his head. "Warning you now, sugar, I'm not backin' off." He could be just as stubborn as I could.

"If you don't, you'll get us both killed." It was a low blow, but desperate times and all that.

"Bullshit."

I ripped my arm free and stepped back, trying to hide the anger I really felt. "I need my partner to watch my back, not be on the lookout for the nearest bed to get me into." It was as much a warning to him as it was a reminder to me.

He continued to watch me with an unsettling intensity as he folded his arms over his chest. "First, I'll always have your back. That doesn't ever change. Second, I know how to separate emotion from the mission just as well as—if not better than—you, sugar."

Metaphoric feathers ruffling, I opened my mouth to snap something snarky but remained mute when he lifted a hand and kept going, proving he knew me better than most. "Third, there was no good time to open this can of worms. I choose now because what we're facing is dicey as hell. And as you said earlier, games aren't your thing, so I'm not wastin' another minute not being straight with you." He dropped his hand and closed in until his mouth was right next to my ear. "And for your information, I don't limit myself to beds."

There was no way to ignore the fire that his starkly carnal threat evoked, but before I could snap back, he straightened and moved to the counter. He grabbed his bag and slung it over his shoulder, settling the strap across his chest, before turning back to me, his jaw hard and his game face firmly in place. "Get your poker face on, *cher*. It's time to ante up."

I curled my hands into fists and gritted my teeth, knowing anything I said at this point would be easily used against me. I settled for glaring at him, but instead of dropping dead at my feet, he shot me a wicked grin and a flick of fingers before strolling down the hall and striding out the door.

Chapter Five

JINX

My frustration and worry were locked tight in the little box where I stashed all the messy emotions Rabbit stirred up. Granted, that was probably an unhealthy solution, but it was necessary. Not that Rabbit was poking around, stirring things up. In fact, he was all about the mission, and if I hadn't still been reeling from his declarations and trying to deny the revelations they dragged to the surface, I'd put the whole thing down to a hormone-influenced hallucination. Fortunately, there was a vast list of items to accomplish to make sure this mission went off without a hitch, and since I was working under a deadline, it was easy to shove the emotional mess into a corner. No doubt about it—I was living proof that denial wasn't just a river in Egypt.

Barefoot, with another torturous set of heels in hand, I pulled my rolling carry-on out of the bedroom and into the open space that included the living room and kitchen. Stopping next to the couch, I set one shoe on top of the luggage and braced my other hand against the back edge of the couch. *Time to begin the toe torture.* I slipped a heel on and was reaching for the other when my cell phone buzzed on the granite countertop.

I quickly limped to the counter and snagged my phone, catching *Mercer* scrolling across the screen before I tucked it between my ear and shoulder. "Hello?" I leaned against the counter and slipped the other heel on.

"I'm downstairs," Rabbit said. "Do you need me to come up and get your bags?"

"No, I'll be down in just a minute. Is our ride here?"

"Not yet, but we're a bit early."

In his role as Mercer, there was no sign of his accent, and I found myself missing it. "Did you get my coffee?"

"Have I ever disappointed?" While his borderline tease carried hints of the Cajun charmer, it was more in line with Mercer's supposed role in Elena's life.

"Lovely. I knew there was a reason I kept you around."

"Just one?" His voice carried a wealth of innuendo.

Playing my part with scary ease, I gave a soft hum of appreciation.

He chuckled in my ear. "Right. Hustle down here before it gets cold."

"Be right there."

It was the innocuous but flirty conversation of a woman and her partner preparing for a business trip—exactly what was expected should anyone be listening in. Once Rabbit had left the condo and Mercer hit the stage in earnest, Jinx and Rabbit were gone, and the game was on. This meant that three days before, roughly an hour and a half after Elena had been dropped off, she reappeared at the curb in front of her condo, where Mercer picked her up in a sleek sedan. From there, she headed out for her afternoon appointments with an unhappy-looking Mercer at her side.

After the meetings, Mercer hustled Elena back into her condo and didn't reappear until he opened the door to claim a dinner delivery from a nearby Indian restaurant. The next morning, the two lovers poorly disguised as business associates left the condo together and hit the small but well-heeled private office before reappearing to meet with a couple of key clients throughout the day. Then it was back to Elena's condo, where Mercer left for only a handful of hours—just long enough to close down his apartment before returning, luggage in hand, to spend another night with Elena.

Zane's directives hit Elena's inbox midafternoon that first day, complete with embedded traps designed to take over the recipient's operating system. Thanks to Rabbit's devious bent when it came to technological viruses, he knew the second the traps went to work. In pure Rabbit fashion, he slipped around the nasty programming and launched his own much more devious counterattack that would leave the server crippled once he was certain he'd managed to mine all the data he could. It was slow going and would implode the server within a week. The viral traps, with their detailed architecture, left an elaborate electronic trail. Add in the wafting fumes of money required for the price tag of such a customized virus, and we knew we were dealing with an extensive network funded by deep pockets.

Once Rabbit was certain the email was cleared of threats, we turned our attention to the actual directives. At the end of the forty-eight-hour time limit Zane had given Elena to get her affairs in order, a driver would arrive at the condo to pick up her and Mercer. From there, we would be taken to a private airfield, from which we would be whisked away to our unnamed location. Rabbit took what little information we had and narrowed down our location options to the nearby private airfields. His theory was that neither Zane nor his employers would risk utilizing public flights, as that would threaten their control over Elena. Rabbit struck gold when he found a fly-in community with Zane Seward, vineyard owner, as a listed member. Digging a bit deeper, Rabbit tied a shell corporation to a plane's tail numbers that matched one bought by Cedar Creek Winery six years previously.

Those afternoon meetings with Elena's clients served as a screen for a flurry of activity as Rabbit and I coordinated our best plan of action for the op with our team and Delacourt. Since our final destination was up in the air—pun intended—the team was limited to tracking our movements via the cutting-edge skin tags Rabbit guarded like gold. On top of that, mini trackers—another bit of Rabbit-modified tech—would be used on the vehicle picking us up.

We discussed dropping a tracker in the plane but in the end decided against it. Delacourt was not keen on being kept blind, and because she was determined to trace every possible thread, up to and including the routes of extraneous vehicles, she was willing to risk leaving a tracker on the car picking us up. But when it came to tracking Rabbit and me, since we couldn't do subdermal GPS—something Rabbit confirmed existed—the skin tags were our best bet. They were undetectable when not active, so we had to be careful when and where we used them.

When Mercer went back to his apartment, he returned to Elena's condo with specialized luggage with hidden compartments impervious to most scanning technology. While packing an arsenal might be conspicuous, we could fill our bags with the necessities, including garrotes, a couple of thin blades, and the small conceal-and-carry nine millimeters—Glock 43 for me, Walther CCP for him—not to mention the secondary laptop that Rabbit would use once we managed to set our hook inside Falcon's network. With less than two days to prep, we were as ready as we'd ever get.

Heels on, phone in hand, I snatched up the oversized sunglasses and nabbed my rolling carry-on. Taking one last look around Elena's condo, I found I was not the least bit sorry to be leaving. The place creeped me out, probably because it reflected its owner, who was pretty but soulless.

I stepped out of the elevator to find Rabbit waiting in the lobby in full-on Mercer mode—wearing neatly pressed dark-gray dress pants and a steel-blue collared shirt covered by a matching unbuttoned gray jacket. His hair had been ruthlessly tamed into a short, neat style. A black rolling case that matched my blue one sat at his side. He looked like the epitome of a successful businessman, and unless you knew to notice, you'd miss the keen mind assessing everything and everyone around him. The intelligently ruthless man under a deceptively attractive mask was a combination detrimental to my peace of mind.

Still, I was a professional, and as such, I pulled my shit together and let Elena's personality reign supreme. With an attitude that made it clear I was a woman who always got what she wanted when she wanted it and how she wanted it, I held his gaze and crossed the floor, my needle high heels helping the lazy sway of my hips. It was a show designed to make every male take notice.

It didn't fail me now. As I got closer, his hazel eyes darkened, and his lips curled up in an appreciative grin. He pushed off the wall he was leaning against and waited for me to approach. When I got close, he offered me one of the cups he held.

Taking it, I tilted my head so he could brush his lips over my cheek and murmured, "Thank you."

He lifted his head, a humor that belonged to Rabbit sparking in his eyes as he waved his cup toward the lobby doors. "Shall we?"

"If we must."

I sipped my coffee while he grabbed his carry-on with his free hand. Then I led the way as he followed me out the lobby doors. Pausing inside the entrance, I released my case and dropped my sunglasses into place. On the sidewalk in front of me, morning commuters rushed by, their heads down, attention aimed at their phones. Miraculously, they managed not to run into each other. All in all, it was just another busy weekday morning in the city.

Rabbit stepped up to my side, his shoulder brushing mine, his eyes hidden behind a pair of dark sunglasses. He raised his coffee and said, sotto voce, "Incoming."

A dark town car slid through traffic with sharklike grace and came to a stop in front of us. We waited as the driver got out and rounded the hood. The driver's black pants and white shirt did little to hide the build or the posture that all but screamed *ex-military*. In contrast, "Ms. Drake, Mr. Somers?" emerged in a melodious baritone.

Rabbit lifted a chin in acknowledgement while I offered a polite yet distant, "Yes?"

The driver opened the back door then motioned to my luggage. "I can take your bags."

"Thank you." I left my carry-on for him to grab and turned back to the open door of the car.

The driver said, "Sir?" and I turned to see Rabbit

keeping hold of his bag and following the driver to the trunk.

My attention was caught by the rattle of wheels against concrete, which was quickly followed by startled exclamations from nearby pedestrians. I shifted on my heels, one hand on the door's edge, and I spun around as a teenager zipped through the crowded sidewalk on a skateboard. People scattered, and someone bumped into me hard, knocking me off-balance.

I braced the arm with the coffee against the side of the car as liquid sloshed in the cup, but thanks to the tight lid, it didn't spill. A hand wrapped around my arm, steadying me, and the male business professional who'd fallen into me offered a rushed apology. Once he was sure I wouldn't fall, he let me go.

I palmed the tracker he'd pressed into my hand and murmured, "I'm good, thank you."

With a nod, he hurried back into the wave of pedestrians and disappeared.

The entire exchange took less than thirty seconds. I turned back to where Rabbit and the driver were half-hidden by the raised trunk and slipped the tracker under the lip of the rear wheel well as I took a sip of the coffee. Tracker in place, I slid into the back seat and pulled my door closed. I settled in, putting my coffee in the cup holder that divided the back seat before tucking my skirt under as I crossed my legs. When Rabbit opened the door facing the street and joined me, I was enjoying my coffee.

The driver wasn't far behind. Once settled behind the wheel, he smoothly pulled into the street and made his way through the morning traffic. Conversation between Rabbit and me remained superficial and sporadic. Neither of us bothered asking the driver any questions, knowing it was pointless. Instead, I watched the cityscape slowly thin into rolling hills scarred by recent wildfires.

Close to an hour later, my coffee was a memory, and the driver was turning down a long, lonely stretch of paved road. For a moment, I wondered if he was planning on dumping our bodies in the middle of nowhere, because our surroundings certainly fit the bill. Luckily, before my imagination could set land-speed records, the first signs of life shimmered in the distance and morphed into the roofline of a hangar. As we got closer, a corporate jet joined the hangar, its nose aimed down the single runway unfurling toward the horizon.

The car slowed, turned, and came to a stop just inside the wide-open doors of the hangar. The driver shut off the engine, got out, and opened Rabbit's door before rounding the trunk. I took my time gathering my things while I scanned what I could of the hangar's interior from behind my sunglasses.

On the far edge, two men, obviously mechanics, stood leaning against a cluttered workbench. Two others were doing a stellar job imitating bookends just beyond the car's hood. Off to the side sat a table complete with a scanner for the luggage, the kind normally seen at airports. Oh yeah, money was definitely involved. This kind of setup wasn't the norm for a private airstrip.

Rabbit beat the driver to my door, opening it without sparing the other man a glance. A wave of heat chased away the AC's cooler temperature. I got out of the car and took a moment to smooth away a line at my hip. The driver dragged our cases over to the bookends, who were standing at parade rest, arms clasped behind their backs. Rabbit and I followed. Behind the screen of my sunglasses, I noted the revealing bumps along their ribcages. The marred lines of the tailored clothing indicated both were carrying weapons. *Ah, the joys of a private hangar and armed guards.*

Rabbit's hand curled around my wrist in silent warning. I slowed my approach. He didn't let go even as the guard on the left stepped forward.

"Ms. Drake."

I came to a stop, feeling Rabbit do the same, his hand brushing my palm before he shifted, putting a few more inches between us.

The first guard's gaze did a quick once-over, clearly dismissing me as a threat, before concentrating on Rabbit. "Mr. Somers. Welcome."

I watched the driver hand off our luggage to the second guard, who shifted the bags to the table and began unzipping them. "Is there something in particular you're hoping to find in our luggage?"

My question earned a hard glance from the one about to dig through our stuff and a flat smile from the one in front of us. "It's protocol, ma'am."

Protocol, my ass. I kept the second guard in my peripheral vision as I faced his partner, knowing good and well that our stuff was being tagged.

The verbal guard shifted, motioning toward the table with his arm. "If you don't mind making your way over, we'll get this taken care of before boarding."

Since refusing wasn't an option, I headed toward the table, Rabbit and the first guard at my back. I stopped at the opposite end from where our luggage was being searched, not missing the two empty plastic bins and the scanning wand lying in wait.

Sure enough, our first guard said, "If you don't mind putting your electronics in the bins, please."

I set my phone and iPad in one while Rabbit dumped

his phone and laptop in the second bin. The first guard motioned to one of the mechanics, who headed over. When he collected the bins and went to take them away, I revised my assessment. *No mere mechanic, then.*

"Excuse me." My voice came out sharp and stopped the supposed mechanic in his tracks. He turned toward me, and I aimed a glare at the first guard, who was reaching for the wand. "I'd prefer that those don't leave our sight."

Tension snapped into place, and the one searching our luggage stilled, while the man holding the bins swallowed hard, his glance darting between me and the first guard, who held the wand.

"They won't leave this building." Wand Man stepped away from the table, and behind him, the guy with the bins beat a hasty retreat. Unruffled by my temper, Wand Man motioned toward the clear space at the end just beyond the table. "If you don't mind?"

Since Elena wasn't one to take attitude, no matter how politely thrown, I dished it right back. Instead of heeding his directions, I held my spot and propped my hands on my hips. "Actually, I do."

Wand Man's mouth tightened, and he failed to completely hide his irritation. He opened his mouth, but whatever he was going to say was silenced by Rabbit's low but biting "Elena."

I spun on a heel, giving the guards my back, and faced Rabbit. With my jaw clenched, spine stiff, and hands fisted on my hips, I leaned my torso toward Rabbit, the picture of a woman on the verge of losing her shit. "It's bad enough they're pawing through my clothes"—my voice came out on a low whip of anger—"but I'll be damned if I'm going to stand here and let them do the same to me. No job is worth this."

Rabbit gave a sharp shake of his head, moved around me, and held his hand out to the first guard. "Give it to me."

The guard took a moment and looked indecisive, but in the end, he handed the wand to Rabbit.

Rabbit took it and turned back to me. "Better?"

I dialed back the attitude and heaved an irate feminine sigh. "Fine."

His lip twitched, but since he was facing me and his back was to the guard, it didn't matter. He kept up the hard-ass routine. "Hand over the glasses."

I pulled my sunglasses off and slapped them into his hand. He handed them over to the guard behind him while I assumed the pose—arms out, legs hip width apart. While Rabbit ran the wand over me, I glared over his shoulder at the guard, who managed to stifle a disgusted grimace before it became more than a twitch.

Inwardly, I smiled. Oh yeah, Elena's bitchy attitude would be reported, but so would the fact that Mercer kept her in check. That kind of dynamic would follow Zane's expectations beautifully.

But that wasn't the only reason for my temper tantrum. The wand's hum stayed steady even as it drifted up my shoulders and over my head. Getting the wand into Rabbit's hands wasn't necessary, but it was helpful, especially since Rabbit could override its programming in his highly unique way. While the chance of it detecting the skin tags was low, it was better not to tempt the odds.

Scan complete, Rabbit stepped back and returned the wand to the guard. "Here."

"Thank you." The guard held out my glasses in exchange.

Rabbit took them with a nod. Then he turned away,

pulled his sunglasses off, and handed both pairs to me. "Hold this." He didn't wait for an answer before turning away and heading back to the guard.

I put my glasses back on and waited while Rabbit took his turn under the wand. I wasn't surprised when the guard decided to follow up the wanding with a thorough pat-down. *Yep, they definitely consider Mercer the bigger threat.*

While Rabbit kept the first guard busy, I watched the second one finish up his search of the luggage. When he finally flipped the lids down and zipped them closed, the low-level tension tightening my shoulders eased a notch. Fortunately, the specialized bags did their job, and our secrets were still carefully tucked away. By the time Wand Man was done with Rabbit, his partner was setting our bags on the floor.

I didn't miss their quick visual exchange followed by a barely there headshake from the silent one. *That's right, other than some seriously pricey undies, not much of interest in those bags, buddy.* Much like Elena, I wasn't keen on having a stranger paw through my underwear in the first place, but in this case, there wasn't much I could do about it. Now I was stuck watching our bags get rolled away, presumably to the jet waiting outside the hangar.

A rush of feet over concrete heralded the arrival of our electronics. The bins were set on the table with a clatter. Wand Man and Mechanic exchanged a few words, but their voices were too low to catch. I had to wonder exactly what they did to scan our devices, because they didn't have them long enough to get anything useful—not to mention that unless they knew what to look for, they'd be wasting time and fishing blindly. Add in Elena's technical reputation, and the difficult task of hacking her electronics graduated to impossible. There wasn't anything worth worrying about on those devices anyway, but maybe Zane's people were more concerned that we would try something stupid like taking down the plane. Of course, if we wanted to do that, we wouldn't need those electronics, just Rabbit.

Wand Man gathered our phones and laptop from the bins and brought them over. Once we collected our items, he said, "If you'll follow me, we'll let you get settled in. We'll be taking off shortly."

Rabbit and I followed Wand Man out of the hangar and to the waiting jet. At the stairs, Wand Man stepped aside and gave another one of his empty smiles that did nothing to soften the hard lines of his face. "Enjoy your trip."

Maybe it was just me, but I could have sworn there was a thin layer of menace in his voice. *Hmm, I must not have made a good impression.*

Before I could form a response, Rabbit's hand landed on the small of my back and nudged me up the stairs. Once inside the cabin, a dark-haired woman greeted us and helped us settle in, asking for drink preferences. I went with water, and unsurprisingly, so did Rabbit. We picked the set of seats in the center facing each other over a small table.

The woman headed toward the front of the cabin. As I set my iPad up in front of me, Rabbit said in a low voice, "Elena." I lifted my head to meet his gaze. "Did you get in touch with Mark at Baron's?"

Dipping my chin in acknowledgement, I answered, "He was out when I called, so I left a message with his assistant."

"Good. I didn't have time to return his call yesterday." He sat back, relaxing into the chair. "Since you've run me ragged these last couple of days, I'm taking advantage of our downtime."

"Poor baby, did I tire you out?" The question came out as a husky purr and earned me a knowing look.

That was the extent of our conversation, since we were almost certainly being monitored. As Rabbit closed his eyes, I went back to my iPad, scrolling through a few of Elena's files, making minor adjustments. No matter how many times they replayed the inconspicuous exchange, there was no way they'd be able to decipher its meaning.

I'd just confirmed to Rabbit that the tracker on the car was in place, thanks to the handoff by Ricochet back on the sidewalk in front of the condo, an exchange that hadn't even raised an eyebrow. Such casual encounters barely blipped anyone's radar. It always came down to expectations and perceptions. The driver wouldn't have considered that we might risk a handoff in broad daylight and under his nose. Nor would he have taken into account that a random act, like a teen on a skateboard, could be engineered so as to have a faceless young businessman stumble against me.

The reality was that it was a well-coordinated and exacting plan involving a payoff to a random teen while our lethal sniper took on the role of a random businessman. The success of deception, whether it was a con game or a covert operation, all came down to precise execution, including the smallest details. The guards considered Mercer more of a threat than Elena, an impression deepened by her temper tantrum and Rabbit's interference with the wand, all of which ensured that the skin tag nestled behind my ear remained undetected, dormant, and secure. People's predictability never failed to amaze me, but it did come in handy.

Fifteen minutes later, the rumble of the plane's engines kicked in, and we were soon taxiing down the runway. As the jet gained altitude, I shut down the iPad and settled back to watch the familiar landscape of San Diego disappeared under a layer of white clouds. For the first time that morning, I let my muscles uncoil, my body settling deeper into the seat.

Across from me, Rabbit's eyelids lifted. "You good?"

Am I? Getting past the first hurdle wasn't much of a challenge. Yeah, the sleight-of-hand tricks were fun, but in the overall scheme of things, that would be the easiest part. What lay ahead was trickier, not just because of the mask I wore or the nuances of our undercover roles but also because of the threat posed by Rabbit, who was watching me with disconcerting intensity. For the moment, though, I could keep my personal feelings for him at a distance. While I normally preferred running my cons solo, I was extremely glad for Rabbit's presence. He brought a crucial set of skills to the mission, and having him at my side made me feel safer.

God, I'm in such trouble.

Chapter Six

RABBIT

Early afternoon, the plane slipped below the cloud layer, and the blue of the ocean was replaced by the purples and grays of mountains. Before long, the plane rolled along another private landing strip next to a handful of hangars. It came to a stop next to another anonymous sedan, this one with its trunk open. The amount of effort Zane's crew had expended to stay under the radar made me think someone had spent too much time watching action flicks. They were determined to wipe their footprints away, and that amount of dedication was worrisome and over-the-top cautious.

When the attendant finally allowed us to disembark, I took the lead, ignoring Jinx's frown. As I stood in the open doorway, the cool air hit me, bringing the scent of fir and snow despite the bright sunlight. We made our way across the tarmac to the waiting car and its driver.

"Welcome to Denver," he said as I deftly stepped in and helped Jinx slide into the seat.

Jinx flashed the driver one of Elena's coolly professional

smiles and made an indistinct murmur as she settled in. One of the ground crew hustled by with our luggage, its wheels rattling over the tarmac. He set them inside the trunk and slammed it closed before hurrying off into the nearby hangar.

I straightened, feeling the moment the driver's attention shifted from Jinx to me. I turned my head and stared into the dark lenses hiding his eyes. The hair on the back of my neck rose in primitive warning. I shifted back to close Jinx's door. This man wasn't as obvious as the one who'd picked us up outside Elena's condo, but he was definitely an operator. He turned to face me. It wasn't his build, which was more like mine, but the way he adjusted his balance that gave away his training.

As Elena's bodyguard, I had a point to make, so I stood there, silently holding his gaze, waiting for him to get in before I left Jinx's door. The seconds ticked by as we engaged in our silent standoff. With the barest dip of his chin, he relented and yanked his door open. Only when he was in the car did I walk around to the passenger side and join Jinx in the back seat.

As I clipped my belt into place, the driver aimed a glance through the rearview mirror, his jaw tightening, before his attention moved forward. I kept my grin to myself, knowing exactly what worried him. From the back passenger seat, I held the ideal position should we no longer need his services. I wasn't planning on making that move, but he didn't know that.

We left the landing strip behind. Roughly three-quarters of an hour later, after navigating through downtown Denver, we left the busy tree-lined road and turned into the covered entryway of a six-story brick building. A couple of high-priced sedans were parked in the adjacent lot, but otherwise, it was quiet.

Our car stopped at the lobby doors, and as the engine shut off, a valet stepped forward to open my door. "Welcome to Paradiso Plaza."

I stepped out, psychically tagging the discreetly placed cameras. The valet moved to the trunk and pulled out our cases as the driver trailed Jinx around the bumper. He stayed to speak to the valet, his voice too low to catch, while Jinx came to my side. The valet nodded and motioned a hovering bellman over to collect the luggage then closed the trunk, took the keys from the driver, and moved to the driver's seat, leaving the bellman to hustle over with our bags.

Once the hospitality dance ended, our driver joined us. "If you'll follow me, I'll show you to your condo."

We followed him into the comfortable but luxurious lobby, which was a perfect blend of casual money and elegance. Sunlight streamed through the art deco windows that stretched two stories and framed a panoramic view of Denver's skyline. We followed the driver across the starburst pattern set in the veined tiles and passed the massive fireplace. The front desk was discreetly tucked to the side. A grand staircase, complete with a wrought-iron railing, curved toward the second floor, creating a unique nook for the elevators underneath.

Our driver headed straight for the elevators. We followed. The bellman's spiel started up as he kept pace with us, barely taking a breath as we piled into the elevator. He ran through the condo's amenities, his list ending just before the elevator's doors opened on the sixth floor.

We stepped out into a plush carpeted hallway. The bellman helpfully explained that there were only four private residences on this end of the hall. Elena's new employers were far from cheap bastards if they provided accommodations like these.

As we walked, I loosened the hold on my psychic ability just enough to pinpoint the security cameras lining the hall and monitoring the elevators, their active electrical signatures holding a steady vibration. We were being watched or, more likely, recorded. No surprise there. Moving about without attracting attention could be challenging, but then, I was always up for a challenge. Maybe I'd carve out some time and dig up the building's blueprints, just in case I had a sudden urge to visit the security offices.

We stopped at the second-to-last door on the left. While the bellman waited off to the side, our driver punched in a code on the electronic lock. He pushed open the thick door, stood aside, and waved us in. "After you."

Jinx and I stepped through and followed the hardwood floors, which swept by a kitchen with gleaming stainless steel set against warm earth tones into an open-concept floor plan. Jinx set her phone and sunglasses on the granite ledge of the bar-height island and slowly walked into the living room. The combined dining room and living room was impressively huge. Light spilled through the doors leading to a private balcony and spread across a subtly patterned area rug.

An inviting leather sofa sectional and two armchairs surrounded a custom-made, burnished, low-slung table that sat in front of the show-stopping fireplace. Slate ran from the mantel to the ceiling high above, turning the wall into a statement piece.

I tossed my sunglasses next to hers and followed her as she went to the French doors leading to the balcony. When she stepped outside, I was right behind her. We left our driver and bellman standing in the living room.

I joined Jinx at the railing. I hated to admit it, but the place was damn impressive. From where we stood, we had an uninterrupted view of the mountains against the blue sky, while a carpet of green, interspersed with the downtown district's glass-and-steel profiles, spread out below. Even more impressive, the balcony stretched along the entire side of the apartment, a partial wall separating us from what I was betting was the bedroom portion of the deck.

Next to me, Jinx murmured, "God, it's gorgeous."

"Ms. Drake, Mr. Somers," the driver said from behind us, "if you don't mind, I'll show you the rest of the condo."

Jinx took her time leaving the balcony. I stayed at her side as we both headed back inside. Our driver led us through the rest of the space, explaining the condo's concierge services and the plethora of nearby shopping, dining, and entertainment options available in Cherry Creek.

I'd revised my assessment of *huge* to *fucking huge* by the time he was finished. The condo was almost as big as a house. I understood that this place was meant to impress, and it most certainly did. In the real world—the one where people didn't make their livings from criminal investments —shelling out for a place like this was all about appearances. Once a visitor got past the astonishment at how this place looked, there wasn't much to it. It was as devoid of personality as its owners were of morals. Hell, my childhood home might have been an older shotgun house down south, but it held more personality than this showstopper.

When the driver's practiced spiel wound down, Jinx

made her opening gambit. "Please be sure to thank Mr. Seward for his generous accommodations."

Knowing her the way I did, I didn't find her comment unexpected, but it took the driver off guard. His polite mask slipped for a second, revealing a flat, predatory consideration that set my hackles on end. He quickly got his shit together and managed a pleasant response. "I'll be sure to do that." No doubt, he'd waste no time reporting that Elena had identified Zane as her benefactor. "If there is nothing else I can assist with, I'll leave you both to settle in." When neither Jinx nor I said anything, he gave us a nod, turned on his heel, and walked down the hall, the bellman trotting in his wake.

After the door latched with a soft click, I turned to Jinx. "Shall we unpack?"

"Sounds good." She reclaimed her phone and headed down the hall toward the bedroom.

I grabbed our luggage from the entryway and joined her. As I walked through the condo, I decided to check on just how close an eye was being kept on Elena's activities. One of the benefits of my ability was being able to use it without showing any telltale signs. Unlike my initial scan of the hall, this time, I wanted confirmation of exactly what we might be facing. For an in-depth scan, I would need to do more than simply loosen my psychic grip. This kind of job required dropping the mental gate between me and the unseen world of energy generated by all things electronic.

Lowering my mental wall, I braced myself as an overwhelming barrage of electronic noise rushed in like a deafening wave. Only a lifetime of practice enabled me to withstand the initial impact while I adjusted the volume. Once I was able to navigate the interference of everyday electronics, pinpointing the distinctive signals spread throughout the condo wasn't hard.

The unique signals hit my senses like mini-novas, lighting up my nerve endings. There was one near the entryway, one in the kitchen, and two in the main living area that, based on their differing electronic signatures, were spaced at opposite sides of the room to ensure coverage. Tightening my focus, I took my time to carefully scan the hall and the bedroom even as I continued to put clothes away. Jinx took our toiletries into the bedroom's en suite bathroom. I stretched my senses, unsurprised when the hall came up clean. When I pulled my senses into the bedroom, a cold anger settled in my veins. I counted four devices there.

Why in the hell did they put that many in a highly private space smaller than the living room? It was overkill, unless there was another reason for the excessive coverage. Being the type of male who occasionally drifted into less-than-polite thoughts, my icy anger shifted into a primitive, possessive fury. No way in hell was that going to fly.

A warm hand landed on my back, followed by Jinx's soft "Mercer, are you all right?"

Her touch unlocked my frozen position over the open luggage. A pair of pants was crushed in my white-knuckled hands. "I'm good." I forced my hands to relax and gave her a smile. "Did you want to set up in the office?"

Jinx was no one's fool, and standing so close to me, she wouldn't have missed my tension or my less-than-amused smile. She studied my face. "Sure, but let's finish here first before we check out what we'll be working with."

Ruthlessly controlling my urge to fry the eavesdropping electronics, I held tight to my role. "Because heaven forbid we leave anything unpacked."

Jinx gave one of Elena's husky laughs. "You know how crazy it makes me if things aren't in order."

"Yeah, I do. Let me hang these up, and we'll get on that." Pants in hand, I turned away and stepped into the oversized walk-in closet, calling back, "I think we should enact zeta protocol while we're here." I draped my pants over the hanger.

"You sure that's wise?" Her voice was close.

I turned to find her at the door of the closet. She raised a brow in silent question, and I did a barely there head-shake. The closet was clear of surveillance, which gave us some privacy.

"Considering how hard they're working to keep you in the dark, yes." I shifted my gaze to the room behind her and lifted four fingers, giving her a number. When I met her green-tinted eyes again, a hardness lay under them. *Yeah, she got my message loud and clear.*

"How many times have I told you, there is no such thing as anonymity?" She didn't move back as I stepped forward. Until she decided to move, I wasn't getting through the doorway.

Left with little choice, I stopped in front of her. I swore I could feel a sharpening in the attention behind the electronic bugs. *Oh yeah, someone's a voyeuristic bastard.* Not sure how obvious she wanted to make Elena and Mercer's relationship, I folded my arms. "It's not me you have to convince."

"Oh, I know." She tilted her head back and reached up to curl a hand around the back of my neck. Acceding to her gentle pressure, I lowered my head until she could brush her lips over mine. My hands went to her hips, and I held her close, unable to resist her touch. When she drew back, she brushed her thumb over my lower lip, adding an unmistakable intimacy. Even though I knew it was a deliberate play for those watching, my body's reaction was all too real.

Unfortunately for my peace of mind, she wasn't done making her point. She turned, moved back into the bedroom, and picked up her phone from the dresser. I followed, wrestling my hunger into a contained ball. I stopped to lean against the doorjamb of the closet and watched as she gave the space a leisurely visual scan. Her fingers swept over the screen of her phone as she did a deliberate circuit of the room.

I wasn't surprised that when her attention came anywhere close to one of the bugs, the signal went quiet, the psychic nova dimming to barely there. The person monitoring was trying to remain undetectable and would have succeeded if it had been anyone but me on the opposing side. When Jinx's attention came back to me, her fingers stilled over the phone's screen. Heeding the warning in her eyes, I reached out and wrapped my psychic hand around the electronic trail of each bug.

She sashayed to the spot directly in front of me and held up her phone, her thumb poised over the screen. "Let the games begin." Her thumb pressed down.

I tightened my psychic grip and, with ruthless satisfaction, snapped the electronic cords to the bugs, dousing the starbursts into nothing. To the ones watching, Elena had just blacked out their bugs.

In front of me, Jinx kept her back to the room and murmured, "Are we clear?"

I did a psychic sweep for confirmation and came up clean. "Yeah," I answered in an equally low voice. "Still have eyes and ears in the main room, kitchen, and entryway."

She tossed her phone on the dresser and turned away to pace. "We don't have much time."

She was absolutely right. I predicted it would be maybe two minutes before her phone rang or someone knocked on the door. "So far, they're following expectations. I'm not sure how much longer that will last. No matter what, we don't separate."

She turned to me. "You're worried about whatever test they're going to throw at us."

I didn't rush to answer, because the words rising to be freed would spark an argument I had no hope of winning. *She's your partner, not your lover.*

The reminder did nothing to ease my concerns. The minute we'd started this game, I left *worried* behind and began moving toward *highly concerned*. It didn't matter how much I trusted her abilities as an agent— something about this situation brought to mind the butterfly effect. One tiny mistake could blow this whole operation straight to hell, taking both of us with it.

It was bad enough that we were forced to juggle a variety of unknowns, but my biggest worry was that Jinx's extraordinary ability couldn't mimic the real-life decisions of a near-genius immoral hacker. Considering what I knew of Elena from her files and interrogation videos, she had no compunction about the fallout from her creations and wouldn't even blink at whatever test Seward and company threw her way. Loss of innocent lives didn't factor against the almighty dollar.

No matter how much Jinx looked like Elena, under the surface, she couldn't scratch that level of soullessness. If Jinx balked even the barest breath at the test—and no doubt, there would be a test—Seward and his bosses would be all over her ass.

She stopped pacing and placed a hand on my arm. "I've got this." She squeezed. "We've got this."

Where the hell is your head, boy? After crowing to Jinx that I could keep my emotions out of this, I was failing in a spectacular fashion. The middle of a mission was not the time or place to give emotion-fueled fear the field. Rabbit, the man, had no place in this room. Wyatt Tessier, the operative, needed to step the fuck up. Hell, these asinine thoughts hadn't even surfaced during my partnership with Jinx until I let my dick get in the way. She was damn good at her job, and questioning her skills at this point was a lethal kind of stupid.

Kicking the mental mess aside, I blew out a breath and gave her a grim smile. "Yeah, we've got this."

She searched my face long enough to make me want to squirm. I managed not to give in, and fortunately, her phone rang. She went to the dresser and picked it up. "Yes." Her gaze came to mine, then her eyes narrowed as her jaw tightened. "There is no reason to monitor my bedroom." Clearly, whoever was on the other end had picked the wrong tone, because there was enough ice in her voice to shrivel a male's pride and joy. "I agreed to work for Mr. Seward, not be a star in his or his employer's prurient fantasies." Her fingers whitened on the phone. "You go ahead and do that, and while you're tattling, I'll be making other arrangements as I'm no longer comfortable here." She paused, listening to whatever excuse they spouted, before cutting in. "I wasn't asking for permission." Another pause. "No." A longer pause, this time accompanied by the drumming of her fingers against the dresser's top. "No, no driver. We'll get our own transportation." Then finally, she said, "Two hours."

She hung up, a satisfied gleam in her eye. "We've been

invited to dine with Mr. Seward so he can offer a personal apology for the unfortunate oversight in his surveillance."

That's one way to label it. "An oversight?" I straightened but stayed in the closet doorway as I studied her.

She nodded.

"So that's what they're calling it?"

She curled her lip. "I'd rather call it like I see it—insulting."

And Elena would find it highly insulting, so much so that she would easily walk away from this deal that she wasn't completely sold on in the first place. Unfortunately, unlike Elena, we needed to stay in the deal, which left Jinx navigating a shaky line. And based on the crafty consideration in Jinx's face, she had a plan—something that would fit with Elena's natural disdain for Zane and his employers.

"You're going to make them work for it," I said.

She arched a brow, her smile more of a sneer. "Of course I am." The hard, arrogant lines in her face eased into something more natural. "But before I do that, you are going to be the voice of reason and talk me into hearing Mr. Seward out."

Curious, I asked, "Is that so?"

"Who else would make sure I don't lose sight of the strategic advantage to this particular deal?" The look she gave me was all Jinx. "That is, of course, why you work for me, isn't it?"

At her comment, her ploy came together. For someone like Elena to consider Mercer a partner, he would need to offer more than his skills in the bedroom and office. Perhaps he would be the voice of reason for a woman who was prone to arrogance and theatrics. Those skills would be vital, say, if she discovered she was being spied upon and threw a temper tantrum that threatened to derail a rather lucrative deal. That kind of drama would force Mercer to showcase his skills and talk her off the dramatic ledge. It was the perfect scene to ensure that those watching grasped the importance of keeping him at her side. It was manipulative as hell, but it just might work.

As much as I admired the play, I couldn't help but wonder how much it irritated Jinx, who tended to view the male sex with a jaundiced eye, to play such a submissive role. But that was something to ponder when our asses weren't hanging out there. Refocusing, I searched for the best stage to play out our scene. "Head to the living room."

Confusion wrinkled her brow. "What?"

"Storm into the living room, then call on your inner drama llama and start ranting and raving about trust in professional relationships." I nudged her toward the hall. "I'll be right behind you, talking you back into calm rationality."

Her confusion cleared. "Got it."

I caught her hand before she hit the hall. "Remember, make me work for it."

She shot me a wicked look over her shoulder. "Don't I always?"

Chapter Seven

JINX

The address we were given was remarkably close to our condo, but as we stopped outside an exclusive neighborhood guarded by an impressive security gate, it became clear that the only thing the two addresses shared was possibly a zip code. After Rabbit punched in the code we'd been given, the gate rolled back, allowing entrance.

"Well, at least the car won't stick out like a sore thumb," I murmured as Rabbit drove our high-end rental sedan through the opening.

"Did a little checking before we left," Rabbit said. "The average house here goes anywhere from four to seven million."

I gave a soundless whistle. "I'm suitably impressed."

Rabbit's attention stayed on the road, but his lips curved up. "I think that was the point."

Considering where Zane had chosen to hold our initial meeting and his need to play lord of the manor, this second location would no doubt be just as blatant in its show of money and power. As we heeded the low speed limit and cruised through the neighborhood, we passed large lots that stated clearly that the homeowners were not keen on rubbing elbows with their neighbors. If the community's designers were hoping to transport the owners of these houses to another world, they'd definitely succeeded. Long driveways curved inward while brick walls flanked by trees allowed the barest glimpses of the homes sitting deep within the lots' interiors. Dense and green, the foliage was a verdant curtain separating those inside from the drab real world rumbling outside the gates.

It was difficult to reconcile this lush oasis with the everyday buzz of urban life zipping along on the other side of the walls. A person didn't live here just for the pricey showpiece home. Nope, it was obvious what the ultimate prize was—privacy.

The lifestyle was tempting for those who could afford it. Once upon a time, I would have done anything for that kind of peace and quiet, especially after growing up in over-crowded urban centers where space and privacy were luxuries few could afford and necessities were earned the hard way. Only after I'd survived a number of missions that took place behind similarly guarded walls was the wish to live in this kind of neighborhood finally snuffed out. Some of the dirtiest secrets swam behind the bright smiles and picture-perfect lives. When light dispersed those shadows, the ugliest truths were revealed, wearing the shine right off of my rose-colored glasses.

Now when I looked at this neighborhood like this, draped in all its gorgeousness, all I could see was a disturbing kind of beauty. "Creepy."

I didn't realize I'd spoken aloud until Rabbit asked, "What's that?"

Turning away from yet another mini McMansion, I answered, "This place gives me the creeps."

Lines appeared in Rabbit's brow as he shot me a quick look. "So, you're not into the posh mansion-on-the-hill lifestyle?"

"At what point did I ever give you that idea?" I didn't wait for his response. "This isn't normal." Not wanting to get into the dark demons nibbling at my mind, I waved a hand at the immaculate yards and chose one of the minor examples of creepiness. "What do the landscaping people do—use a damn ruler on the lawns? Make sacrifices to the lawn gods?"

"And what kind of sacrifice is required to appease a lawn god?" Rabbit teased.

I shrugged. "I don't know. Maybe an abundance of compost? A rusted rake? A pile of weeds, complete with bared roots, thrown into a stone-lined fire pit? Blood of those who dare to overwater?" Even as Rabbit snorted, I kept going. "I mean, everything is just so… perfect. It's creepy." A tiny shudder ran down my spine.

Rabbit chuckled and shook his head. "Seriously?"

"Yeah, seriously. If we're greeted by a smiling wife and two kids or some manic scarecrow-looking dude, I'm bailing."

Rabbit laughed at my overly dramatic but heartfelt comment. "I don't think we have to worry about the Stepford family being part of tonight's entertainment or a horror-film reject taking us out. I'm fairly certain the picture-perfect yards are an HOA requirement, not the result of arcane rituals."

"Maybe." Poking fun at the weirdness created by a homeowners' association alleviated some of the low-level tension that followed us from the condo.

Rabbit's hand found mine and squeezed. "You okay?"

Guess my distraction attempt failed. I squeezed his hand back. "I'm good." With our final location looming closer, I got back on track. "Were you able to link Zane or Falcon to this address?"

Rabbit shook his head. "I didn't have enough time to unravel the ownership records before we had to leave."

"You think it will be that easy to find?"

His hands tightened on the steering wheel. "Probably not. The owner's buried pretty deep, so someone's hiding something."

I sighed. "And that never bodes well." I looked back out the window, trying to ignore the low-level disquiet sitting like a rock in my gut. In the world of lies and shadows, proof tended to be as elusive as a unicorn. "I know it's early in the game, but it would be nice to know who we're really playing against instead of assuming it's Falcon."

"It would," Rabbit agreed. "But until that happens, we go with what we have."

"Which is?"

"The property is currently held in a trust."

I shifted in my seat. "Is that normal?"

Rabbit nodded. "For an exclusive property like this? It's not unheard-of. Most of the time, it's part of estate planning —especially when the homeowner is trying to bypass tax liabilities incurred with inheritance taxes."

It was my turn to snort. "I don't think anyone's worried about taxes."

"Probably not," Rabbit said. "But it's also a great way to mask ownership."

That didn't ease my tension. "Which means anyone could be lying in wait for us tonight."

"I don't think it'll be that dire, but…"

I prompted, "But?"

He shot me a look, his face dark, before he turned back to his driving. "But you know how I warned you that they'd test Elena before giving her the actual job?"

I nodded.

"That does worry me."

It didn't take a genius to follow his thoughts, because those same concerns had kept sleep a stranger for the last couple of days. God only knew what we'd be asked to do and how far we'd have to push our personal lines to keep our cover intact. *Or how far I'll have to stretch mine.* I shoved the dark thought aside. "Yeah, me too."

We fell silent as Rabbit made a right into one of the driveways. It coiled around, and when he took the last curve, a house appeared ahead, a modern take on the English manor. As expected, it was a showpiece. Towering trees stood guard around the light stone structure, adding shade to the arched windows but not brushing the gray peaked roofs.

The drive bypassed the front entrance and wound around to what appeared to be a small carriage house. Rabbit parked and shut off the engine. An oversized wooden door decorated in wrought iron swung open, revealing a human-shaped shadow. Thanks to the angle of the slowly sinking sun, I couldn't make out details.

Rabbit said in a bare murmur, "Ready?"

"As ready I'm going to get," I responded just as quietly.

Rabbit got out and came around to open my door. I took the hand he offered and kept it as we moved toward the waiting figure. At that point, considering our latest play to our host, there was no sense in hiding Mercer and Elena's supposed romantic relationship, especially as we wanted to cement the necessity of keeping Mercer close to her.

Rabbit and I were aware that tonight's dinner was the opening move in a very dangerous game. Zane or his bosses, or both, would test Elena's skills. I tried not to think too much about exactly what that test would entail. Considering the immoral bastards we suspected we were dealing with, I had a feeling it would leave a mark. Hopefully, it wouldn't be as deep as some of the ones I already carried.

"Elena, Mercer, welcome."

Rabbit and I came to a stop. Recognizing the voice, I answered with a polite but tight "Zane."

"Come in, please." He stepped aside and waved us in.

I held my position and Zane's flat gaze. "After you."

Zane gave a sharp smile, tilted his head in acknowledgement, then turned on his heel to lead the way. With Rabbit at my back, I followed Zane through a house meant to elicit oohs and aahs. Alert for unseen threats, I was unmoved, which was a good thing because the glitz wouldn't faze Elena in the slightest. Hell, she would expect it.

Exchanging the typical pleasantries, Zane led us into what was obviously the study—from the stone fireplace to the high-gloss-polished bar and the cluster of leather chairs. The paneled walls held portraits, landscapes, and medieval weaponry. We strode by a full suit of armor. Thanks to my childhood training at spotting a fake—a necessary skill when running a con—I could tell it was a damn good replica. Most obviously, it was too tall. The armor was an expensive replica, for sure, but not priceless. All in all, I could tell that someone was highly enamored of English aristocracy.

"What can I get you to drink?" Zane took a spot behind the bar like the good host he was mimicking. "Elena, an old-fashioned for you?"

"Please." I settled into one of the chairs, unsurprised when Rabbit chose to remain standing.

Zane's attention shifted to Rabbit. "Mr. Somers?"

"It's Mercer," Rabbit corrected. "Whiskey neat."

"We have Auchentoshan '78 or eighteen-year-old Glenmorangie." Zane set out the glasses and grabbed the nearby bottles.

"Auchentoshan."

He paused in his pour and shot Rabbit a small smile before going back to his task. "I prefer the Glenmorangie myself."

If Zane was expecting Rabbit to reply, he was bound to be disappointed. He spent the next couple of minutes preparing our drinks and bringing them over. I took mine with a murmur of thanks.

Zane handed Rabbit his and motioned to a chair. "Sit, please. Make yourself comfortable. Dinner will be ready shortly. I hope you like beef." He heeded his own advice, dropping into a chair before taking a sip of whiskey.

As Zane and I did the polite dance of small pleasantries, Rabbit took his time sitting as Zane and I talked for a few minutes.

"Will anyone else be joining us?" Rabbit finally asked.

"No, it will just be us tonight, I'm afraid." Zane met my gaze. "I'd like to offer my sincere apologies for the scene earlier today. That condo is one commonly used for various guests, some of whom require delicate handling."

I gave a soft snort of disbelief and set my drink aside. "Don't soft-soap things, Zane. Those cameras are there to blackmail your guests. While I understand the necessity of acquiring leverage, in this case, I find it highly offensive as you came to me, not the other way around."

He half hid his anger behind an uncomfortable grimace. "I understand your anger and can only reassure you that the situation has been remedied. I hope it doesn't impact our relationship moving forward."

Prior to arriving, Rabbit and I had agreed on an approach. Zane's rote apology gave us an opening, and I took it without hesitation, setting us on our predetermined path. "If I'm being truthful, I was more than ready to leave. However"—I shot a look at Rabbit before switching my attention to Zane—"I was reminded of the potential advantages of your proposed partnership."

"Again, I can only offer my regrets and assure you that your privacy is no longer an issue."

Oh, he's good. There was enough sincerity in his voice that if I hadn't known about the bugs still active in the other parts of the condo, I might have believed him. "We shall see." I didn't miss the flash of frustrated anger at my disdainful comment. To ensure that he understood that Elena had claws of her own, I added, "Fair warning, Zane. Should a recording of tonight's interactions surface at some point, that program that fried your little spies will be a cakewalk compared to what I do to your network."

Zane's fingers on his glass whitened even though he managed to hang on to his pleasant expression. "A threat, Elena?"

I gave him a sweet smile that I knew damn well didn't reach my eyes. "I don't make threats, Zane. They're a waste of my time."

Zane's jaw tightened as he held my eyes.

"Elena," Rabbit murmured, breaking our staring contest. I lowered my eyes, eased back, and reclaimed my drink.

Zane turned to Rabbit. "Mercer, tell me about yourself."

Rabbit swirled his whiskey, his gaze sharp. "I'm sure your investigators uncovered all the high points."

Over the rim of the glass, I watched the two men verbally circle each other and fought to hide my grin. Rabbit's skills at baiting targets would make this interesting if not downright fun.

"Yes, you have quite the list of accomplishments," Zane said. "You're a Berkeley grad—top of your class, in fact— and had a highly decorated career in the navy. With all that drive, I find it curious that you ended up as Elena's assistant."

A lash of derision colored the last word, and my hand tightened on the cut crystal.

Rabbit didn't pause before responding, "She offers excellent benefits."

At his deadpan delivery, I barely managed to choke off my snort of amusement.

A sneer crept into Zane's pleasant expression. "Well, your skills are obviously valued, as Elena made sure to nego- tiate your presence here."

Unmoved, Rabbit held his gaze. "A smart move on her part, considering…" He tilted his glass toward Zane.

His dig hit its mark, and a flush colored Zane's face.

This time, I didn't bother to stifle my laugh. "Enough, Zane. Baiting Mercer won't end well. If you continue to do so, it will only upset him, which in turn will upset me." I set my drink aside and rose. "As dinner isn't ready, show me your home."

Backed into a corner, Zane gave in to manners. We spent the next thirty minutes wandering through the house. Through well-chosen random questions, I found out Zane considered this his winter home. Unfortunately, I wasn't able to pry anything more helpful out of him before we all sat down to dinner.

Conversation during the meal was like a walk through a minefield. For the most part, our talk was confined to surface gambits and remained civil. But something about the Mercer persona kept ruffling Zane's fur, so much so that he continued his not-so-subtle digs. Each one shoved the underlying tension higher, yet Rabbit showed no sign of snapping. The longer the dinner went, the more I wondered at Zane's behavior. Needling Mercer wasn't smart unless there was a specific reason behind it.

Before I could figure out what that reason was, the remains of dinner were whisked away by a silently efficient server I recognized as our airport chauffeur. Rabbit wasn't the only one with multiple talents. Obviously, Zane wasn't as comfortable with us as he appeared—hence, the bodyguard-driver doing double duty as a butler.

With the table cleared and a full pot of coffee in front of him, Zane finally shifted the conversation to the matter at hand. "It's my understanding that congratulations are in order."

Not quite sure where he was going with this, I asked, "Are they?"

Zane inclined his head. "Your influence with the Areñas situation was quite inspired. It was actually what convinced my employer to approach you."

I did a quick mental review of Elena's file. It didn't take me long to place the name. Elena had delivered a customized virus program to a black-market weapons runner who was pissed when the Areñas cartel shorted him on his profits. Although the Areñas cartel was a relatively small fish swimming in an ocean ruled by one of Mexico's bigger sharks, Los Zetas, Elena's take-home pay for the job had been three million dollars.

"Is that so?" I said. "And here I thought it was the general's recommendation that caught your attention."

Zane pushed back his chair, angling it so he could stretch out his legs. He cupped his hand around his coffee cup and raised it in a half toast. "Not directly. Granted, the general heard about the fallout down south first and did some digging, but when he ran out of leads, he brought it to our attention. It took an impressive bit of research for us to find out the particulars, including your role, and that"—he pointed a finger at me without letting go of his cup—"was what actually fascinated us." He sipped his coffee.

I wasn't sure that kind of interest was a good thing. "*Fascinated* is an unusual word choice."

"But it fits." He leaned in and set his cup on the table. The look he shot me was filled with speculation. "You managed to redirect a weapons shipment Areñas promised to their allies—a rival gang, in fact. You did it while padding Areñas's financials. When the unhappy and empty-handed buyer found the money in the Areñas account, he was highly displeased."

That was putting it mildly. Areñas had managed to cultivate a partnership of sorts with a local gang, Diablos de Sangre, or DDS. When the weapons shipment failed to show, DDS went after Areñas's number-two man, Luis Rivera, because of the financial trail Elena had laid. Thanks to a last-minute itinerary change and an unknown affair, DDS's hit squad not only eliminated Rivera but the wife of Areñas's leader as well. It was a Machiavellian move that would have been admirable if not for the people it involved. Next to me, Rabbit angled closer, his arm stretching over the back of my chair, obviously concerned about where this was heading.

"The cartel is still scrambling to regroup, trying to excuse the poor behavior of their now-dead lieutenant." Zane cocked his head. "Whose idea was it to frame Areñas's lieutenant?"

Clever boy, but it takes more than that to trip me up. Stepping around his question, I used the details from the classified file I'd committed to memory. "Rivera was notoriously tight-fisted, so it wasn't hard to redirect a few funds into a hidden account. Add in his proclivity for taking what didn't belong to him, and it was an easy sell."

"And you still managed to stay in the shadows while pocketing a pretty profit." He lifted his cup. "Well played."

All this ass-kissing was getting on my nerves. It was too calculated to ring true. "As much as I appreciate the compliment, I'm here and listening, so there's no need to convince me to work with you." Propping my elbows on the table, I interlaced my fingers and rested my chin on top. "Why don't we get down to why I'm actually here? What exactly do you expect my help with?"

The muscles in Rabbit's arm tensed against my shoulders, but he maintained his casual pose, legs sprawled, one hand holding an after-drink and the other playing with the tendrils of hair along my neck.

"Refreshingly blunt." The slight stiffening of Zane's shoulders belied his amicable observation. "What a nice change."

Mustering a soft but audible sigh, I sat back. Rabbit's fingers brushed over my shoulder, a subtle reminder to tread carefully. I took my time crossing my legs and smoothing out my skirt. "I find it best to keep discussions focused. Games are a waste of both time and money." I lifted my eyes to

Zane's and kept my face blank and my gaze hard. "I don't like wasting either of those things."

Zane's mouth curved into an all-out grin. "And that puts me in my place, doesn't it?"

In keeping with Elena's cucumber-cool reputation, I lifted an eyebrow and managed to a droll response. "If that's how you want to view it." I waited for his chuckle to die down before I asked, "Now, shall we discuss whatever it is you want me to do?"

Zane shook his head, his humor draining away. "Nothing as elaborate as the Areñas job. In fact, this should be rather straightforward for you."

I sipped my coffee and waited.

"We'd like to request an identity verification."

That was not the kind of job I was expecting. For one, it was way too simple. Background checks, even deep ones, were easy enough to do with a modicum of technical expertise. Frowning, I lowered my cup to the table. "You kidnapped me, demanding exclusivity of both my time and skills, for a background check?" I didn't bother masking my disbelief.

Zane's pleasant expression took on a hard edge. "This goes well beyond a background check."

My curiosity was sparked. "How so?"

His attention shifted between Rabbit and me, but instead of answering my question, he explained in an empty voice, "Recently, there have been some questionable coincidences during specific business transactions that share a common denominator."

Translation: someone was interfering with Zane's illegal dealings. My first thought was, *Well, boo-fucking-hoo.* My second was, *Which transactions?* Considering that neither could be shared safely, I kept my mouth shut.

Rabbit didn't. "Let me guess. The common denominator is the individual you want Elena to investigate." It wasn't a question.

Mouth tight, eyes dark, Zane replied in a strained voice, "Yes."

I wasn't sure what part of Rabbit's statement was upsetting Zane, but as I had explained earlier, I wasn't into games. "What's the name?" My question cut through the rising tension and redirected Zane's attention back to me.

"Amalia Black." Zane sat up and turned to call out, "John."

As if he'd been waiting for the summons, Zane's jack-of-all-trades reappeared, carrying a file. He made his way to Zane and handed it over. Zane took it and tapped a corner against the table as John disappeared into whatever corner he'd been hiding in.

"This is our initial check." Zane pushed the file across the table.

I pulled it close and opened it, angling it so Rabbit could read over my shoulder. The initial report was impressively detailed, like any good deep-background check. I scanned through the pages until I hit a photograph. Pulling it free, I studied the target.

A sable-haired woman was caught in profile, her eyes hidden behind sunglasses and her attention on someone off to the side and out of frame. The casualness of the shot meant she hadn't been aware it was being taken. Something about her seemed familiar, but with a strangely tense Zane sitting across from me, this was not the time to play footsie with my memory.

I set the photo facedown with the previous pages and continued flipping through the rest of the report. By the time I finished, I had an idea of why this was Elena's first job. It was probably a pretest of sorts, because there was something off about Amalia that I couldn't put my finger on. Yet.

For appearance's sake, I asked, "Considering how detailed this report is, what exactly are you looking for?"

"Who she really is." Zane's strange blank expression was a dead giveaway that this went beyond professional and dipped right into personal.

My guess was that he was heavily involved with this woman. I tapped the file absent-mindedly, watching him, and asked a question that was more me than Elena. "How close did she get to you?"

Zane's gaze flickered, and when it steadied, it carried an edge of anger. "Close."

The brush of Rabbit's fingers against the nape of my neck refocused my curiosity and triggered a curl of heat that had no place in this situation. My voice emerged a bit lower, which I hoped Zane would attribute to the delicate nature of my questions and not Rabbit's touch. "How long has she been with you?"

The hand Zane had on the table curled into a fist, his knuckles whitening. "Close to two years."

Oh yeah, Zane is not a happy camper. An unhappy Zane could not be good for this Amalia chick. I almost felt sorry for her. Almost.

"Two years?" Rabbit asked with a hint of cynical disbelief. "And you're just now asking questions?" He shook his head slowly, his gaze never leaving Zane's. "Either she's a hell of a game player, or you're about to make a big mistake."

"My mistake to make." Zane's smile was tight and grim. "And should your research prove it is a mistake, she'll never know it was even a question."

I swallowed a snort of disbelief. Boy, Zane was delusional if he really believed that Amalia wouldn't find out. In my experience, things like this tended to backfire in a big, damaging way.

"And if she's playing games?" Rabbit pressed.

Zane gave an elegant shrug. "If that's the case, I'll deal with it as needed."

"But," I said, regaining Zane's attention, "you expect me to find proof she's betraying you."

"As I've said before, I don't believe in coincidence."

Rabbit shifted, set his drink on the table, and folded his arms. "Not to mention this is a test. Yours or your boss's?" There was no missing the challenge in his voice.

A muscle in Zane's jaw tightened, but he said nothing.

His. Definitely his. In keeping with Elena's professional ego, I let my lips curl with amusement and lifted the folder. "This is your idea of a test?" I tossed it on the table and shifted my smile to a sneer. "I was expecting something more… challenging."

Zane's expression—something dark and indefinable lurking in his eyes—made me feel a niggling unease. "Don't worry, Elena. Consider this the first of your… exams." He slowly uncurled his fist and flattened his palm against the table. "Something tells me this will be a worthy challenge for your skills."

Uneasy, I tapped a finger against the file, reviewing what little information I had. I was missing something important. To mask my concern, I murmured, "Your people made a good start." I met Zane's surety with cool arrogance. "I can work with this." I handed the file to Rabbit. "What's our deadline?"

Zane's expression turned smug. "Forty-eight hours."

I shared a look with Rabbit. "Saturday it is."

Chapter Eight

I didn't breathe easy until the iron gates of the ritzy neighborhood rolled closed behind us. In the passenger seat, Jinx was quiet. I wasn't in a rush to break the silence, but I wanted some distance between us and that cocky bastard, Zane. My mind buzzed with questions I couldn't ask until we were sure the car was clear of surveillance. Considering that the dinner lasted close to four hours, there'd been more than enough time to bug the car.

To play it safe and because I needed time to do my thing, I asked Jinx, "You want to head back?"

When she turned to me, I did a quick headshake.

Fortunately, she followed my lead. "Actually, why don't we find something that's open? Maybe get a drink somewhere?"

"Sounds good to me. How about we check out what's around Cherry Creek? I've heard they've got some great spots."

"I'm game." She fell quiet as I headed toward Cherry Creek and its bevy of bars and dining options.

Knowing that if we were being listened to, our silence would raise suspicions, I came to a stop sign and looked at her. "You're awfully quiet."

She shifted in her seat and tilted her head. "Just thinking." Then she mouthed, "Bugs?"

I nodded and watched her mouth thin. I hit the gas and, conscious of our roles, went with Mercer's obvious next question. "Worried about the job?"

"No, not the job."

"Seward?"

"More like his employers," she corrected, doing that finger tapping she'd taken to doing in her role as Elena. "I don't like being kept in the dark about who I'm working with, not to mention that this background run he's requesting is awfully mundane. As a test, it's negligible."

"I'm betting this has nothing to do with his boss and everything to do with him."

She rolled her eyes, indicating that she was quite aware of that, but said, "What do you mean?"

"Did you catch his reaction about this Black woman?" Catching her nod, I added, "This is highly personal."

"Personal enough that he's willing to keep it from his boss?"

"Think about how it would look if Seward was being screwed."

"In more ways than one," she muttered.

Her dry humor left me shaking my head. "That's not something someone like him would want his bosses to know."

She made a sound of agreement.

"Wouldn't be the first time we've dealt with someone taking advantage of your skills."

"True," she murmured.

"Got to admit, it leaves me all sorts of curious about this woman."

"You and me both," she said.

We left it at that as we turned into a more populated area where the buildings started to rise and spread along the streets. People wandered by storefronts dotted with colored lights. Traffic slowed as we moved deeper into the area.

Jinx leaned forward. "What about there?" A bustling group was gathered in front of what looked like a combo bar-and-music club. "Let's check that one out."

"Looks good to me." I kept an eye out for parking options. Finally, I drove around the block and found a parking lot tucked behind a building.

Parking underneath one of the lights, I grabbed the file, closed my door, and waited for Jinx to join me. Once she did, she took the file and tucked it into the oversize purse she carried. We walked away as I activated the car alarm. We were a few hundred feet out, at the edge of the lot, when I turned and wrapped my arms around her, pulling her in close. Not expecting my move, she flattened her hands against my chest as she made a startled noise and stared up into my face.

Even though we weren't close enough to be overheard, I dipped my head down until my mouth brushed her ear. "I need to check the car."

She hid her face in my neck, her breath warm against my skin. "Got it."

With Jinx in my arms, slumbering hunger stretched awake. I pushed through the familiar physical reaction and closed my eyes. Focusing my attention on the car behind us, I couldn't help but breathe in her uniquely warm spicy scent. It curled through me, brushing against the ever-present need to soothe the ragged edge of its demand.

My mind relatively clear, I stretched out that unique ability that was all mine and wove through the tapestry of electricity emanating from the parked vehicles. Once I identified the stable electrical pattern of our car's alarm from the low-level buzz of the surrounding alarms, I narrowed my concentration to the sedan. The sensation was like threading a needle. Slowly, I scanned our car from bumper to bumper, unsurprised when I hit an anomaly tucked under where the hood and front windshield met. *Yep, Zane tagged us.*

Identifying what kind of bug it was took a little more finesse. As I slid a little deeper into the psychic realm, my sense of self faded into the background until I was riding the electrical current into that sphere where only the hum of energy existed. Using the electronic traces as my guide, I navigated the minute signals, parsing out the purpose of each one—not an easy task, considering the refined nature of the bug.

It was a fairly sophisticated creation serving a dual purpose as both a tracker and a listening device. The bug was designed to identify audio waves by utilizing the sonic vibrations of the glass. Most people didn't understand the lethal and benevolent aspects of the highly complex world of sound. In this case, we could have turned on the radio to cause a low level of interference, but it wouldn't have been enough to mask the conversation completely, especially if someone had access to a good audio program designed to isolate various wavelengths. And Zane no doubt had the right tools if he was using this kind of tech.

The brush of heat against my jaw pulled me back from my fascination and reminded me that I was more than another energy signature—I was attached to blood and bone. A soft feminine murmur hit my ear. "Rabbit, come back to me."

Her words and her soft touch replaced the mesmerizing draw of energy. I blinked my eyes open, only to wince when a sharp spike of pain lanced behind my left eye. I drew my head back. "Ow."

Jinx reached up and cupped my jaw, holding me still as she studied me, concern clear in her gaze. "You went too deep."

"Yeah." I rubbed a temple. "Damn, I hate when that happens." One of the drawbacks to my ability was not being able to tell when I went too deep after what I was tracking. It was easy to get lost among the electrical currents when surfing the electrical world. Tracing those signals as they swam through the currents was like riding a lightning bolt—I never realized how dangerous it was until it burned my ass. *C'est la vie.* Trial and error was a bitch, but it was all I had.

Fortunately, she didn't ride my ass about it. "I take it you found something."

"Bastard tagged and bugged the car." I dropped my hand to her hip, keeping her close. To anyone watching, we were just another couple taking a moment to talk.

She let my face go and rested her hands against my chest. "Did you leave it active?"

"Yeah. No sense in letting them know we found it." *Safer to keep Zane comfortable in his arrogance.*

She sighed and shifted back. "All right, let's find somewhere we can talk."

Wrapping my arm around her waist, we made our way back toward the busier streets. The sidewalks weren't crowded, but people were definitely out enjoying the evening. We headed toward the club we'd first noticed but decided against going there when the noise level hit us two doors down. Instead, we chose a tucked-away restaurant that offered a much more subdued atmosphere and booth seating near the back.

The sounds of the other patrons as they enjoyed their food and conversation created a soothing white noise as we settled into our seats. For appearance's sake, we both ordered dessert. The waitstaff was quick and efficient. Our drinks and dessert—coffee and cheesecake for Jinx, soda and mud pie for me—hit our table within minutes.

Once we were alone, Jinx dug out the file and handed it to me. "I would've thought he'd give us this information on a flash drive instead of going old-school."

I set it between us. "Actually, I'm not surprised. No way would any self-respecting hacker use someone else's drive."

She grimaced. "I hadn't considered that."

"Don't worry none. That's why you've got me, *cher*." I opened the file. "Shall we?"

We started going over it in closer detail, passing pages back and forth as we read. I had to give Zane credit—his initial investigation was damn good. Amalia's background seemed fairly straightforward. She was born to an addict mother, father unknown, bounced through the system until ten, at which point she ended up with an older foster couple. She held her own during her time with them, other than a couple of hiccups. There were some noticeable blank spots, including her earlier life and a short span in her early twenties, but that was a given as most people didn't start to leave a real trail until their teens. But the lack of information about her twenties struck me as either a sloppy data wipe or a deliberate mislead. It would be interesting to discover which one was in play. Once her foster parents passed away due to health complications, when she was seventeen, things took a turn. It wasn't the worst case I'd seen, but it wasn't all fluffy kittens and rainbows either.

"She didn't catch many breaks."

"Doesn't seem like it, but that's how it goes sometimes," Jinx murmured. She pulled out a page and gave it to me. "No surprise, but looks like she hooked up with a bad boyfriend after she lost her fosters."

I read through a list of minor charges ranging from shoplifting to a couple of incidents of vandalism, all done shortly after her home life imploded. I noted a domestic dispute on file, right about the time the boyfriend disappeared from her life. "Didn't take long for her to clue in."

"Sometimes once is all it takes." The bitter certainty in Jinx's voice caught my attention.

"Hey." I waited until she was looking at me. "What was that?"

She gave me an uncomfortable shrug and dropped her eyes back to the papers in front of her. "A bad memory."

That unexpected glimpse into the past that Jinx normally kept under lock and key made me want to push, but heeding the closed expression on her face, I kept my mouth shut. Deciding to take us out of treacherous waters, I slid over a copy of a police report. "Did you see this?"

Jinx took the papers and read through them, her mouth tightening. "The boyfriend was murdered."

Maybe, or maybe I'm a cynical bastard for thinking the same. "You think the report has it right or…?" I let the question hang for a moment.

"If she was behind the boyfriend's murder, she was smart about the setup."

Warped dick that I was, I found it comforting that Jinx had no problem following my vague theory. "Yeah, hard to claim a mugging as premeditated murder, especially if your victim is an all-around shit involved in shady deals."

Amalia's boyfriend was gunned down in a neighborhood

known for its gang activity. In fact, he'd been arrested twice in that same area for dealing, so it was feasible that he'd been taken out in retaliation for something he'd done. The thing was, Amalia was with him and witnessed the whole thing. She escaped with a few bruises and scraped knees from hitting the sidewalk when the shooting started.

The unknown assailants sprayed the sidewalk, yet Amalia managed not to get nicked? The story felt off, and I wasn't the only one who thought so, because the police dragged her in for interviews multiple times, but with no evidence to indicate her involvement, she walked away.

"Still, there's something not quite right about this."

"True, but there's something… where was it?" Jinx riffled through the pages and laid out two more sheets. "Here, look at this."

Pulling the pages close, I started to read them. "He's the first of three incidents. That's the start of a pattern, not a run of bad luck."

"If she's involved with Zane, she isn't exactly on the side of angels."

As I read through the notes, I muttered, "And that slide into darkness had to start somewhere." I flicked a look at Jinx. "Why not start by getting rid of the first person who dared to harm you?"

Jinx lifted her fork, tipped it my way in agreement, and took a bite of her cheesecake.

I went back to the pages she gave me. Five years after the death of the abusive boyfriend, Amalia and her grad-student fiancé were involved in a car accident. Amalia spent a month in the hospital, and the grad student ended up six feet under. According to various friends, the two of them adored each other and were blissfully planning their upcoming nuptials. With nothing to indicate foul play, the case was closed as nothing more than a tragic vehicular accident.

Then six years later, twenty-eight-year-old Amalia was once again caught up in an investigation involving the death of her mentor and friend, a philanthropic multimillionaire during a group ski trip. This time, the investigation started for insurance purposes, not because of criminal charges, but that death was eventually chalked up to a preexisting heart condition. Interestingly enough, she got a fifty-thousand-dollar gift from her mentor.

"You think Amalia's playing black widow? And what? Zane's her next target?"

"Maybe." Jinx ate another bite of her dessert.

The trail of dead male companions wasn't Amalia's only peculiarity. "Then she's a busy bee." I pulled out a list of financial transactions and passed them over. "From what Zane's people found, she makes quite a tidy profit from creative financing." While Jinx went through the numbers, I took a big bite of my mud pie then tapped the handle of my fork against one of the pages. "She's got three offshore accounts. Altogether, they total up to about eight million and change. I'm betting if we dig a little deeper, we'll find more."

"What are these?" Jinx shifted the paper around so I could see what she was looking at.

Taking in the five- to six-digit deposits that didn't follow any recognizable pattern, I shook my head. "They could be anything. Our best bet is to trace these back to the origination point."

Jinx set her fork down, propped her elbow on the table, and rested her chin against her palm. "Considering our deadline, how far do you think we'll get?"

Taking care to keep my voice low, I leaned in and held

her gaze. "*Cher*, did you forget who you're workin' with here?"

"As if I could." She stared down at the papers between us. "As much as I hate to admit it, Zane's right."

"About?" I sat back and took another bite, enjoying the mix of chocolate fudge and vanilla.

"Amalia. This"—she waved her hand at the papers strewn between us—"doesn't ring true."

"Considering who we're discussing, it shouldn't be that surprising. Neither of them is completely aboveboard in business or with personal dealings."

"Maybe." She didn't look convinced. "But it bothers me."

"Which part? Zane using this as his test of Elena's skills or that a woman's life depends on what we uncover and decide to share?"

That earned me a nose wrinkle. "Both." She took another bite and chewed it thoughtfully, before adding, "I can't help but wonder…"

"What?"

Her attention dropped the file. "It's too neat." She met my gaze, her face serious. "Could be a setup."

"For us or her?"

"I don't know."

"Yeah, I get that," I said because I hadn't missed the smug gleam in Zane's eye when he handed this task over to Elena. Something else definitely lay underneath the narrative we'd been handed, and it might be enough to blow our whole operation sky-high. Unfortunately, the only way to defuse the situation was to get in the dirt and start digging. "Until we work through Amalia's information, we're fishing in the dark. Once we have something concrete to work from, we can figure out our next move."

"So we wait and decide what to share with Zane?" She pushed her dessert around the small plate. "I don't know, Rabbit. That's a hell of a risk. What if he already has information and what we share doesn't match?" She turned to me, a cloud of worry darkening her eyes. "We fail his test, and the repercussions might be more than we bargained for."

I got her concern because my sense of being played was very real, but indulging in what-if games was just as dangerous. "We do the check, just as we would if this was a legit request. I'll take us as deep as I can, and once we unearth whatever the story is, we'll make the call on what we share. To be fair, there's no way Elena would show all her cards to Zane, nor would Zane expect her to. Aren't you the one who told me the best way to outcon a con was to stack the deck?" I waited for her reluctant nod. "Then we stack our deck. Deal?"

The worry in her face didn't soften, but she relented. "Deal."

Chapter Nine

RABBIT

"No fucking way." I stared at the information on my screen, wondering if my lack of sleep was finally kicking in. I had set up shop in the second bedroom and now pushed away from the desk with enough force to send the empty water bottles scattering across the surface until they bumped into the half-filled coffee cup.

The chair's wheels rattled over the tile, rousing Jinx from where she half dozed, slumped on the futon. "What?"

"I think I found out why Amalia Black doesn't add up." I spun around and rubbed my burning eyes before dragging a hand through my hair. "She doesn't exist."

Jinx's long lashes fluttered as she blinked herself awake and sat up, lines of confusion joining the lingering marks from the futon's cushions. "Wait, what?"

"Amalia Black isn't really Amalia Black." Hearing the words out loud, even I had to admit they sounded overly dramatic, but after spending the last ten hours scouring the cyberverse and the mind-numbing lines of data, it was the scenario I kept coming back to. Hell, at this point, if a little green alien popped up with a fresh pot of coffee and an offer for a galactic space ride, I wouldn't blink.

When we got back to the condo the night before, the first thing I'd done was make sure the second bedroom, which served as an office, was surveillance-free. Then I got down to business. The first few hours were spent repeating exactly what Zane's investigation had uncovered. But there were blips in Amalia's story that slipped under my skin and irritated the hell out of me, so once the preliminaries were out of the way, I had Jinx work on backtracking the money in Amalia's various accounts as I trekked through the less legit areas of cybernetic information. While I stayed on my trail, Jinx managed to find two other accounts linked to Amalia, and considering how much work it took to unravel those threads, that had been an impressive find.

Jinx set her laptop on top of the papers piled next to her and uncurled her legs. "What are you talking about?" She stood up and stretched, a dangerous choice, considering what the movement did to the thin material of her tank and yoga pants.

Watching her, my body shoved exhaustion aside and perked right the hell up. *Merde*, she was better than any coffee.

"Rabbit."

The sound of my name in a purely exasperated feminine tone jerked my attention up to her contact-free brown eyes, which sparked with laughter. Heat climbed my neck, and I used both hands to scrub my face hard, feeling the heavy scrape of scruff against my palms. "Sorry." I dropped my hands and spun back to my computer. "Come see."

She came over and stood next to me, her hip brushing my shoulder as she leaned over to see the screen. "What am I looking at?"

"This here is the report surrounding the death of her supposed fiancé. And this…" I tabbed between windows. "This is a traffic incident with the same date. What do you see?"

She read silently, reaching out to shift between windows. It didn't take her long. She turned and looked at me. "Where did you find the incident report?"

"Let's just say that the chain of evidence wouldn't hold up in a court of law." *Mainly because the way I accessed it was nowhere near legal.* "But there's more." I pulled up a couple more files. "This is the insurance report on the millionaire mentor who's tied to Amalia Black. The one on the right is older by about six years, and the names don't line up, but notice the details?"

She shifted her stance as she read the screen. Giving in to temptation, I wrapped an arm around her hips and drew her down until she was sitting in my lap. As her weight settled against me, I swallowed a groan, but there was shit-all I could do about the telltale stiffness.

She shot me a half-lidded look over her shoulder, her mouth curved in a secret smile. "Brave man, aren't you?"

Her unexpected tease had my hands tightening on her hips. I used my chin to move her hair back from her shoulder. "Is this where I say, 'Danger is my middle name'?"

She snorted, turned back to the screen, and relaxed against me. "Okay, Mr. Danger, tell me what I'm looking at."

I reached around her and clicked through files as I explained. "The initial search was confined to legit channels and would normally survive an impressive background search."

"Like Zane's?"

"Exactly like Zane's. I went deeper into the major incidents noted, looking for initial or corroborating reports. Once I found those, I dove into the metadata attached to the files and noted a strange pattern. The access dates on the files were staggered around the same time, which is not normal if these incidents occurred years apart."

"Shouldn't Zane's people have found this in the initial background check?"

"Nope, because most background checks don't go that deep into the weeds. Drilling into the metadata is problematic for most."

"Okay." She drew out the word. "So, does this mean the files were created at the same time?"

"Close." I brought up another screen, this one filled with text on a black background. "See this list?" I pointed it out and waited for her nod. "The original content of all of these files was modified."

She frowned. "I know I'm tired, but isn't being modified the same thing as being created?"

I shook my head. "Not in this case. Here, it's a microscopically thin line between modification and creation. It's an indicator that the information we're seeing was altered just enough to fit whatever narrative Amalia needed."

"Someone changed the original records and… what? Zane's people didn't catch these other files you found?"

"Got it in one." Considering just how deep and far I'd gone to find those other files, my success had been more due to luck than skill. "To be fair, it wasn't easy, and those alterations? They weren't obvious enough to be caught on the first or fourth sweep, but yeah, they were definitely changed. And it wasn't just these items. Once I knew what to look for, I found traces of modifications on her social media and various other points that I checked." I didn't mention that those traces had taken me down paths that would result in my arrest if my footprints were ever found. But I was good at playing ghost. "On top of that, most of her supposed history is a jigsaw puzzle of other stories, all of which were woven together to create an impressive whole."

She shifted so she could see me. "That sounds expensive."

I held her gaze. "Or it's a hell of a cover."

She stiffened in my lap before her eyes narrowed. "Cover?"

I nodded grimly. "This type of modification, buried this deep—I've seen it before."

I'd found discrepancies like this in the type of files the government didn't like to admit having. Of course, I could only go digging so far without sending up flags that would bring more problems down on us than we needed. Since I didn't want Delacourt or the US government riding my ass, I'd made sure to keep my presence virtually nonexistent.

It didn't take long for Jinx to piece it together. "Could she be Delacourt's mole?"

"If I was a gambling man, I'd be placing a sizable bet that she is."

"Shit." She scrambled out of my lap.

Suppressing a groan, as her move left a certain part of me aching with unfulfilled expectations, I used my foot to spin around and watch her pace. "That's one way to put it."

She dragged a hand through her hair. "How sure are you?"

I shrugged. "At this point? Eighty, eighty-five percent."

"Which means we could be wrong." She resumed her pacing.

"It's possible. But our other option isn't much better." That brought her to a stop in front of me, so I obliged her with more information. "The criminal element isn't without its savvy operators." When she continued to frown, I added, "Those two accounts you found—did you find out where the money in them came from yet?"

She grimaced. "Not yet." She wrapped her arms over her stomach. "Nothing in her background indicates Amalia has the kind of expertise needed to pull this off."

I cleared my throat, and when she looked at me, I said, "We both know that's not a hard thing to hide, especially if she's working for some other criminal element—say, one that has it out for Falcon." I watched my suggestion sink in. "We have firsthand knowledge of just what kind of bastards they are, so it isn't that big of a stretch to think they've managed to piss someone else way the hell off with some sort of dirty deal."

"True." She rubbed the back of her neck. "I'm guessing your contacts couldn't confirm or deny if Amalia's tied to our side?"

I used a foot to swivel my seat from side to side. "Didn't ask." When that earned me a questioning look, I explained, "Too risky. I was pushing things as is."

"Which leaves Delacourt as our only way to confirm Amalia's allegiances." She made a couple of passes before she stopped. "Not that it matters whose side she's on, because if Zane's starting to wonder about her identity, her time is limited."

There was no arguing with that assessment. "If she's who we think she is, we can't leave her ass hanging out there, yeah?"

"No, we can't." She sighed. "Do you think this is what Zane was trying to trip us up with?"

Since that was a scenario I'd considered, I answered, "I think he knows there's more to her than what's coming up, but this much detail?" I shook my head. "I don't think he has that."

"If he does—"

"If he did, she'd already be dead."

Darkness slipped through her eyes. "How do we know she's not?"

"We don't. But what does Zane gain by having us investigate a dead woman? Besides, you saw him when he gave this to us."

Her gaze dropped, and she rubbed the back of her neck again. "You're right. This is highly personal to him, but he's not completely sold on Amalia's loyalty." She lifted her head, her mouth a tight line. "We can't risk moving one way or another until we know which side she's on. We need verification from Delacourt, and to get that, we have to share this information."

I leaned back, folding my hands over my stomach, which made my chair groan. "Okay, and we get that in less than"—I craned my neck to note the time on the computer—"twenty-four hours how?" When she turned to me, I added, "Reaching directly out to Delacourt is too damn risky at this point. Not with all the eyes and ears on us." I tapped behind my ear to indicate the tags. "This has limited range, and we're already taking a risk when we run them. Then there's getting a response in such a tight time frame, which is damn near impossible."

"What about your super-secret back doors? Can't you use one of them?"

I shook my head. "If we had more time, maybe, but not in this situation. Plus, I'm not comfortable sharing information like this over an open network." It was better for all involved if we used a closed system, like a flash drive, to get this information to the colonel. That way, I wouldn't have to live with risking a possible operative's life.

She moved toward me. I shifted my legs to give her room to step in. She took it. As with Pavlov's beloved canine friend, having her that close triggered a riot of reactions, all of which would take us somewhere we couldn't afford to go—not here, not now. Tension zipped through me as I battled back the urge to pull her closer.

Oblivious to my personal fight, she covered my white-knuckled hands with hers. "We need to know who we're dealing with."

Staring up into her face, I couldn't miss the fact that she was hell-bent on making contact with Delacourt. I understood her motivation, because whenever an embedded operative's cover was blown, the fallout was catastrophic. In this case, it wouldn't just be Amalia paying the ultimate price—our asses were hanging out there as well.

I blew out a hard breath. "I'll figure something out and see if we can get a meet of some kind set." Her hands tightened on my mine even as some of the lines around her mouth and eyes eased. I kept my tone cautious. "No guarantees we can do it before Zane's deadline."

She bit her lip, her expression changing too fast for me to guess what she was thinking. "You said a cover like this could be utilized by a savvy criminal element, right? Maybe someone with a grudge against Falcon?"

I dipped my chin in acknowledgement.

"Why don't we stick with that? Maybe we could add a few pieces and skew a couple of others just to help create the right picture—just enough to appease Zane but not enough to convict her. Maybe use one of the accounts I found to help sell the story. Is that possible?"

I thought through what that would entail. Melding

misinformation, both financial and factual, might work, but I'd need at least three more hours to make it happen. And maybe another pot of coffee.

"Yeah." I drew the word out. "But I can't guarantee it'll withstand serious scrutiny."

She flashed me a smile—one that managed to slip through the cracks and worm its way into places better left alone. "It just has to give us enough to keep Zane happy that Elena's done her job and buy us some space to figure out our next steps with Amalia."

I shook my head. "How do you plan to sell this to Zane? We tell him Amalia's possibly working for another criminal organization, and it's no different than exposing her for a spy."

"Not if we spin this right."

"Spin it for me, because I don't see a happy ending here."

"The best lies are the ones based in truth." Her expression clouded, but she blinked, and it cleared. "We don't have to confirm she's working against him. We explain that we've found a few inconsistencies with Amalia's information."

"And when he asks what kind of inconsistencies?"

"Elena is all about leverage, and this kind of information is the kind of leverage she'd exploit to keep Zane on his toes. She won't share the information without gaining something from it."

The way Jinx's mind worked was something to behold, but this… this was going to be tricky as shit to pull off. "A power play? You think that's wise?"

She didn't back down. "In this case, I think it's the only option we have."

"*C'est fou.*"

"It might be crazy, but do you have another option?"

She had me there. Blowing out a hard breath, I straightened in my chair. "Fine, but if we're doing this, you're on coffee duty." I nudged her back so I could turn back to my screen and get the ball rolling.

She came up behind me, wrapped her arms around my shoulders, and squeezed. "Thank you."

The sensation of her cheek pressed against mine and her arms around me landed like a velvet punch to the gut. I closed my eyes, savoring the moment. My voice was rough when I replied, "Anytime, *cher*."

Chapter Ten

JINX

It was early afternoon on Saturday, so Rabbit and I were back in Zane's pseudo-English study, awaiting the inevitable fallout from sharing our modified report.

"Inconsistencies?" Zane stood staring into an empty fireplace, his voice devoid of any revealing emotion. Unfortunately for him, his rigid posture and the unconscious curling of his hand into a fist at his side exposed how hard he was struggling with the information we'd shared about Amalia Black. He was clearly unhappy with it, even though it wasn't anywhere near as incriminating as what we'd initially suspected.

If I still harbored any doubts that this test was solely Zane's brainchild, they were fizzling out under his revealing reaction. Exerting that much control spoke to a depth of emotion that was difficult to fake. If this had come from someone higher up, he wouldn't be so personally invested, which meant that if he was working for Falcon and was the pyromancer we feared he was, I had to hope his control was such that we wouldn't suddenly find ourselves turning into human candles. A visceral memory of the gruesome aftermath of our last run-in with Zane arose. I'd stood frozen on the threshold of a smoke-filled Vegas penthouse, staring at a gray layer of ash that had once been a person. Rabbit had managed to usher me out before I could take it all in, but the scene still made appearances in my nightmares.

Zane finally turned to look at me, a merciless light shifting his brown eyes to a paler bronze. A strange bend in the air wavered around him. "What kind of inconsistencies?"

Next to me, I felt Rabbit shift, angling his body closer, neither one of us missing the unspoken menace hovering around Zane. Refusing to quail under that hard, eerie stare and invisible threat, I kept my body and voice relaxed. "The kind I refuse to share until I'm certain of them."

A muscle in Zane's jaw jumped, and that cruel light flared bright before fading back into brown. "And when you're certain?"

Channeling Elena for all I was worth, I continued to hold his gaze, matching his fury with icy disdain. "If it's worth sharing, then I'll share."

Zane's eyes narrowed, and the smile curving his lips carried more cruelty than humor. "And if I request that you share regardless?"

Not missing his implied threat, I returned it with one of my own, except mine carried the surety of well-deserved arrogance. "You'll find I'm not easily manipulated, Zane."

When he deliberately looked around the room and opened his mouth, it didn't take a genius to know what was coming next. "Aren't you?"

I refrained from rolling my eyes. "Do you believe that I would be here, dealing with you and your"—I let my lip curl —"employers without having done my homework? And I can promise you, your little test doesn't come close to what I do when I'm personally invested in a situation." Since I refused to look away, I didn't miss the flicker of doubt he couldn't douse. *That's right, asshat. Secrets are a bitch, eh?* Assured that my message had been received, I said, "Now, you tasked me to find out what your people missed. I did just that."

He pushed away from the fireplace to pace, his hand opening and closing at his side. Oh yeah, I was pissing him off. *Good.* Maybe if we kept him focused on me, Amalia would take a back seat long enough for us to find out what her real role was in this mess.

"You gave me hidden accounts with millions—" he started, a hot layer of anger in his voice.

"Earned from unverified business transactions," I added in a bland tone.

"But you won't confirm who she may be working with?" He stopped and faced me, his typical smoothness replaced by sharpness.

"Because I deal in certainties, not assumptions." Maybe if I said it enough times, he'd finally listen. I dropped my gaze and smoothed out a nonexistent wrinkle from another one of the hip-hugging skirts Elena liked so much. Linking my hands over my knee, I looked back up. "Theorizing about Ms. Black's possible business partners is not something I'm comfortable with as it can generate unwanted attention. As I explained, I'm still gathering facts. Once I have those, then I'll be happy to discuss the ramifications with you."

The flush of anger riding his cheekbones was a clear indicator that Zane wasn't happy with my answer. "How long will that take?"

Unperturbed, I shrugged. "As long as is needed."

My answer appeared to fray the hold Zane was trying to maintain on his temper, but before it could snap, Rabbit redirected his attention. "Seward, don't be an idiot."

Zane shifted his glare to the man sitting at my side. "Excuse me?"

Rabbit stretched and slowly stood. "You're pissed because it's starting to appear that you were right to think that this woman is playing you."

Zane's mouth tightened, but he didn't say anything.

Undaunted, Rabbit walked over to the bar and set his empty glass on top. "Until you know for sure, it's stupid to start kicking at rocks and riling snakes unless you're left with no other choice."

Zane's glare eased, but edgy anger still burned the air around him. "You picked an interesting analogy, Mercer." He turned away and gave us his back. "And if she decides to strike before you find your confirmation?"

Rabbit shook his head, exasperation clear on his face as he came back to his chair next to me. "She's been with you for two years. I doubt she's planning on taking you out in the near future. Just watch your back."

Zane's shoulders tightened. "I always do."

For a fraction of an instant, I felt for him, because there was something in the grim resolution of his voice I understood—an isolation that eventually crept in when a person's whole world was built on illusions. Shaking off the weird moment, I decided to start leading Zane away from his darker suspicions about Amalia. "May I make an observation?"

At my politely worded request, Zane turned to look over his shoulder at me before giving me the barest nod.

"Maybe she's working with someone, maybe she isn't. While I can't confirm or deny your suspicions, I can tell you that the inconsistencies I found could be easily explained as information she would rather not have widely known. In our line of business, there are…" I paused, choosing my words with obvious care. "Certain transactions and situations that are best left anonymous for all parties involved. Ms. Black's situation may fall into this category."

While I spoke, Zane turned away from the window and walked over to where we sat, looking far from convinced. "Yes, but such anonymity can be detrimental, the repercussions far-reaching and long-lasting."

"If you're that worried," Rabbit drawled as he straightened his legs and crossed them at the ankles, "I'd suggest keeping her from your more delicate dealings for now."

Not bothering to respond, Zane took a seat in the nearby chair, and the edgy tension in the room began to dissipate. He fiddled with the flash drive we'd handed over with our padded investigation, turning it end over end against the armrest.

Reading the speculation on his face and remembering what Rabbit had shared the night before, I said, "The drive is safe to use."

His restless movements stopped.

I inclined my head toward the drive. "You can put your team on what we found, but you'll be wasting their time and your money. I guarantee they won't find the answers."

"And you will?"

"It might take a couple more days, but yes."

"So certain of your skills?" The bite in Zane's tone indicated that he might be backing off, but he was far from happy.

I refrained from snapping back that he was the one who'd all but blackmailed me to be here, and instead, I went with the less confrontational approach. "It is why you hired me, isn't it?"

He lifted the flash drive and tilted it in my direction. "Touché."

His response made me wonder if our suspicions regarding the real power behind this mess were spot-on or way off. *What if there is no boss or higher-up? What if Zane is Falcon?* It was a startling thought, but at that moment it took a back seat to more important worries. We needed to buy ourselves more time to confirm Amalia's identity, which meant feeding Zane's uncertainty about her true motives.

"You know I am curious, though," I said.

Zane settled back in his seat, the drive disappearing into his fist. "About?"

I held his gaze and started laying breadcrumbs. "Who is it you're really worried about?"

Confusion marred his face. "Excuse me?"

I dropped the first crumbs. "For all her colorful history, Ms. Black doesn't strike me as a stupid woman. To believe she would be working against you doesn't make sense. What would she get out of it? You two seem to travel in the same circles. I can't see where she would profit by sabotaging you. Unless there's something you're not sharing." I studied him. "Did you betray her somehow? Another woman perhaps?"

A burst of laughter escaped Zane, catching me by surprise. When it faded, he said, "If you knew Amalia, you'd get why that is not an option."

"Ah, a woman after my own heart, then," I murmured.

"As for gaining something from turning on me, no, I can't think of what would be important enough for her to risk such reprisals." For the barest moment, the real Zane peeked out, and I caught sight of the merciless predator lying under the charming host. His shoulders rose and fell as his mask resumed its position. "As you stated, Amalia is not a stupid woman."

Before I could form a response, a bell rang through the house. We all fell silent, our attention shifting to the empty doorway. It wasn't long before footsteps approached and John appeared. "Mr. Seward, Ms. Black is here to see you."

"Thank you, John. Escort her in."

Rabbit looked at me. "Speak of the devil," he murmured.

Zane shot us a sharp glance. The distinct sound of heels over tile grew closer, and John reappeared, this time with a brunette trailing him.

Zane rose from his chair and moved toward the woman stepping around his majordomo. "Amalia, this is unexpected."

That's one way to put it.

Next to me, Rabbit rose to his feet, but I stayed seated, unobtrusively taking in the woman who was most likely a double agent but might or might not be on our side. Her hair held hints of red and gold that shifted the brown—the color from the photo—to sable. Arranged in a tumble of casual curls and held back by the sunglasses perched on top, it framed an intriguing collection of angles and curves that turned Amalia from pretty to captivating. As someone familiar with just how deceiving appearances could be, I noted the sharp assessment that was there and gone, hidden behind a polite smile, as her gaze flickered over Rabbit and me before landing on Zane. As fleeting as it was, like recognized like.

Oh yeah, there's much more to Amalia than a pretty face. It would be interesting to see how she would choose to play her part.

"I'm sorry, Zane." She met him halfway, her hands outstretched. "I should've called."

He took her hands and drew her close, brushing a chaste kiss over her cheek. "No apologies needed." He pulled her into his side, and despite her high heels, her head barely brushed his shoulder. "May I introduce Elena Drake and Mercer Somers. Elena, Mercer, this is Amalia Black."

Amalia wrapped an arm around Zane's waist and leaned forward, offering Rabbit her other hand. "Pleasure to meet you, Mr. Somers."

I rose to stand next to Rabbit as he responded, "And you, Ms. Black."

She gave him a charming smile. "Just Amalia, please." She turned to me, her hand out. "Ms. Drake."

"Call me Elena," I murmured, taking her hand.

She gave a quick firm clasp and then was pulling back, her hand going to Zane's stomach as she looked up at him. "I didn't mean to interrupt, but my meeting ended earlier than expected."

"We were just finishing up our conversation, darling. No harm." Zane smiled down into her face, no sign of his earlier temper or suspicions in evidence. It was disturbingly eerie how attentive he appeared to a woman he'd so casually discussed eliminating only moments earlier. "We were just finalizing a few details on a possible business venture. I'm hoping to gain their agreement to join us on our upcoming project."

Despite the shiver of nebulous dread crawling over my skin, I didn't miss Zane's pronoun use and filed it away to discuss with Rabbit later. It hinted that maybe Amalia's involvement in this mess was deeper than we'd anticipated. I shifted the tiniest bit toward Rabbit, who didn't hesitate to curl his arm around my waist and pull me close to his side.

Amalia remained relaxed in Zane's hold. "Oh?" The weight of knowledge behind that one word revealed that despite her act, Amalia knew exactly what type of business Zane meant. Her attention shifted to us then returned to Zane. "Is this the possible solution you mentioned?"

"She is." He led her over to a chair, waiting until she sat before heading to the bar. His every move was the epitome of masculine indulgence, an affectation that left me fighting my urge to sneer.

Recognizing my strained patience for the warning light that it was, I forced my frustration down and tightened my focus on the mission objectives. Rabbit and I needed to appear as relaxed as the two of them. We retook our positions on the sofa as Zane poured Amalia a drink and brought it over to her.

She took it with a soft smile. "Thank you."

He gave her a nod and reclaimed his previous seat to her left.

With everyone once again seated, her attention shifted to me, the friendly pretense of her smile altering the tiniest bit to reveal the shrewd mind underneath. "You're not quite what I expected when Zane mentioned that he was considering utilizing your skills."

At her unexpected attack, delivered with a lethal smoothness, I blinked. Staying true to Elena, I said in a cold tone, "Oh?"

"You have to admit, you're not quite what one expects when they picture a hacker." Her eyes widened, and she brought her hand up to her mouth as color rushed under her skin. She skated a quick look between Zane and me. "I'm so sorry. That came out mortifyingly awkward."

I had to give her credit. She was damn good. Although her expression and tone conveyed dismay bordering on chagrin, something about her reaction didn't ring true.

She turned back to me and murmured, "No offense meant."

Rabbit sat so close that I caught the tension coiling through him at Amalia's not-so-subtle barb, but he kept quiet, leaving the field to me.

"None taken." I held her gaze and decided to answer with a swipe of my own. "In our line of business, sometimes it's best not to cater to expectations, don't you think? They can be devastatingly disappointing when they fail to match reality."

Amalia's expression didn't betray any reaction, but I knew—with that instinctive skill honed by years on the streets and studying my marks—my hit had landed a solid blow. Cradling the heavy cut glass in her palms, she managed an embarrassed laugh even as she sipped her drink. When she lowered the glass, there was no way to miss the appreciative light in her eyes. "I think I'm going to like you, Elena."

Strangely, she sounded sincere, but I couldn't return her sentiment. Not yet. I had to know whose side she was really on—Zane's, ours, or hers.

Before I could come up with a pithy reply, Zane stepped in. "Elena, I owe you a thank-you."

Amalia quickly stifled a jerk as she turned to him, but with my attention on Zane, I couldn't see why. I asked, "For…?"

He straightened a crease in his slacks and looked at me from under his lashes. "Your earlier help."

It took a lot of effort not to look to Amalia and instead incline my head in acknowledgement. *Why in the hell is he pulling this now? Is he baiting Amalia? Baiting me? What does he expect to gain from such a play?* There were too many unanswered questions and murky motives, making it hard to determine his game. But if he wanted to make the first move, I was happy to play along.

Conscious of Rabbit's arm stretched along the couch's edge behind me, I set my hand on his knee. "Does that mean you plan on giving me a real challenge at some point?" In keeping with the cat-and-mouse game that we all seemed to be engaged in, my question carried an edge of attitude. Against my nape, Rabbit's fingers stilled in warning or surprise—I wasn't sure which—but I kept my gaze locked with Zane's.

Something disturbing swept into Zane's pleasant expression. "Oh, I think that can be arranged."

Despite my unease, anticipation raced under my skin. I continued to hold his gaze. As if that sign of defiance was the trigger, Zane's pleasant mask dissolved, leaving behind a dark, calculating enjoyment. There was no doubt that he considered himself the cat, and we were all just poor, foolish mice.

That arrogance rubbed me the wrong way, and I refused to drop my gaze. The reaction was very much me and not Elena. My stubbornness held until Rabbit interfered, tightening his hold on the back of my neck in an unmistakable warning. Gritting my teeth, I looked down, ceding this victory to Zane.

A sharp sound broke through the strange tension as Amalia clapped her hands and turned to Zane, her voice perky enough to make me wince. "Honey, I have a great idea. Why don't we take Mercer and Elena to dinner tonight?" She turned back to me and leaned forward. "Think of it as an apology for stepping in it earlier."

Zane's smile didn't disguise the irritated tightness

around his eyes and mouth. Whether he was reacting to Amalia's suggestion or the situation in general was a mystery. "How about it, you two? Do you have plans for tonight?"

Even knowing his question was purely for show, I played along and shared a look with Rabbit, catching a rising intensity in his gaze. He braced an elbow against the arm of the couch and rested his head against his fingertips as he considered. Then he gave the barest dip of his chin in agreement.

I turned back to Zane. "What time?"

"Say, seven at Santiago's?"

Recognizing the name of a Michelin-starred restaurant, I inclined my head. "We'd be happy to join you."

Rabbit gave an exasperated snort as he pulled his arm from around my shoulders, sat up, and leaned forward. "Well done, Seward. You've given her an excuse to go shopping."

It took a moment for my brain to process Rabbit's comment, because he was more than aware of how much I abhorred shopping. Just the idea of trudging through the mass of bags and bad-tempered shoppers made me shudder. Hoping there was a reason for his insane comment, I shot him a look from under my eyelashes. "I was unaware an excuse was ever needed."

Rabbit grimaced, which earned a laugh from Amalia. "If you'd like some suggestions, I have some great shops I'd be happy to share."

Not wanting to commit to any specific spot, in case Zane decided we needed shadows, I gave her an apologetic look. "I appreciate it and may take you up on it, but a friend of mine mentioned a couple of stores I was hoping to check out. Considering we only have a few hours, I'll start with those."

"Start with?" Rabbit asked with the perfect touch of impatience and indulgence.

I patted his knee. "Don't worry. It won't take long."

He heaved a sigh and stood up, offering me his hand. "Where have I heard that before?"

Zane rose, and Amalia followed suit. Taking Rabbit's hand, I let him help me up before turning to exchange air kisses with Amalia. We did the polite back-and-forth of goodbyes as the men shook hands.

Amalia hooked her arm through mine as we headed toward the door. "Truly, Elena, if you don't find anything, text me. I'll send you the names of a couple of great boutiques."

It was disconcerting how sincere she sounded. If she was working undercover, she was damn good, because she had the socialite routine down pat. If Rabbit and I hadn't spent the last several hours tearing apart her history, I'd never have guessed at the depth of cunning running under her mask.

"Sounds good." Dutifully playing along, I stopped, freed my arm, and pulled out my phone. "Oh, should we exchange numbers?"

Before I could register what she was doing, she took my phone, punched in a string of numbers, and handed it back, all without blinking. "Here you go," she said with a smile.

Taking it from her, I kept my smile in place. Her unexpected move layered my anticipation with caution. *Is she for real? Does she have any clue what a hacker can do with her number?* Searching her face, I found nothing to work with. I didn't dare look at Rabbit. "Thanks again." I pocketed my phone as Zane opened the door.

With Rabbit's hand at the base of my spine, I was about to take a step when Zane chuckled and said dryly, "I wish you luck," to Rabbit.

There was something so patronizing about his reaction that I was left gritting my teeth, but I managed to hang on to my smile through sheer will as we did a final round of goodbyes. *This damn well better be a move on Rabbit's part to get us an unobtrusive way to make contact.* If it wasn't a strategic move, I was going to make my partner pay in very painful ways for his chauvinistic play.

Chapter Eleven

RABBIT

Jinx was in a hell of a temper as we left Seward's house, and I was pretty sure why, but we were stuck in a monitored car, which was not the place to brave the decidedly stormy waters. "Where to first?"

Despite the thunderclouds on her face, her voice remained unruffled as she casually gave the name of a high-end store in Cherry Creek. We managed to maintain a conversation by staying on topic with our upcoming shopping trip. I was working through how best to block the surveillance on the car and get in touch with our team when road construction slowed us to a stop in bumper-to-bumper traffic.

Taking advantage of the unexpected opening, I caught Jinx's attention and made a rolling motion with my hand, silently indicating that she should keep up her conversational end enough so that I could get away with the occasional "uh-huh" or "sure." She raised a brow but followed my lead. It took just over a minute to activate the skin tag behind my ear and shift the signal's frequency enough to make it invisible to the eavesdropping bug on the windshield. I could have done it while driving, but splitting my attention like that wasn't safe for me or anyone else on the road.

Once the tag went active on my end, it would signal our team to listen in. With only a few hours available to exchange the information we had on Amalia, we had to work fast. First up, we had to let the team know where we'd be. I turned into the sprawling Cherry Creek Mall and began prowling for a parking space.

"There." Jinx pointed out a spot in front of Neiman Marcus.

As I pulled in and parked, an unmistakable one-two click sounded in my ear. Now that someone was listening, I started the ball rolling. "I thought you wanted to start with that White House place?"

"White House Black Market," she corrected. "But Neiman Marcus works too." She met my gaze as she undid her seat belt, and mouthed, "Are we live?"

I gave her a nod as I opened my door. She did the same on her side, and we left our unwelcome ears behind and headed into the dubious safety of the mall. As we crossed the lot, I caught her hand and pulled her up short.

She turned and aimed a narrow-eyed glare at me. "What?"

Instead of answering, I reach up and tucked a strand of hair behind her ear, using the move to not only touch her but activate her tag as well. I drew my hand away slowly, careful not to pull on the few strands that refused to let go, relishing the sensation of the silk brushing through my fingers and the warm skin of her delicate jaw. It was the most careful of touches, but it was enough to calm her. Jinx's earlier irritation faded, replaced by a poignant softness as her head tilted the slightest bit. We stood there, locked in some indefinable moment. Then she lowered her eyes. It took me a minute to realize her hand had caught mine and tugged it down until we stood with our fingers loosely linked.

"Come on. Time to spend some money." Despite the husky timbre, her voice carried a heated edge, but whether that was due to temper or something else, I wasn't sure.

Still grappling with the unexpected moment of intimacy, I kept my mouth shut. She pivoted on her heel and headed in. Since she kept possession of my hand, I went along, lengthening my stride to keep up with her irritated pace.

We hit the automatic doors, which slid aside, emitting a blast of frigid air. The artificial chill inside the mall acted like a slap, jerking my head out of my pants and back onto the job. Jinx finally let me go as she wove her way through the maze of racks and displays, doing her best to avoid the other shoppers. Not that they got in her way. I wondered if she noticed how they stepped aside as she moved through the cluttered space.

Watching her jerk through another rack and hearing the painful squeal of hangers against metal, I winced. Okay, I knew she didn't like shopping, but I was starting to think she really hated it. When she finally came to a stop toward the end of the women's department, her movements had become smoother, and I figured it was finally safe to approach.

I came up behind her, stepping in close enough to keep my voice between just the two of us. "You okay?"

Without turning, she made a noncommittal hum and continued moving the hangers along the metal rack. I wanted to grin, but since that was liable to get me smacked, I didn't give in. Instead, going with a more dangerous approach, I closed the minor gap between us, curled an arm around her waist, and brought her against my front. Ignoring how her spine stiffened as her hand clenched an intriguing slip of purple, I lowered my head until our cheeks were level.

Undaunted and determined to tease her out of her pique, I said, "I like that one. You should try it on."

She leaned to the side enough that she could look at me but not break my hold. Color rode high in her cheeks, and as close as we were, I couldn't miss the tiny starburst of anger that even her contacts couldn't hide. "Don't!" It came out as a near hiss, probably because she was trying not to draw attention.

Unfortunately, my mere presence in the women's department was garnering curious looks. Conscious of nearby shoppers who were trying to listen and watch without being obvious and therefore were completely obvious, I let her go. She instantly moved away, leaving me to follow.

Returning a sympathetic smile from an older woman who'd witnessed our exchange, I shoved my hands into my pockets and trailed along. Knowing Jinx, she just needed space to burn out her frustration. So I gave it to her, dutifully following as she meandered through the store.

She stopped here and there. Fifteen long minutes later, she still hadn't tried anything on, but the prickly edge she'd carried was gone. When she finally deigned to acknowledge my presence, she said, "Let's grab a coffee."

Since I was getting bored, I was all for it. We hit up one of the many coffee stands, got our drinks, and took a seat on a bench. I gave it a minute before I tried again. "You ready to share?"

Her shoulders rose and fell as she sighed. "Please tell me

you're putting me through this hell so we can make contact."

The resignation in her voice made my lips twitch. "Aww, *mouche à mielle*, why would I deliberately torment you with the one thing I know turns you into a menace?"

She paused with her cup in the air and gave me a droll look. "Um, because you're crazy."

I waited till she lowered her cup before I gently bumped her shoulder with mine. "True, but this time, there's a definite reason behind my madness."

"Good." She kept her attention on the people strolling by, bags in hands, some pushing strollers filled with more bags and the occasional child. "Because I'm not sure how long I can last in here."

"Then I'd best not waste time, yeah?"

She arched a brow. I leaned forward, arms braced against my knees and my cup cradled in my hands, and kept my head down, not because I truly thought we were being watched but because caution was an ingrained habit. Next to me, Jinx appeared to be scrolling through her phone as she sipped her coffee.

My eyes on the floor and my mind focused on something completely different, I murmured, "You online?"

A soft double click confirmed that our safety line was alive and well. "Time estimate?"

A series of long and short clicks answered. Translating the Morse code, I noted the time. We had twenty minutes before intercept.

"White House, Black Market dressing rooms." Jinx's response was nearly as quiet as mine.

We got a double click in confirmation. Jinx angled her phone so I could see her screen. "Think you can do something with this?"

Noting the name attached, I committed the string of numbers to memory. "If it's legit." I sat back, bringing my cup up as well. "She just gave it to you?"

Jinx met my gaze, her eyes wide as she sipped her coffee. She nodded.

What the hell? Why would Amalia give her number to a known hacker? Is it a test to see how far Elena will go with it? I downed a hefty swallow, and the caffeine hit the knot in my gut. Maybe there was something I wasn't seeing.

I didn't doubt that I could use that number to get access to her phone and maybe set up a little gem that would allow me to listen in on her conversations, but trusting what we found would be the real test. This was what I hated most about working undercover—the constant questioning of motives. Overthinking things was a real risk. It was enough to drive a person batty. In this case, until we knew who Amalia really was and what she wanted, we had to treat her easy divulgence of her number as both a trap and a panicked SOS.

What a mess.

Jinx got to her feet, gaining my attention. She dropped her phone back into her purse and shifted her coffee to her other hand. "Come on." She held out her free hand. "Let's get this done. I have a dress to buy."

Taking her hand, I let her lead, content to walk at her side, fingers tangled, as we made our way to our final destination.

Chapter Twelve

RABBIT

When we got to the store, there were a handful of customers wandering about. Jinx headed toward the displays. I trailed along, just another long-suffering male accompanying his woman.

Jinx managed to politely warn off the smiling store assistant by murmuring, "Just looking for now."

She flicked through outfits, pulling some out, keeping one, discarding another. Leaning against one of the nearby pillars, I split my attention between her and my phone while unobtrusively watching who came and went. Fifteen minutes later, Jinx had gathered quite the collection of outfits and the avid attention of one of the saleswomen.

When Jinx finally paused in her culling of clothes, the saleswoman swept in. "Would you like a dressing room?"

"I'd love one, thank you."

Bringing up the rear, I followed in Jinx's wake as we were led toward the dressing area. We were steps away when a handful of customers hit the store's doors. They scattered like ducks after crumbs, but a flash of color caught my eye as a short, curvy redhead made a beeline for a display clustered with flower-print dresses.

The saleswoman motioned to one of the padded benches tucked inside the dressing room. "Why don't you wait here?"

In keeping with my role as patient male companion, I heeded her advice as she led Jinx to a private changing room. Once she was assured that we were settled, she left us to it. I tried to find a comfortable position but finally gave up and simply leaned forward, arms on my knees, phone in hand, and eyes on the screen, while Jinx began the marathon of costume changes.

I did a quick psychic sweep. The good news was the only camera I pinged was discreetly aimed at the entrance to the dressing rooms. That meant visuals would be limited to comings and goings, not what was happening inside. *Good enough.*

When Jinx emerged wearing a little black number, I let out a low, appreciative whistle. "Now that's something."

I might not be the biggest fan of shopping, but I had to admit that having Jinx model various cocktail dresses wasn't exactly a hardship, especially since the styles she chose were more in line with Elena's sophistication than Jinx's normal casual preferences.

She turned and twisted in front of the trio of mirrors, a frown on her face, as she eyed her reflection. "I don't know. Maybe it's a little too formal?"

"I think it'll work."

Her gaze lifted and met mine through the mirror while her hands went to her hips. "Do you not remember the first rule of shopping?"

"We do not talk about shopping?" I misused a favorite movie quote.

She bit her lip, but some of the lingering frustration faded from her face, and her tone was lighter when she said, "We don't buy the first thing we try on."

"Uh, must have missed that one."

She shook her head and headed back into the dressing room. I was bent back over my phone when a familiar voice echoed in my mind. *Heads up, Rabbit.*

My fingers paused for half a second then went back to mindlessly fiddling with my phone. With the ease of practice, I sent my telepathic response back: *Wolf, my man, nice to hear you.*

Heard you have a pickup for us.

You heard right. Need an identity verification ASAP.

What level? he asked.

Top.

There was a pause. *No guarantees, but we'll do our best.*

An ache started up in my temple, a typical occurrence when I worked with Wolf. Something about his telepathic ability and my electronic one tended to clash.

Meli's heading your way now, he added.

That was not the name I'd expected. Wolf's fiancée wasn't psychic. She wasn't even a member of the team.

The downside of working with a telepath like Wolf was that nothing stayed private, and he easily picked up on my concern. *We're not exactly heavy on the female bench, and Falcon knows about Cyn and Risia.*

Got it. There was no sense in getting defensive, because even though Wolf was very careful not to overstep his bounds, things sometimes spilled over. *They only have one camera at the entrance. Otherwise, we're clear in here, so I can pass over the flash drive.*

We'll reach back out as soon as we have the info.

Understood, I said.

"What about this one?" Jinx's question made me pull my head up. She was back in front of the mirrors, this time in a fluttering white skirt topped by a silky blue blouse.

The bit of whimsy hinted at by the skirt was definitely not something sharp-edged Elena would wear. "Pretty, but I like the black better."

She wrinkled her nose. "Agreed."

"Those just came in the other day." The voice of the perky saleswoman was coming closer. "That blouse would make a great match with those capris." Jinx and I both turned as she led Meli—who was toting a collection of clothes—toward an unused dressing room.

Jinx and Meli exchanged a polite smile and nod, but the saleswoman already had the door unlocked and open on one of the cubbies. "Why don't you take this one?"

"Thanks," murmured Meli as she stepped inside.

The saleswoman turned to Jinx. "That's lovely."

"Thank you." Jinx brushed the skirt. "Unfortunately, it's not quite what I had in mind."

"Is there something else I can get you?" Ms. Helpful offered.

"No, I've got a couple more to go through, so I'm good."

"Great." The woman flashed another smile. "I can take that back if you'd like."

Jinx blinked, probably taken aback by her enthusiasm. Before Jinx could formulate a response, I stood up and moved between the two. "How about I bring it out to you? We don't want to keep you from your other customers."

Based upon the saleswoman's startled expression, that was not the response she'd expected, but her professionalism kicked in. "I appreciate it. Just let me know what I can do to help."

Jinx wasted no time disappearing into her room, and left with no other option, the saleswoman headed back out. For a second, I stood there wondering what exactly she thought we would do if left alone. The images that popped up were not fit for mixed company and had me quickly thinking of less scandalous things. I did not need Wolf getting a prime viewing of my fantasies.

A muffled giggle came from behind Meli's door. "Smooth move."

That earned a soft snort from Jinx's area. "Don't encourage him."

"Aren't you two a laugh a minute." We were keeping our voices down just to be safe. I went over to Meli's door, palming the drive from my pocket. "You decent?"

"I'm always decent." She opened the door, and I handed over the drive. She took it and slipped it into her jeans pocket. "Thanks."

I gave her a nod. "Stay safe, yeah?"

That earned me a mischievous grin. "Don't worry. I've got my own big bad wolf on guard."

Unable to resist, I sent out a telepathic hail. *Hey, big bad wolf. Handoff complete.*

Don't make me show you my teeth, Rabbit.

Aw, now, it's cute. I turned away, hearing Meli's door click shut behind me.

A low growl echoed in my head as I went to Jinx's door. Satisfied that I'd distracted Wolf enough to make him miss anything incriminating my frustrated psyche might leak, I shifted back into work mode. *Once Jinx gets an outfit, we'll head back out. You should be clear to move after that.*

Roger. You two watch your backs.

Always do.

Standing outside of Jinx's room, I said, "Better hand over that outfit, *cher*."

"Give me a second." There was some rustling followed by a bit of cursing then the rattle of a hanger. "Here." The fluttering skirt flew over the top of the door, along with its accompanying hanger.

I caught both before they hit the floor. "This it?"

Her answer was to toss over the blouse.

"Hanger?"

It flew over the door.

It took a minute to get the blouse on the hanger right. Then I headed out to pass both items to Ms. Helpful. When I got back, Meli was in front of the mirror, doing that twisty turning thing while modeling a pair of white pants that stopped short of her ankles and a flowing blouse that rippled with every move.

"Cute." When my compliment earned me a frown, I asked, "What?"

From behind Jinx's door came her tart "A man of your charm should know 'cute' is the death knell for any outfit."

"*Cute* is for your baby sister," Meli chimed in.

Holding up my hands in surrender, I retook my seat on the bench. "Apologies. How about I take back the cute comment."

"Too late." Meli headed back to her room, a flounce in her step.

As her door clicked shut, I wondered how in the hell I ended up in these situations.

Better you than me. Wolf's amusement came through loud and clear.

Deciding turnabout was fair play, I tugged Wolf's tail. *Oh, I don' know about dat, my man, because the view in here has its perks.*

Go ahead, geekmeister. There was a hint of a growl in his mental voice. *Reach out and see how fast my redhead will singe your ego.*

As much fun as it was to ruffle Wolf's fur, it was best not to tempt those teeth. *C'est bon. I got me a Jinx to head off any trouble.*

Please. Jinx carries trouble in her damn pocket.

I could all but hear Wolf rolling his damn eyes, but since he was spot-on with his assessment, there was no way to argue. Not that I'd try. Hell, I liked that Jinx brought a bit of the unexpected to all that she touched.

Jinx's door opened, and she stepped out. "What about this one?"

An invisible fist nailed my gut, and I stared at what Jinx called a dress as she moved to the mirrors. *Merde.* That was no dress. It was temptation, pure and simple. The depth of my reaction had me throwing up every block Wolf had taught the team. I needed to keep him blind to the images cascading through my mind.

The deep-bronze material adhered to every delectable curve with loving dedication. That color against the golden hue of her skin turned it a pettable shade of honey. The tailored skirt that hit midthigh combined with the metallic-bronze heels turned her bare legs into a mouth-watering visual. *Oh yeah, this dress is nothin' but trouble.*

"Well?" A curvy hip bump interrupted my dazed fascination. She sounded exasperated.

Shifting my gaze away from her unintended enticement, I managed a semicoherent answer. "That one works, *cher.*"

Color rose in her cheeks, and she looked down and smoothed her hands over her hips. "I didn't think I would, but I kind of like it."

"Get it. You look good, and it works for tonight's

dinner." Hunger had a chokehold on my vocal cords, and my voice came out rougher than intended but didn't make the words any less true. The dress carried the sophistication of Elena and the fire of Jinx, so yeah—it was perfect.

She looked up and studied me. I didn't know what she saw, but I could guess. All those tricky emotions—fascination, curiosity, want—were shoving against the cage I kept them in, rattling the bars and making demands.

Her eyelids fluttered as the color on her cheeks deepened. "I guess this is the one, then."

"Good." Knowing that if I stayed, whatever control I had might snap, I got to my feet, wincing as certain parts of my anatomy protested. "I'll meet you out front."

I left the dressing room and arrowed to the doors, stopping a few feet away. Shoppers split and moved around me like water around a stone. It took a couple of deep breaths before I could think beyond the chaos of my libido. With the cage door closed once more, I angled myself so I could keep an eye on the store and the mall traffic at the same time.

As I scanned the mall, I tagged Wolf sprawled in a chair two storefronts down. With a baseball cap pulled low enough to shadow his face, he was just another guy whiling away his time checking scores or reading headlines on his phone. He did get a couple of glances from women and even one or two from other guys. No surprise there. His wide shoulders and broad chest left many thinking he was a football player or weightlifter.

Something bumped my legs. I looked down to find I'd been caught by a three-foot bundle of curiosity. "Hey, little man." I reached down to help the kid steady his balance. "You okay?"

Bright eyes stared back, accompanied by a big smile

outlined in orange that matched the color dripping from the stick in his hand. "Hi!"

"Jayden! Leave the poor man alone." A harried young mom rushed forward, bags rustling, hands outstretched to reclaim the runaway. Capture complete, she turned her attention to me. "I'm so, so sorry."

I grinned. "No harm, no foul."

"Say sorry, Jayden."

"Sorry." He gave me a wave as his mom led him away.

I looked back into the store and saw that Jinx was at the counter. Near the dressing room, Meli was chatting with the saleswoman as they headed toward another rack. It looked like poor Wolf would be here for a bit longer.

Jinx strolled up to me, her gaze sweeping through the mall, and only because I knew why did I note the slight pause when she spotted Wolf. She handed me the bags. "Here, I found the one for tonight." She took my arm and turned us away from Wolf and the store. "We can consider this trip a success."

"Does that mean you're done?" I matched my pace to hers. *Just another couple out shopping.*

Her husky laugh made me seriously wonder how bad it would really be if I just stopped and kissed her the way I needed to. She teased, "Not quite. Just a couple more stops."

"I thought you hated shopping?"

"Jinx loathes shopping, but Elena likes her little luxuries."

The emphasis on the last word took my mind on an indecent side trip. "Oh, joy."

She sent me a wicked sideways glance. "I'm sure you'll survive."

Swallowing my groan that was equal parts frustration

and hunger, I gave in. She managed to spend nearly an hour meandering in and out of shops. For a woman who claimed to hate shopping, she was a natural. I managed to keep an eye open, but other than an occasional uncomfortable niggle that I could attribute to the passing crowds, we appeared to be surveillance-free. Not that it mattered—we both understood the crucial need to stay in character.

By the time we headed back to the car, I vowed to sit out the next mission that required shopping of any kind. We were crossing through the lot when that sixth sense instilled in every soldier pinged. I didn't stop, but behind the lenses of my sunglasses, I did another sweep of our surroundings. There were others here and there—some arriving, some leaving, and a couple dropping bags in trunks—but nothing that explained the visceral warning I felt.

I wasn't the only one picking it up, because Jinx took a couple of the bags, giving me a chance to free my hands, and put enough space between us that we both could move if we needed to. As we got closer to the car, I used the remote to unlock the doors and pop the trunk. I stayed on Jinx's six as she dumped the bags into the trunk. I pushed the uneasiness down, still scanning as she got in. As I made my way to the driver's side, I did another unobtrusive scan and came up frustratingly empty.

Inside the car, I started the engine, not missing Jinx's movements as she did the same sort of scan. "Anything?" I asked.

She shook her head. With an arm around her headrest, I twisted around to watch as I backed out—backup cameras were sweet, but I trusted my own eyes more. I'd gotten us out of the mall parking lot when Jinx asked, "Mind if I turn on the radio?"

Since it would help mask our conversation, I said, "Go ahead."

Jinx turned on the radio, letting the music fill the car. The niggling worry downgraded but didn't disappear as I started putting distance between us and the mall. Unable to settle, I kept my attention on the traffic even as I started up a conversation. "What time do you want to head out for dinner tonight?"

Jinx shifted in her seat, angling toward me. "If dinner's at seven, I say we leave about six, six fifteen. Does that work for you?"

I checked the dash clock. We had about two and half hours to kill—enough time to get a couple of programs started on that number Amalia had given Jinx. "Yeah, that should give us plenty of time."

Conscious of our eavesdroppers, we kept our conversation casual and unremarkable for the rest of the drive. We got to the condo and made our way up. As I punched in the code for the door, I did a psychic sweep of the condo, checking the status of the electronic surveillance inside. Other than the known bugs we had left in place, the sweep came up empty, but it didn't ease the knot in my gut.

My hand was tightening on the knob when Jinx wrapped her fingers around my wrist. I turned to find her watching me with a questioning look. Frowning, I gave a half shake of my head to indicate that something was off. She let me take the lead as we entered.

We hadn't gone armed to Zane's. It seemed pointless to give him a reason to confiscate our weapons, so we'd left them locked in a biometric safe in the bedroom. Moving through the condo's entry hall with Jinx at my back, I did a visual sweep. No lingering shadows, no torn-up furniture—

everything seemed to be exactly where we'd left it. Still, I couldn't shake the impression that something was wrong.

Mindful of the ears on us, I asked Jinx, "You want the shower first?"

"Sure." She set the bags on the counter and watched me with a frown.

I motioned with my hand for her to keep up the conversation as I cleared the rest of the condo. Part of me kept an ear open to her voice, noting the change in pitch when she required an "Uh-huh" as I did my sweep. Together, we moved through the condo.

The tension riding my ass eased a bit as each room came up clean. Then I hit the office, and two steps in, I stopped, my attention on the chair in front of the desk. Used to working in tight confines, I had a deeply ingrained habit of shoving my chair in whenever I left my workstation. The chair was still in front of the desk, but it sat back by about a foot. Not where I'd left it.

Behind me, Jinx's voice cut into my dark thoughts. "Is that okay?"

"Sure." I had no idea what I was agreeing to, but it didn't matter. I did another psychic sweep, but no unusual electronic visitors pinged. The office was still clean, but someone had been in here.

She came up behind me, leaning in close and keeping her voice low. "What is it?"

I motioned to the chair. "We've had a visitor."

"Bugs?"

I shook my head then turned and ushered her toward the bedroom, where we were ensured some privacy. As I closed the door behind us, she moved toward the discreet wireless speaker near the dresser. I headed toward the closet.

"I'll try not to use all the hot water." She connected her phone to the speaker, and music filled the room. It took her a few seconds to adjust the volume to something that would cover our conversation.

Inside the spacious master closet, I headed straight for where our weapons and my laptop were hidden. There were no signs of disturbance or tampering. Some of my uneasiness disappeared. Whoever had been in the condo had failed to find this stash.

I joined her by the dresser. She dropped her sunglasses on top of it. "You sure we're clear in here?"

"Yeah."

Jinx turned so she was facing me and crossed her arms, leaning a hip against the dresser. "Did they bug the office?"

"Nothing was active when I scanned."

"But?"

"But that doesn't mean jack if they're using keylogging tech." *Which would also mean they managed to infiltrate the laptop we left out as a decoy.* I rubbed my neck, trying to relax the tight clutch of muscles at the base of my skull. "You go ahead and start getting ready. I'll go double check the office and computer."

"Didn't you lock up the laptop?"

"The decoy one, yeah, but it wouldn't be that hard to crack the lock and get to it." Mine—the one I didn't want Zane to know about—was safely hidden in the master closet.

She narrowed her eyes. "And if they managed to access it?"

I gave a shrug. "Then all the better for us."

"What did you do?" The lines of worry around her mouth eased as she studied me.

"What do you think?"

Her lips twitched as she shook her head. "You set a trap."

"Of course I did, *cher*."

"Well, let's go see what you caught, shall we?"

Chapter Thirteen

JINX

Following Rabbit to the office, I was caught by the way he moved. He had a predatory grace that tended to hide in plain sight, and when it caught me unawares, it took my breath away. It didn't help that the hot-as-hell look he'd given me at the mall haunted my thoughts. Like his first earth-shattering kiss, it blew through the crumbling wall I'd hastily erected so I could deal with the mission. Even worse, twined in the emotional rubble was the echo of his vow not to back off. My worry that he wouldn't be able to keep his emotions separate from the job was a slow rising dust cloud drifting off over the horizon. To be honest, during the last few days, he'd handled things way better than I had.

That damn kiss had left me wrecked on an unseen level. It haunted my dreams, leaving me tossing and turning and irritable as all get-out. It had demolished the comfortable boundaries I'd erected around our friendship and kept tempting me to explore what lay beyond. As the days passed, that temptation grew, dragging me closer to the inevitable edge. Not only did I want more, but curiosity about just how good it could get was driving me nuts. It was like there were two women stuck inside me, the practical one who warned that getting involved with Rabbit was a surefire way to destroy a cherished friendship and the uninhibited daredevil willing to dash into the unknown and indulge in bliss. Hell, that woman even provided detailed visuals of what lay in wait. Thank God we'd spent the previous night combing through Amalia's file because otherwise, thanks to the enforced intimacy of our sharing a bed, sheer desperation would have forced me to do some seriously intimate explorations despite my wariness.

Honestly, I wasn't sure how much longer I could withstand the combined pressure of Rabbit's determination and my curiosity-edged hunger. While I might hate myself the day after, I had no doubt I'd enjoy every magnificent moment of my fall from friend to lover. It was becoming difficult to even argue that lust wouldn't be worth the risk. The wisps of possibilities slipped through the cracks in my shield of pragmatism, completely ignoring the blaring warning signs, and showed me tantalizing glimpses of promised beauty.

I stayed on Rabbit's heels as we hit the office. When he dropped into a crouch in front of the locked cabinet by the desk, I stayed at his side. His shoulders pulled his shirt taut, and I found myself curling my hand into a fist so I wouldn't give in to my need to touch.

"I can feel you starin', y'know."

Although my cheeks heated, I couldn't ignore the teasing challenge, so I decided to brazen it out. "So?"

He turned his head, locking me in his gaze, the luscious velvet brown of his eyes bright and hungry. "So? You know you're playing with fire."

That look made my blood run hot and my toes curl.

The daredevil inside shoved the practical me into a corner and slapped duct tape over her mouth. I reached a little deeper into the flames, enjoying the burn. "You started it."

A flash of something—surprise maybe—was quickly replaced by a disconcerting intensity. "And you're going to —what? Finish it?"

Yes. I realized that I was tired of fighting a losing battle. Maybe it was time to surrender. I lifted my white flag. "Maybe."

At my husky response, Rabbit stopped. We stared at each other as a tide of awareness swept between us, threatening to take us both down. "*Mouche à mielle…*" His voice was gravel rough. "You're goin' drive me to my grave, you keep looking at me like that."

His sexy-as-sin accent was back and wreaking havoc. The urge to reach for what he offered was almost painful, but the fear of how that would change us—me—held me back, freezing me in place. Practical me got back up and shoved daredevil me hard before tearing away the impromptu gag. If I gave in to whatever this was, I risked losing my best friend for a momentary indulgence. It wasn't like it would last. Relationships that started out with an attraction this strong never did.

That harsh reality check had me jerking my gaze away, freeing us both. "You've got this?"

"Yeah. You go and take your shower. By the time you get out, I should know something."

I managed a curt nod, spun on my heel, and made my escape.

I stayed in the safety of the shower long enough for my fingers to wrinkle and the water to lose its sauna-like heat. Wrapped in one of the oversized towels, I finger combed my hair back from my face and tried to remember where I'd put my clothes.

A quick scan confirmed they weren't in the bathroom. *Dammit.* I'd been so focused on getting away from Rabbit that I forgot to bring them in with me. Ensuring that the towel was secure, I opened the bathroom door. Thanks to the condo's air-conditioning, an arctic blast swept through the humid warmth, bringing goose bumps to my arms and shoulders.

My things were on the edge of the bed, right where I'd left them. A quick check showed the bedroom door opened halfway but no sign of movement. Deciding to chance it, I dashed out and grabbed the pile of silk and lace, holding it against my chest. I was turning to go back to the haven of the bathroom when my luck ran out. Rabbit came through the door, looking at the phone in his hand.

I must have made a sound because his head came up, his attention locking on me. We both froze. His gaze dropped to the material in my arms and heated. There was such depth to his speculative expression that I found it hard to breathe, much less make my voice work.

He tossed his phone onto the bed and stalked toward me until he was close enough to touch me. Then he did. He ran a finger along my exposed collarbone. His simple touch left a line of searing fire in its wake that made my pulse pound and released the hold on my voice.

"Wyatt." His real name came out somewhere between a warning and an invitation.

"Right here, *cher.*"

I swayed just the tiniest bit as that husky drawl swept through my faltering defenses like a velvet glove, clearing a path. When a revealing glint of male satisfaction flashed in those eyes, I lost what I wanted to say.

His gaze dropped to the shivery path he was tracing. "So soft," he murmured as he continued his devastatingly gentle caress. When his eyes came back to mine, what stared back at me—hunger, need—tore through all my self-imposed arguments. "You goin' to bite if I take a taste?"

He was too close, my desire too demanding, and the combination broke through my wariness. "Maybe."

"Worth it." Then he kissed me.

This time, there was no tender lead-in. Instead, it was pure male demand layered in heat and want. The storm of it crashed into me, leaving only sensation behind. And I loved every minute of it. His mouth moved over mine with seductive demand, wiping away all rational thought. Caught in the wildfire, I let the flames sink deep until he was the only solid thing in my world.

I pressed against him, my hands curling into his shoulders, trying to drag him closer. He helped, widening his stance until I was surrounded by the solid strength of him. His hands went to my hips and then slid around to my ass. I sank my hands into his hair, holding on for dear life even as heat settled low. Despite the barrier of the towel and his pants, I couldn't miss the fact that he was hard. His hands on my ass tightened, and as that hardness pressed deeper, my hips moved with mindless demand. Against my aching breasts, his chest vibrated with his answering groan. The burn went white-hot, and my world dissolved until only his taste and touch remained.

A steady beep began to penetrate the sensual haze. I

would have ignored it, but Rabbit eased us both back from the crumbling edge of need, ending the destructive kiss. I gripped his shoulders, my forehead pressed into his sternum, eyes closed, as I relearned to breathe and waited for my world to right itself. He said nothing as he cradled my head, gently massaging the tension at the base of my skull.

The beeping noise continued unabated. I didn't bother moving from my position. "What is that?"

"That would be proof of our uninvited visitor." His hand left my neck and stroked down my spine.

Enjoying his touch, I stayed in place but opened my eyes. The first thing I noticed was the spectacular results of our shared kiss on Rabbit. My fingers curled into his biceps, mainly so I wouldn't do something reckless like reach down and stroke.

I blinked, shifted my gaze lower, and realized I was staring at my forgotten lingerie. Something about seeing the tangle of lace and silk on the floor between our bare feet added another fracture to my deteriorating emotional defenses. At that moment, I knew the battle was well and truly lost. I admitted to myself that I wanted to discover how deep this thing between us was, and I wanted it badly enough to risk ruining everything.

Not ready to share that with the man holding me, I scrambled for something to say. "You'd better check it."

The stroking hand stilled at the base of my spine. "You gotta let me go first, sugar."

I reluctantly dropped my arms and took a step back, and he let me go. Of course, I had to grab at the towel that had loosened when I moved. Tightening it, I tried not to flinch when it rubbed against sensitized flesh.

Rabbit crouched down and gathered my fallen clothes.

With him in that position, my brain short-circuited. I didn't realize what I was doing until my fingers were buried in his hair, stroking through the thick strands.

He looked up with a devastating grin. "I like the way you pet me."

Staring into his face, I could only shake my head. "Crazy man."

"Nothing wrong with being a little crazy." He handed me the pile of silk and lace then straightened and turned to the beeping phone on the bed. He picked it up and sat on the edge of the bed. "Well, now…"

"What?" I shifted my stuff to one arm and angled myself so I could see what he was looking at.

"Looks like our visitor left behind a nifty little bugger." Despite his casual tone, he was frowning.

"You recognize it?" I sat next to him, brushing shoulders with him, his heat beating back the artificial cool of the AC.

"Sort of." He scrolled through a string of text and symbols. "It's actually a modified version of a data-collecting virus. Ran across one of these a couple of years back."

"Data collection? So… what? It's sharing all our information?" That would not be good. Even though it was the decoy laptop, there was still enough damaging information on it to cause us problems.

"Essentially, yeah."

"Can you figure out who's on the other end?"

"Maybe?"

"You don't sound sure."

He looked up and met my gaze. "Because I'm not. Whoever did this, they're good—scary good."

I did not like the sound of that. Rabbit was damn good at what he did, to the degree that there weren't many out there who were better. Instead of feeding into his doubts, I fell back on a proven approach—one I'd discovered by accident—and challenged his competitive streak. "You're telling me whoever did this can outplay you?"

Predictably, he snorted. "It's not that. It's the time component. We're already working against a tight clock. Trying to unmask this one"—he held up his phone—"might take longer than what we have."

"Okay." That made sense. We could only fight effectively on so many fronts. "Well, if we can't unmask them, maybe we can trip them up—make them come forward."

His eyes narrowed. "You're thinking we feed them false information."

Since that approach was currently working with our situation with Zane, we might as well stick to it. I nodded. "If you hadn't been here, would this intrusion be caught?"

He paused, thoughtful. "Probably not."

"So, it's a viable option, then, right?"

He gave a slow nod. "It might work."

I looked down at the phone he held, worrying my bottom lip. Whoever had set this up would have had to get into the condo undetected. Considering the security, I wasn't sure such a thing was easily accomplished. "Do you think it's Zane?"

"Got to say no." When I sent him a questioning look, he said, "The brain behind this level of sophistication would have found the discrepancies we did with Amalia."

That was not what I wanted to hear. "Then who else are we dealing with?"

He cocked his head. "I know one way we can find out."

It didn't take much to follow his logic. "The security cameras in the hall. Can you access the feeds from here?"

"Won't know until I try."

I grabbed his hand and angled the phone toward me. "Do we have enough time?" We were down to an hour and twenty minutes before we had to leave.

"Maybe." He tugged his hand free. "You finish up, and I'll see how far I can get."

Chapter Fourteen

JINX

Thanks to Rabbit's insistence on accessing the security feed, we made Santiago's with five minutes to spare. Both of us were edgy by the time we stepped into the restaurant, me because I didn't like cutting it so close and Rabbit because the security feed had been a bust. Whoever broke into the condo had managed to take the cameras offline, so all we'd had to confirm their presence was a twenty-eight-minute window of missing footage.

After giving our names, we were ushered through the restaurant's hushed elegance to a semiprivate alcove in the back, where Zane and Amalia were already waiting. We exchanged greetings and got settled, small talk fluttering around while a server took our drink orders. Conversation remained casual, and Amalia skillfully kept it flowing as our orders were delivered and we began to eat.

Only after our server cleared the table, refreshed our coffee and drinks, and left us alone did Zane finally decide to get to the point. From his relaxed position across from me, one hand cradling his preferred whiskey, the other playing with the back of Amalia's necklace, he lobbed the opening salvo. "Elena, what do you know about the Boyau project?"

The seemingly casual question sent a shockwave through me. The last thing I expected to hear was the name of the highly classified communications project that had almost killed Risia and Tag in Vegas. I blinked, thinking fast. "It was proposed by a developer out of Nevada as a fix for a fault in the Department of Defense's encrypted communication system. However, rumor has it he tried to double-cross the DOD. Didn't end well for him, and the DOD managed to plug their supposed holes." I picked up my coffee and gave a tiny shrug. "Or so I heard." I took a sip and set my cup aside. "Why?"

For a long moment, Zane watched me without revealing any reaction. Next to him, Amalia appeared relaxed, but the tense line of her arm as it disappeared under the table, where she presumably had her hand on Zane's knee, betrayed her strain.

Finally, he said, "The project we asked you here for shares some similarities."

That wasn't good, not even a little bit. The initial Boyau project was designed to not only fix the flaw in the DOD's communication server but to also create an undetectable back door that granted access to secured files relating to covert operations. In fact, the developer, Rawlings, had managed to nab a list of embedded operatives and was in the midst of conducting a private auction for said list when everything went to hell. Zane had been at that auction as Alexander Spires. And he hadn't been alone. His female companion had been a curvy blonde.

One of the pieces that had been nagging at me finally fell into place. The hair color might be different, the curves not as pronounced, and the angles of the face softer, but chances were damn good that Amalia and the blonde were one and the same. I didn't know why I hadn't thought of it before, but that kind of transformation wouldn't be hard to pull off, especially if she had the same ability as me, which wasn't as big a stretch as one might think. In fact, those who excelled at taking on roles—whether as actors or operatives specializing in undercover work—had some trace of the ability. In my case, and probably Amalia's, that ability was supercharged, but it came with a downside. Once someone realized it was an illusion, the truth would eventually leak through. And now that I knew the two women were the same person, Amalia's illusionary impact would begin to fray.

I fought to keep my attention on Zane. "I'm listening."

"We'd like you to confirm that the holes have been well and truly plugged."

"You think they aren't?" Rabbit shifted next to me, and while his body language remained relaxed, an invisible intensity brushed against me.

"I'm sure whatever weaknesses were identified have been corrected, but if it worked once, why not twice?"

Is he really that delusional? I didn't bother hiding the scorn in my voice. "Because the US government is highly territorial about their classified programs. Once they were made aware of the flaws that allowed Boyau to infiltrate their systems, those same systems would have been locked down tight."

Zane leaned in, his eyes bright. "It took Rawlings three years to develop the program. I'm sure you, with your considerable skills, can do better and faster."

If he thought pandering to Elena's ego was going to work, he was in for a big surprise. It didn't matter how good

Elena was. What he was asking for would take a hell of a lot more time than the month allotted for Elena's trial run. But unfortunately, this was a situation where saying no outright could end badly.

"Do you think you're the first one to ask for something like this?" I shook my head.

"Because you aren't," Rabbit broke into the conversation, his voice hard. "And I'll tell you what I told the last interested party who asked her—if you're keen on putting a target on your back, go ahead, but she stays clear."

Zane scowled, but I used Rabbit's defense and bolstered it. "I haven't gotten this far in my career by being stupid, Zane. Accessing that list is akin to getting your hands on the Holy Grail. Add in the fact that they're still on high alert from the first bungled attempt, and the risks versus rewards aren't even worth considering."

Amalia spoke, her voice calm in contrast to the vibrating tension at the table. "We understand that the initial target is under scrutiny, which is why we don't want the list."

For the first time, I turned to Amalia, and sure enough, the pieces of the blonde merged with the brunette, skewing the illusion. Fortunately, her unexpected comment helped the sincerity of my startled reaction. "What do you want?"

"Something a little less volatile but quite valuable to us." There was a mercenary edge to her expression.

I kept quiet, curious, despite myself, about what could be more valuable than the identifying list of operatives.

Amalia continued, "There are indications that the back door Boyau was to exploit might still be accessible. We're hoping you can answer that question."

Rabbit shifted, his foot tapping mine under the table. As if I needed the warning. I knew if that door was still open, we needed to close it, and fast. "And if it is?"

Zane smiled like an evil Cheshire Cat. "We'd like to commission you for a customized program."

"Customized how?" Next to me, I could feel Rabbit's attention come on point.

"We have extensive global business ties with complex schedules and routes. Having those interrupted tends to create detrimental impacts on our financials. My employers would like to be more proactive in avoiding such future interruptions."

Reading between the lines, I put the clues together. "You want to watch those who are watching you." We weren't the only ones interested in Falcon's movements, especially after the fiasco with Hawes. But there had to be more to this request, because I was fairly sure there were plenty of black hats out there who could create such a program for far less than Elena would demand. "There's something more you want, isn't there?"

Zane exchanged a quick look with Amalia before coming back to me. "It's always nice to work with intelligent people."

"It's not a matter of intelligence but practicality. Spyware isn't much of a challenge. I can think of a handful of people who could create that program for you."

"But they can't do what you do, can they?" There was a subtle menace to Zane's question.

Everything I knew about Elena flicked through my brain, and it hit me what they were really looking for. "You want a skeleton key."

"No, they want more than a key," Rabbit said, cold speculation making him sound like a stranger. "They not only want to open and close that door at will, but they also want unfettered access to whoever's monitoring them."

I murmured, "Because if you know who's watching you

and when they plan to move, you can turn the tables." Acceding to Zane's demand would put the teams going in to intercept Falcon's various illegal shipments at risk and would, moreover, keep Falcon permanently a step ahead of its watchers. "You want a Rosetta program—data collection, encryption key, unfettered control of the system, and undetectable virus."

Zane lifted his glass. "You did ask for a challenge."

It was closing in on eleven when the taillights of Zane's car turned out of the parking lot and disappeared into the night. For the first time all night, I could take a deep breath.

"You okay?" Rabbit asked in a low voice. His palm rested against the base of my spine, the warm weight of it doing little to ease the chill sliding through my veins.

"I don't know," I murmured, questions and worries circling like vultures in my brain.

"I did warn you."

He had, but for some reason, until Zane laid out the particulars of his nefarious test, it hadn't really hit me just how far my personal line would be shoved. "What he wants…" I was unable to put the full ugly picture into any comprehensible words.

"I know." Rabbit's equally grim response didn't bode well. He nudged me forward.

"Can you do it?" That was the real question. This whole mission would be moot if Rabbit couldn't create the program Zane—and by extension, Falcon—wanted.

"It'll be tricky to pull off."

"I hear a *but* in there." I matched my steps to his, staying close so our conversation remained between us even though we were the only ones moving through the lot.

Rabbit shook his head even as he scanned our surroundings. "No *but*—not yet."

Maybe not, but something was happening in that quicksilver brain. "What are you thinking?"

He glanced down at me, his face inscrutable. "I'm thinking I need to dig into the Boyau project before I decide anything."

Since I wasn't keen on having this conversation overheard, I slowed, bringing us both to a stop, hopefully far enough away from the car to be safe. Then I stepped in front of him and put a hand on his chest. "Share."

His hands went to my hips, and his gaze met mine. "This isn't exactly the best place to discuss this, *cher*."

Considering that we had an avid audience in both the car and the condo, I begged to differ. "Isn't it?" I deliberately looked around at the nearly empty lot. Despite the few remaining cars, no one else was around. "Looks like we're about as private as we can get right now."

"Stubborn."

Not about to argue, I waited in silent demand.

Finally, he sighed and gave in. "Back in Vegas, we made a copy of the drive Risia requisitioned from Aether."

"You modified it. Tweaking the encrypted information until it skewed the data so no one at the auction got a usable list."

Rabbit had needed to sell the team on that solution because of the high degree of risk associated with using the actual classified list, which contained the identity of every covert operator and each person's active assignment. Rawlings—Aether's CEO—was determined to earn top dollar with his private, and highly illegal, auction of the data and the back door that granted initial access via the DOD's systems. At that same auction, Zane had made his first appearance as Alexander Spires, and things had gone horrifically wrong for Rawlings and most of the buyers.

"We can do something similar here."

Before he could continue, I was shaking my head. "I don't think that's wise. Don't forget, Zane was there. No way would he fall for that trick twice."

Despite the shadows cast by the sporadically placed lights, there was no missing the exasperation filling Rabbit's face. "Give me some credit, yeah?" Since his question came out with the bite of temper, I kept my mouth shut. It took a lot to get Rabbit riled. His hands left my hips, one to rake through his hair and the other to make a fist at his side. "The type of program he wants, he's going to want to test it. When he does, it has to work."

That did not sound good, especially considering that Falcon dealt in drugs, weapons, and humans. "You want to give him a clear shot at whatever shipment he's going to test it with, without interference?"

Grim resolution replaced his exasperation. "We don't have much choice."

"No," I said, though I knew better. No matter how much I didn't like it, Rabbit's logic was sound. In the covert world, there was a level of ruthless practicality that dominated the decision-making process. In this case, there was no doubt that the higher-ups would consider the loss of an illegal shipment, and whatever casualties that involved, an acceptable exchange for dismantling a criminal syndicate like Falcon. The win would outweigh the human costs.

It wasn't a new realization. Hell, I'd been in similar situations before—and would be again—but it never got easier to accept. Sometimes I hated our job.

I looked away, wrapping my arms around my stomach and clenching my teeth as frustration boiled. "Dammit, just… dammit."

"Yeah, I know." He stepped in and pulled me close.

For a few seconds, I remained stiff, but Rabbit wasn't the one I was mad at. It was the whole messed-up situation and the bleak outcomes that made me want to scream and rail. I dropped my head against his chest, needing to think, to find some other way out of this mess. But no matter how hard I twisted the facts, I couldn't see my way clear.

Rabbit curled one hand around the back of my neck while the other stroked my spine in silent comfort. It took a few breaths before I lifted my head and made to step back. Rabbit let me go.

I turned away to pace in front of him as I considered our options. I stopped on one of my return passes. "Can't we embed a fail-safe of some kind?"

"We could, but when would we activate it? We still have to let at least one of whatever shipment they identify get through. Otherwise, they'll know we screwed them." He folded his arms as he continued to play devil's advocate. "Trigger it before the transaction is complete, and you blow the entire op. And trigger it after…"

He left the rest unsaid, but he'd made his point. Triggering it after the fact would result in casualties on both sides. And in either scenario, we'd be the first ones blamed, which wouldn't end well for either of us.

"We can't let a team go in blind," I said. "They need to know what they're walking into." Guilt might be a familiar companion, but I still wanted to avoid it.

"We clue in whatever agency is watching Falcon, and you and I both know it'll turn into a total cluster." Rabbit's voice held nothing but cold logic. "The more individuals who know what's happening, the higher the chance of it all going tits up."

I shifted my gaze beyond him and stared sightlessly into the night as personal experiences played out in my mind's eye, leaving me no way to argue his point. Those experiences had factored into my decision to leave the corps and work for Delacourt. My dark thoughts came to a skidding halt, and my gaze snapped to Rabbit. "We keep thinking we have to read in for whatever agency is watching. What if we limit the disclosure on this?"

"To…?"

"Delacourt." Excitement made my words tumble over each other as I retook my position in front of him and pressed my palms against his chest. "We keep this part of the operation in-house."

He frowned. "You want to set up a decoy shipment?"

I nodded. "Complete with a decoy sting team. If we stack the odds in our favor, we have a better chance of pulling this off." Since he didn't appear convinced, I laid it out in rough strokes. "Zane all but told us Falcon's shipments are being monitored, which is why they're requesting the program. So let's use that. I'm sure Delacourt has some in with whichever agencies are currently eyeing Falcon. If she can get them to identify key targets, we can skew the program to focus on those. Then she can set up one of the other PSY-IV teams to play the part of whatever agency Zane currently has eyes on. Even if something slips through, if the shipment is tagged, we can still go in and retrieve it."

He took his time responding. "You realize just how shaky this plan is?"

I did. It was a regular house of cards. With one slipup, the resulting blow would wipe the entire thing out. "You have a better one?"

He grimaced, confirming my guess that we had a slim chance in hell of pulling this off. "We do this, and we'll be dancing with the devil, yeah?"

"Yeah," I agreed, going on tiptoe to press a quick kiss to his tight jaw. "Here's hoping our moves are enough to keep the devil begging for more."

Shaking his head, he wrapped an arm around my waist as we headed for the car. "Wicked woman."

This time, I kept my satisfied grin to myself.

Chapter Fifteen

RABBIT

I wasn't nearly as confident as Jinx about her plan, but it wasn't like I had a better one. She was driven by the same demons who dug their nasty claws into me. Gaining a victory with the blood and lives of good men was not something either of us could stomach. The need to face decisions like this was what kept me away from the more clandestine agencies. If I had to swim in the murky waters of frayed ethics, I'd soon find myself drowning in good intentions gone bad.

Once I got Jinx into the car, she didn't waste time kicking off her heels and drawing one leg up under her. As I rounded the hood, I tested the bug and found that it was still active. Frustrated by the situational restrictions but knowing there was jack all I could do about it, I got in and slammed the door a little harder than necessary, which earned me a raised eyebrow from Jinx.

I shook my head and glanced meaningfully at the windshield. She rolled her eyes, snapped her seat belt in place, and heaved a small sigh. We did the chitchat thing until I got out of the lot, then she turned on the radio, giving us a minor mask of white noise. Eventually, conversation petered out until the only sound was the incongruous pop chords coming from the speakers.

As I navigated through the late-night traffic, my mind worked over the problem Zane's test presented. Creating the initial spyware program would be time-consuming but doable, but masking the double-agent aspect would be tricky. I had a few ideas, but until I could get in front of a keyboard and test them, I wouldn't know which one would pan out.

Before long, the lack of sleep started catching up with me, and I found myself drifting. Stopping at a red light, I turned to find that Jinx had already nodded off, her head lolling against the window. Since I wasn't keen on wrapping the two of us around a light pole, I hit the button to lower the window just as the light turned green. The window didn't move.

"Dammit." Not about to play around with it and piss off the drivers behind me, I hit the gas and tried the button a couple more times. Same result. I didn't want to lower Jinx's window, since she was using it as a pillow, so I went for the next best thing, the AC. I jacked the temperature as cold as it would go. When tepid air emerged instead of the expected frigid blast, I started trying to angle the vents one-handed. *Damn rentals.*

My hand fumbled against the controls as things blurred around the edges. I must have managed to hit something, because the radio blinked off, but there was no change in the AC. The jarring warning of a car horn as I drifted into the other lane brought momentary clarity. I jerked my attention back to the road, automatically overcorrecting my steering. The car rocked in its lane as I regained control, but I felt almost punch-drunk.

"Fuck, fuck, fuck." Something was wrong—really wrong. This wasn't normal. I forced my way through the thickening haze that seemed to cloud my brain. I needed to get out of traffic and figure out what was happening.

A turn was coming up on the right, an escape from the main road. I took it, praying I'd find a place to pull over. Spotting a shoulder, I let off the gas and flicked on my turn signal, but instead of slowing, the car picked up speed. Not only that, but I suddenly found myself fighting the wheel. The tires bounced hard over the gravel shoulder, the back wheels spinning before regaining traction and jumping back onto the asphalt.

A dull thump sounded as Jinx's head hit the window, and she groaned. My alarm rose when that failed to rouse her.

"Jinx, dammit, wake up." I continued to fight the wheel, but it was clear I wasn't regaining control any time soon. The car had a mind of its own. Adrenaline began to clear out the fog, giving my brain a chance to kick in.

Sweat stung my eyes as I white knuckled the steering wheel. I used a shoulder to wipe them clear as I slapped the AC off, since it wasn't doing a damn bit of good. "Jinx." I didn't dare take my eyes off the ribbon of road whipping under the wheels. The street remained clear and straight, but something told me that wasn't going to last long. "Jinx, wake up!"

I gripped the gearshift and threw it into neutral. The engine continued to rev, the speedometer rising in tandem. I gritted my teeth as realization wiped away the last of the unnatural haze.

"What the hell?" Jinx's slurred question meant she was finally awake.

"Someone's hacked the car."

"What?"

I caught her movement out of the corner of my eye. "Leave the belt on!"

She froze as headlights broke the darkness ahead and another car headed toward us.

Fear sank icy teeth in deep as I watched those lights get closer. I kept my death grip on the steering wheel, praying that whoever was behind this didn't want us dead.

"Rabbit?" Jinx squeaked as she slapped her hands on the dash.

My mind spun, information coming in snapshots and generating various outcomes. Staring out the windshield, I realized that whoever was behind the hack had picked the perfect spot to take control.

The road disappeared into the darkness, leading away from the more populated urban sprawl. A narrow ditch lined the left side, empty darkness sprawling beyond it. Cement walls and old-growth trees delineated the neighborhood green spaces on the right, creating a lethal obstacle course. Staying straight worked for me, but I wasn't the one in control.

As if that was the spark it was waiting for, inspiration struck. "Jinx, I need you to take the wheel."

Fortunately, she didn't waste time with pointless questions but instead undid her belt as I shoved my seat back in an effort to give her room. "As soon as you can, send us to the left."

"Got it." She all but climbed into my lap, adding her strength to mine on the wheel and her foot on top of mine on the useless brake.

Not liking the fact that she had no seat belt, I locked my arms across her chest in a human harness, praying it would be enough to keep her safe. As soon as her hands were in place, I shifted my focus, accessing the electronic world that belonged to me. Instead of finding the smooth entry I was used to, I had to fight my way through a distracting screen of anxiety before the car's main computer system came into focus. The energy signals spread out in front of me in dizzying lines of light. Recognizing the familiar signature of the damn bug I had all but forgotten, I didn't waste time cursing. *Who the hell knows how much they picked up?* The best I could do was ensure that they got nothing more. I sent a whip of electricity into its tiny brain and fried it before turning my attention back to the bigger problem.

Despite the loud ticking of my mental clock counting down, I zipped through the electronic freeways, noting the solid presence of the control units running the car's various functions. Signals zipped along in a dizzying race as I swept my psychic eye over the construct. The steady streams of light defined the car's brain as information flowed from system to system, circuit to circuit. That wasn't what I needed.

A spark hit and was quickly followed by another, like firing neurons. Shifting my attention, I waited. When it happened again, it coincided with the vague echo of Jinx's curse and the distant sense of my body swaying in my seat.

Gotcha. As I zeroed in on the hacker's electronic trail, the urgency nipping at my ass had me choosing brute strength over finesse. Energy was the heart of my ability, and manipulation was my preferred weapon. In this case, to break the hacker's stranglehold on the ECU's brain, I needed to land a devastating sucker punch.

Stretching my psychic fingers out, I gathered as much

energy as I could and wound it together until it all but burned through my synapses. Targeting the hacker's last position, I hovered over the information streams. One breath… two. Hair rose on my psychic skin in warning, and I slammed the coiled energy into the stream just as the hacker's interference sparked. The two energies collided in an eye-searing explosion of light.

The electronic freeway went dark. In that same breathless instant, my physical body was wrenched sideways with bruising force that sent pain lancing through my head and left shoulder. A savage spurt of satisfaction followed on its heels as I registered, on some distant level, that Jinx had regained control of the wheel.

But we weren't out of trouble yet. A flicker of light, interspersed with the unique pattern of programming code, heralded the car's electronic systems coming back online. Not about to lose my fragile control, I ignored the bruising sensations battering my body and Jinx's constant stream of curses and began manipulating the now-scrolling curtain of code and redirecting the electronic signals. Before long, the engine control units were mine and locked from any further outside interference.

Then I turned my attention to the hacker, but he or she was long gone. No surprise there. Around me, the process flows kicked into gear as the ECUs all came back online. Since I was still breathing, I took a moment to ensure that there were no missed access points the hacker could exploit.

Confident that the car was mine and would stay that way, I pulled back from the electronic landscape, raising that protective wall that kept my ability in check. Safe in my own mind, the first thing I noted was the merciless throbbing that reverberated from the top of my skull to my toes. That ache was joined by others—along my ribs and the side of my face and radiating down my legs.

"Rabbit? Wyatt?"

Jinx's shaky voice saying my name in a tone I'd never heard from her before had me swallowing back rising nausea and blinking my eyes open. I groaned as even that movement hurt. "I'm here."

"Can you let me go?"

At her question, I realized I had managed to lock her tight against me. *Huh. Guess the human-harness idea worked.* I loosened my hold, giving her room to move. "You okay?"

She gingerly shifted her weight, trying to twist to see me.

My ribs protested. I grabbed her hips and tightened as I sucked in sharp breath. "Hold still for a second."

She froze, and for a couple of heartbeats, only our harsh breaths could be heard.

I did a mental check of my body, and when only muttered complaints came back, I said, "I think I'm good." I let her go.

Her weight lightened, and then hands cupped my face. "Open your eyes."

I hadn't realized I'd closed them. I followed her orders and found that she had shifted toward the center console. My eyes met hers, and I was stunned by the depth of concern I saw. "Hey, I'm okay."

"No, you're not." She studied me with a frown.

When she reached up to turn on the interior light, there was enough ambient light to note the trickle of blood seeping down her from temple to jaw. I caught her chin, stopping her from reaching up, and angled her face so I could see her in the faint light from the dash. "Neither are you."

She held onto my shoulder. "Let me turn on the light."

"I've got it." I reached up, wincing as abused muscles protested, and hit the light. Even though it wasn't super bright, my eyes narrowed against the glare until they could adjust. At first, all I could see was Jinx, eyes dark against her blood-streaked pale face. A bruise was forming along the side of it. Her hair had escaped the neat twist and was tangled around her jaw. She braced herself against the dash then moved off of me and into her seat.

This gave me an uninterrupted view of the windshield, which now sported a spiderweb of cracks. Outside in the inky darkness, the headlights shone into the abyss, the driver's-side light flickering ominously. Considering my angled view of the crumbling edge of the drainage ditch, there was no way we were getting out of this without a tow truck.

Which reminded me… "The other driver?"

"We missed them, but I heard brakes, so they'll probably be here any second." Jinx was digging around the glove compartment. "Yes." She lifted her hand to show off a clutch of napkins.

Taking them from her, I said, "Come here."

She didn't argue but gingerly moved until I could use the napkin against the cut on her temple. While I did that, she was blotting at my face. "I think you have a concussion, probably from when you hit the side window."

I met her gaze in silent question.

"Your pupils are dilated."

"And you've got a hell of a shiner coming up." Taking in the bruising rising along the side of her face, I was grateful that seemed to be the worst of it. "Ribs?"

"Sore, but nothing's broken." She brought my hand up to take over holding a napkin against my nose. "Hold this. It's bleeding."

I held it tight.

She shifted her position, her gaze lowering before she narrowed her eyes. "Your arms."

Without releasing the pressure on my nose, I tried to twist my arms to see what she was staring at. "What?"

"They must have hit the steering wheel at some point." She brushed a careful hand down them. "You sure you're okay?"

Before I could answer, a muffled voice called out. I turned my head, hissing at the tweak of pain flaring down my neck and between my shoulders, to see a shadowy figure picking its way over to us with the help of the light of a cell phone. Using my free hand, I pulled on the door handle, and the door swung open, the hinges groaning, the bottom scraping against dirt.

The figure stopped near the back end of the car. "You okay in there?"

"Banged up and bruised but breathing," I called back. "You?"

The voice came closer. "I'm good." An older man in business casual came over and crouched by the door. The interior light glinted off his glasses, but there was no mistaking his concern when he spotted Jinx. "Ma'am, you okay?"

She managed a wan smile. "I've been better."

He switched his attention to me. "You two want to risk moving?"

"Yeah."

It took some careful maneuvering, and I had to rely on the guy's support to get out, but we managed to limp our way to the shoulder. Eventually, I was leaning against his sedan while Jinx sat on the back seat.

"Emergency services should be here soon. I called right

after you went off the road." He eyed me carefully. "What happened?"

Jinx answered first, injecting a hint of a tremor into her voice. "Something ran out in front of the car."

Since we were about to have police involvement, I chose to weave a believable truth with Jinx's explanation. "We tried to avoid it, but it was like the car went haywire."

The man turned back to me, and I couldn't miss his skepticism, even if he was too polite to call us on it. No doubt he thought I'd had too much to drink. The police would be sure to share that assumption, but fortunately, I'd stayed away from alcohol during dinner.

"Didn't you see it?" Jinx's question regained the man's attention, drawing him in with a note in her voice and holding him spellbound. She gave a delicate shudder. "I think it was something small, maybe a dog or something?"

Her voice twined around my mind, easing the calculating edge of my speeding thoughts. It took me a second to realize what she was doing and erect the necessary psychic barrier so as not to get sucked under. We needed a reason for our erratic driving, and it would be best if both accounts agreed on the main points, such as the story that we were avoiding some animal.

Jinx held the man's gaze as he focused on her, her voice slipping into a soothing murmur. "We're lucky it wasn't something bigger."

He was nodding before she'd finished. "If it had been a deer, this wouldn't have ended so well."

She managed a shaky smile. "Whatever it was, it was fast."

Her damsel-in-distress act had his voice softening with concern. "It was most likely a rabbit."

Even though I'd witnessed this aspect of her ability

before, it always caught me off guard how fast her influence could work. It was a gamble because it didn't always work. She once explained that wielding her ability required delicate handling, because she had to create a shared experience. That was not easy to do unless there was some emotion both parties shared—in this case, relief. Thanks to the near miss of the accident, the man would be more easily influenced, more willing to fill in the blanks about facing a situation that required split-second decisions.

She leaned against the doorframe, and I didn't think her slumped shoulders were for show. "I'm just glad we're all okay."

Unable to help myself, I took her hand and held it tight.

The man turned back to me. "You know, you're lucky the car didn't flip."

Bloodied napkin pressed against my nose with one hand, Jinx's hand in the other, I looked beyond him at the dark hulk of our car. "Yeah, we were." The rear lights blinked with monotonous consistency. "I'm just glad we're upright and breathing." I shook my head, gritting my teeth as my head protested the move. "What a mess. The rental company's going to have a fit."

Catching my wince, Jinx tugged her hand free and patted my thigh. "Hopefully, the police will help us figure this out. Then we'll worry about dealing with the rental agency." She shifted her attention to the man watching us. "Thank you for stopping. Not everyone would."

He looked away as if uncomfortable with Jinx's gratitude. Flashing light cut through the darkness, and I swore there was relief in his voice when he said, "Looks like the cavalry is here."

The next hour was spent answering questions from the police and fielding the pokes and prods of the EMTs. By the time we were bundled into the ambulance, my nose had finally stopped bleeding, and stiffness had set in. Jinx wasn't much better. In the harsh light of the ambulance, her pale face was bordering on gray.

We hit the emergency room, and despite the fact that it was oh-dark-thirty, the place was packed. Noise and smells hit, making my stomach curl, but I swallowed it down and kept walking alongside Jinx's rolling cot. I'd earned that position with my adamant refusal to be wheeled in despite the EMT's insistence that I might have a concussion.

As the charge nurse gathered information, I asked the nearest EMT, "Is it always this crazy in here?"

"Saturday nights are a special kind of crazy. But this is actually not too bad."

Before I could argue, the nurse was leading us to a room. "You two will have to share. We're a bit tight on rooms."

"Works for me." *Especially since I'm not keen on leaving Jinx alone.*

It took another half hour or so to get through the laundry list of questions. Thank God our cover identities were solid. In between the hospital's Q and A session and another round of "Does this hurt? What about this?" I managed to get off a quick request for assistance to the team via the customized chat app. Eventually, the hustle and bustle waned, giving us a small window of privacy. Stretched out on a bed, I laid my arm over my burning eyes.

"Told you so." The sleepy murmur came from Jinx, who was resting on her side in the bed next to me.

I lifted my arm and turned my head to see her blinking valiantly in an effort to stay awake. There was a bandage on the cut just below her hairline and an ice pack covering the side of her face. She'd lost the gray cast to her skin and the pinched lines around her mouth, probably because the painkillers were kicking in. Seeing her like that made me want to crawl into the bed and hold her tight. Unfortunately, neither one of us was in any condition for that.

"Told me what, *cher*?"

"You have a concussion."

"Well, at least we match." I kept my voice quiet, hoping she'd give in and let sleep take her.

"Scared me."

I barely caught her whisper. "Me too, but we're safe."

"For now," she murmured.

Her eyes finally closed, and her breathing evened out as she succumbed. I lay there, watching her sleep, while images of just how horrifically wrong tonight could have gone played through my head. *Could still go wrong if that damn bug on the windshield managed to catch the use of our names during the initial hack.* I hadn't had time to do more than fry the thing, but I couldn't recall if it was active or not. *Nothing I can do about it now.*

I focused on who would have gained by taking us out of the picture, because this hack wasn't just a scare tactic. If I hadn't managed to block that last command, we would have turned straight into the oncoming car. At that speed, I wasn't sure if anyone would have walked away.

No matter how I turned things around and over, I couldn't fit Zane in as being behind the hacker's attack. Even Amalia didn't really fit. Considering the manner of attack, the only possibility I could come up with was that it was the same bastard who'd managed to break in and infect the laptop.

What the fuck did we stumble into? It was bad enough we were playing footsie with Zane and Falcon. We needed to figure out who our unknown third was and quick. Since the hacker was focused on me and Jinx, it made me think we'd inherited an enemy of Elena's. *Just what we need.* When pain shot through my jaw, I consciously unlocked my teeth and forced the muscles in my shoulders and neck to relax.

Movement at the door caught my attention just as a steel-haired man in a white coat spoke. "Mr. Somers, I'm Dr. Addison."

"Doctor." I went to sit up, but he waved me back.

"Best you remain lying down, son." He did a quick check of Jinx and her monitors before pulling a chair between the two beds and angling it so he could face me. "I'm glad you're awake."

Something in his voice set my alarm bells ringing. "I take it you found something?"

"I'm afraid so." He set his iPad on the bed, his expression grave. "Based on the information regarding your accident, I decided to run a couple of extra tests."

When he stopped, I prompted, "And?"

"And I'm afraid you and Ms. Drake are suffering from carbon monoxide poisoning." He tilted his head. "You'll both be fine, but I'm going to have to insist that you two stay here at least until morning."

Leashing the useless frustration and fury curling through me, I kept my voice even. "You'll share this with the police?"

He nodded. "From what I gathered, you were involved in a one-car accident, correct?"

"Yeah. We were coming back from a dinner. I didn't know anything was wrong until I drifted into another lane and realized I was having a hard time staying awake."

"Not a surprise. That's one of the signs of CO poisoning." Sharp intelligence burned behind the medical professional facade. "Do you mind running through what happened once you left your dinner?"

I laid it all out, the sleepiness, trying to get the window down, then turning the AC on, taking the other road, and the mechanical failures with steering and braking. By the time I was done, the doctor's face was carved in stone.

"Did you share this with the police?"

I managed to lift an eyebrow. "I did. They assured us that they'll be pulling the car's black box to review the data." I wasn't keen on that, because I wanted to get my hands on it first. The need to track the hacker down was undeniable. My hands fisted. Maybe it was best the police got to it first. "They think the car may have been hacked."

"Hacked? Really?"

"Like I said, it was a rental so…" I managed a half-hearted shrug despite my protesting shoulder.

The doctor shook his head. "Every day brings something new." He picked up his iPad. "If that's the case, then you're lucky the only things you both are taking away from this are bruises and minor cuts. You'll want to pay special attention to your arms. Both ulnas show deep bruising. Thankfully, everything else checked out."

"And Elena? Is everything okay with her?"

He looked at Jinx and reached over to adjust the ice pack on her cheek. "She'll be bruised for a few days, but it should fade. Our biggest concern is the possible concussions you two have, which is why we want you both here for observation." He rose from his seat as a nurse came in. "I'm going to advise that neither one of you drive home. Is there someone who can pick you up?"

"I'll make arrangements."

"Good." He patted my leg. "Get some rest, and we'll double-check things in the morning, but you should be fine." He gave the nurse a nod and a smile before leaving the room.

I watched the nurse make some minor adjustments to Jinx's monitor before she turned to me. Whatever she saw on my face softened her expression from professional to friendly. "She'll be okay, you know."

"I know."

She ran through a check on my monitors, gave me a gentle "Good night," and left, letting the door close behind her.

I pulled my phone out of the drawer and went to the anonymous chat room that was my emergency link to the team and wrote: *Need ride in a.m.*

Copy. ETA 0600.

I checked the time. *Four hours. Good enough.* I put the phone back, settled into the battle-ready doze perfected by hours on tour, and bided my time.

Chapter Sixteen

JINX

"I've got this, *cher*." Rabbit aimed one of his charming grins at me before he yanked on the wheel of the speeding car, narrowly avoiding the oncoming glare of headlights.

Braced for disaster, I managed an embarrassing squeak and closed my eyes. Instead of the expected explosion of shattered glass and shriek of sheared metal, I was thrown against the door with bruising force as the car swerved and left the road in a bone-rattling shudder. When I pried open my eyes, a terrifyingly steep descent into shades of black and white filled the entire windshield. Outside that thin pane of glass, the blur of the landscape spun in a crazy pattern as the car's headlights danced off objects like light off a damn disco ball.

"Here, take the wheel."

Somehow, I tore my gaze away from my impending death to gape at Rabbit, who let go of the steering to undo his seat belt. The instinct to live had me scrambling for the wheel. "What—"

"Take it, Jinx." With an appalling lack of concern, he reached over, undid my belt and began dragging me into the driver's seat.

Pure instinct had me fighting the wheel to ensure that we didn't hurtle off the edge of the world and into oblivion. With remarkable casualness, Rabbit pulled me into his lap. Heart in my throat, I managed to rasp out, "What are you doing?"

"I need to stop the program."

At his weird answer, I managed to tear my attention away from the death-defying ski ride we were taking down a freakin' mountain and stare at his reflection in the bouncing rearview mirror. "Rab—"

But his grinning face was melting into a stream of indecipherable green code against a black screen that began bleeding through the car.

"*The Matrix*? Really?" That dry question came from the passenger seat, where an unconcerned Ricochet, the team's dream-walker, was staring at me with a bemused look. "I guess it fits, but seriously, Jinx? Rabbit'll be so disappointed."

His presence flicked a switch in my brain, replacing my rush of fear-induced adrenaline with a relieving sense of rationality. "I'm dreaming."

"Yep." Ricochet's calm agreement soothed the ragged beat of my pulse, loosening the tight band around my chest and my grip on the steering wheel.

My surroundings began to drift away like fading fog. When it cleared, I was walking next to Ricochet in a sun-dappled wood. Trees stretched high above us, their grand stature leaving me in awe as we strolled through a thick green carpet. "Wow, where is this?"

"California." Ricochet lifted his face, sunlight and

shadows playing along its sharp planes while a soft breeze rustled the leaves overhead. "Humboldt State Park. I like to hike the trails here."

"I can see why."

He dropped his head, and we continued on in a companionable silence. A well of calm washed away the lingering edge of adrenaline-laced fear. Walking next to Ricochet, my pulse slowed, and the aching stiffness riding my spine seeped away. The hush of a nearby stream trickled in, adding to the sense of seclusion. The hair-raising ride down the mountain faded, replaced by nature's serenity.

I liked this dream, which was a good thing because Ricochet was now the one in control of it, not me. He was a powerful dream-walker, an ability that meant he could influence people's dream states, locking them inside their own minds until their dreams, or nightmares, became their realities. In essence, to anyone in the waking world, the person caught in a dream appeared to be in a coma-like state. In the wrong hands, Ricochet's ability could be deadly because where the mind led, the body followed. If someone died in a dream under the influence of a dream-walker, that person died in the real world as well.

The only reason I wasn't freaking out about this situation was because I knew that Ricochet had my back and always would. Those of us in the PSY-IV teams were more than teammates—we were family. An unusual and scary-as-shit family, but family nonetheless.

Ricochet slowed and stopped next to a fallen tree trunk thick enough to come up to my thighs. "Sit. We have a few minutes. They've got you on some painkillers, but you're getting close to waking up."

"Are you at the hospital?" I scrambled up and sat on top, waiting for him to do the same.

Instead, he braced his elbows against the wood's rough surface and leaned back, stretching his legs out before he nodded. "I'm stuck in the waiting room."

"Why?"

"You've got an officer talking to the nurse, wanting to interview you and Rabbit. So far, she's holding strong, but it won't be long before he gets through. Figured it was best not to draw his attention." He frowned and pushed upright, folding his arms. "I think there's a second set of eyes on you besides Officer Friendly."

I picked at the trunk as I watched him. "Who?"

Instead of answering, he asked, "You recognize him?"

Across the small clearing, a figure with a familiar face appeared. He paced back and forth, completely oblivious to the two of us. My lip curled. "Yep, that would be Zane's right hand, John No-Last-Name. So far, he's played chauffeur and butler." Something poked my butt, and I shifted against the rough surface of the trunk. Whatever it was disappeared, and the surface under me smoothed out. "Thanks."

Ricochet shrugged, but his dark eyes didn't leave John. "Ex-military?"

"That's what Rabbit thinks."

We both watched John do his pacing thing for a few seconds.

"I'll see if we can't get an ID." Ricochet angled toward me, and across from us John blinked out of sight. "Catch me up."

While Ricochet listened without interrupting, I kept to the high points, laying it all out—the program Zane wanted and why, our suspicions on Amalia, the break-in at the condo, and what I could remember from the car crash. Ricochet was a master of the blank face, and it was hard to read his thoughts, but I didn't mind, because it was a relief to share. He made a good sounding board. By the time I wound around to the end, the anxiety dogging me had fallen back, more interested in sniffing the nearby bushes than nipping my ankles. It was a welcome respite.

"I didn't get a chance to talk to Rabbit before they knocked me out, but I'm pretty sure the car was hacked." *Especially since Rabbit had to do his voodoo to ensure that we didn't end up as roadkill.* "I just can't figure out why Zane would try to kill us. Sabotaging the car and putting us in the hospital doesn't get Zane the program. In fact, it delays it. Which makes no sense, considering he seems to have a definite timeline in mind." No matter how I went over the dinner with Zane and Amalia, I couldn't detect any warning signs that we'd given ourselves away.

"I don't think it was Zane."

Ricochet's grim statement, combined with the dark frown lining his brow, had me bracing myself. Amalia's name popped into my head, but I dismissed it for the same reasons I didn't believe Zane was involved. "Then who?"

Ricochet searched my face, but with no idea of what he was looking for, all I could do was stare back. He shook his head and finally answered, "Elena's partner."

That was not the answer I expected. I blinked. "Wait. I thought that was an unconfirmed possibility."

He gave a disgusted grimace. "*Was* is the operative word, in this case." He dropped his arms and pushed off the trunk to pace. "We got word yesterday that they finally confirmed that she was working with someone."

I wasn't sure what to think about his revelation. Having confirmation of a partner could go either way. Granted, Rabbit had created Mercer's role on the possibility of a partner, but the confirmation that there was a real person working with Elena did not bode well for our cover. Rico-chet's agitated movements continued, but he didn't say anything more.

I prompted, "But…?"

He pivoted on his heel and came back to me, stopping in front of where I sat, his gaze somber. "But they have no way to verify the partner's identity."

"If Elena confirmed she has a partner—"

"That's the thing. Elena's not talking."

I tried to make the connection but failed. It was as if he was talking in circles. "Then how do they know she's working with someone?"

Ricochet leaned back against the trunk next to me. "You know how they decided to monitor her electronic safe?"

I thought back to the initial conversations and remem-bered one of the agency people mentioning that they had feelers embedded in an electronic storage file Elena had buried on the dark web. They'd speculated it was where she stored her payments. While they hadn't managed to crack the virtual safe, they were excited to be able to use it as a possible trap.

"Someone tried to access it?"

"They didn't just try—they succeeded."

Okay, that doesn't sound good, not even a little bit. "And they think it's a partner? Not a competitor or someone with an ax to grind with Elena?"

"It's not a competitor."

"How do you figure?"

"A competitor would ransack and destroy, maybe booby-trap it on their way out. None of that happened."

"What did happen?"

"They got in undetected, got what they wanted, and left.

The only reason we know it was accessed was because whoever it was tripped the warning on their way out."

"On their way out?" I might not be up to par with Rabbit's skill levels when it came to technology, but I knew enough to realize just how good someone had to be to get in and move around without raising an alarm. *Good enough that tripping it on the way out didn't make sense, unless…* "They deliberately set it off."

"That's the consensus."

I bit my lower lip. "It's a taunt."

"No doubt. Which indicates they're after more than money." Normally, reading Ricochet was difficult, but it was clear he was just as worried about this development as I was. He watched me carefully. "You said someone broke into the condo and hacked the laptop."

"Right, and they managed to impress Rabbit. He said they not only bypassed Zane's security to get into the condo, but they also managed to install a sophisticated tracking program on the laptop. All without getting caught on video surveillance." Putting the pieces together out loud left me wanting to slap myself for missing the obvious. "Shit. You think Elena's partner is here."

"Yeah, I do, and I think they're gunning for you." He watched me carefully. "They know you're not Elena, Jinx."

Shit damn fuck shit. Dread clamped sharp teeth around my chest and dug in. That was super not good. The fact that Rabbit and I were forced to tap-dance our way through Zane's manipulative web of evil was bad enough, but with Elena's vengeful faceless partner tossed in as well, we were screwed. With one call to Zane, our cover and the mission would detonate like an IED. The fallout would be horrific, not just for Rabbit and me but also for our team and the investigation into Hawes and Falcon.

My mind spun through our options. Sorting through this mess was like looking through a kaleidoscope. Every time I twisted it, another threat popped up. It was beyond frustrating.

"If it helps," Ricochet said, interrupting my whirling thoughts, "I do have one good piece of news to share."

Considering that everything seemed to be going to hell in a handbasket, I was all for some good news. "I'm all ears."

"Amalia Black."

I squashed the flash of excitement and asked cautiously, "She's ours?"

He nodded. "Colonel confirmed just before I headed out to answer Rabbit's request."

Having Amalia on our side should have been a good thing, but I was still grappling with the whole vengeful-partner thing. It took a moment for the last part of Ricochet's statement about Rabbit to sink in. "Wait—request? For what?"

"A ride."

Uh, not the answer I expected. Granted, our car was toast, but Ricochet had been all the way in San Diego. "You flew out to deliver a car?" I shook my head. "That doesn't make sense. Why not have Wolf drop it off?"

He raised a brow, humor lighting the depths of his eyes. "Am I not allowed to join the party now?"

"You know I love having you here, but it seems like a lot to get you out here when Wolf's already on-site."

Completely unoffended, Ricochet shrugged. "First, the colonel's worried about Wolf getting ID'd by Zane or Falcon." He made a valid point. Six foot four, bald, and built like a linebacker, Wolf was hard to miss.

Ricochet continued with his explanation. "Second,

without a car, you'll be dependent on ride shares with unknown drivers. You're being hunted, and that access point is too easy to exploit. It makes the colonel uncomfortable. Hence, my new role as your personal driver. And third…" He pushed away from the tree and stood next to me, his earlier humor replaced by a seriousness that indicated this was the real reason the colonel sent in Ricochet. "If you can't use your friendly neighborhood telepath for an SOS, you go to the next best option." He tilted his head and opened his arms. "Me." He held out a hand. "Come on. Time for you to wake up."

I took his hand and slid off the fallen tree. As my feet hit the forest floor, the trees blinked out, and I found myself staring into the hazel depths of Rabbit's worried gaze. There were dark circles under his bloodshot eyes and that sexy-as-sin stubble lining his jaw. Emotions I wasn't prepared to face clamored for attention. Difficult as it was, I ignored them.

Relief wiped away the fine lines of stress as he managed a faint replica of his normal grin. "Hey, *cher*, you with me?"

My heart clenched, and unable to resist, I lifted my hand and stroked his jaw despite the dull protest of my shoulder. "I'm right here, Cajun man."

He closed his eyes, but not before I caught the rush of gold streaking through the golden depths. He angled his head, covered my hand with his, and pressed a kiss against my palm.

The rough rasp as he held my hand to his face, combined with the unmistakable tenderness of his touch, had goose bumps cascading over my skin. He whispered, "*Merci, Bon Dieu*," with an intense emotion that left an unexpected hot pressure behind my eyes as my stubborn determination not to name what I was feeling took a devastating hit.

I managed to blink back the tears. "Hey, I'm okay." The words came out husky.

A minute or two passed before he lifted his head and brought my hand back to the bed. Instead of letting it go, he wove his fingers with mine. "How do you feel?" His tone was casual, but I knew better.

I thought about it. "Stiff and sore but not enough for them to keep me here."

He studied me, clearly not convinced. "Head?"

"Dull ache but not bad."

"Mmm." It was one of those hums filled with skepticism. "So, if I asked where your pain was on a scale of one to five…?"

"Two."

"So, three, then."

I squeezed his hand. "And if I asked you the same question?"

Finally, I got something close to his normal grin. "Same answer." Without letting go of my hand, he half turned, snagged the nearby chair with his foot, and dragged it closer. He sat down, which put us face-to-face, and then pressed the button that raised the top part of the bed so I was sitting up.

Seeing the signs of exhaustion on his face, I knew he'd stayed up and on guard. "Tell me."

"Car's totaled and at the police impound. No way to get to the black box and figure out who did this."

That was a given. It wasn't like we were in a town where the colonel could reach out and nudge someone into giving us access. This time, we were the civilians. "Not a surprise, but we may not need it."

"You talked to Ricochet?"

I blinked. I didn't expect him to make the connection quite so quickly. "Yeah. How did you know he's here?"

He motioned to the half-filled coffee cup on the table next to him. "Thought I saw him when I went for coffee." He let go of my hand and sat back, and the bed moved a bit as he propped his feet against the bottom rail. "Didn't have time to chat, considering I was trying to stay ahead of the nice officer who was getting off the elevator about the same time."

"Ahhh, so you're hiding out, then." Mindful of the various tubes and wires attached to machines that continued to beep and hum, I shifted. There were some significant protests from abused muscles, but as long as I took my time, I was good.

"Yes, ma'am." In his chair, Rabbit tensed, watching me with an eagle eye. "Pauline was nice enough to keep him busy until you woke."

"And Pauline is…?"

"Your eyes are turning green, darlin'."

I snorted.

Despite his obvious fatigue, Rabbit managed to flash one of his charming grins. "Pauline is our nurse, and she was very willing to inform the nice officer that you were sleeping and he should come back later. She also provided our stylish outfits, since our clothes are a bit of a mess."

I noted the neat pile of scrubs waiting on the bed behind him. I didn't think Pauline's protective streak had as much to do with me as with Rabbit's innate charm. "So, he's gone?"

Rabbit's grin faded. "Yeah, but he'll be back."

Neither of us was thrilled about that prospect, since dealing with the police meant asking for added complications. "Any chance we can get out of here before that happens?"

"Slim to none." He didn't sound any happier about it than I felt.

"Why?"

Rabbit's response was slow in coming. "You know those tests they ran on us when we were admitted?"

I managed to nod even though something in his tone had me bracing myself.

"It seems we were poisoned."

Chapter Seventeen

RABBIT

"Poisoned?" Jinx squeaked.

It was kind of cute but not enough to make up for the yellowing bruise that stood out against her pale face, which served as a visual reminder of how close to death we'd come the previous night. The image of Jinx lying in that damn hospital bed, pale, bruised, and battered, was sure to haunt me for a good long while.

"The asshole who hacked the car managed to divert the carbon monoxide through the air vents." I fought to keep my voice level. The mix of frustration, anger, and fear hovered at a low simmer, but it wouldn't take much for it to boil over.

"Explains why it felt like I was drugged," she murmured, a frown creasing her brow.

"If I could get ahold of that damn ECU, I could reverse engineer the hack and figure out who has a hard-on for us." *And if it comes back to Zane or Amalia, I'm going to enjoy taking their asses out.*

"About that…" Jinx waited until I looked at her before

continuing in a low voice. "There's a good chance the hacker is Elena's partner."

My brain stumbled, and when it found its footing, my mouth moved. "Say it again."

Jinx quickly relayed her conversation with Ricochet. By the time she was done, I had to agree that our hacker was out for blood, specifically Jinx's. I didn't feel any better now that I had a target, especially since that target was still faceless. Even the news that Amalia was Delacourt's mole didn't dispel the coiling tension. Jinx might be reassured, but I harbored some serious reservations regarding Amalia's true loyalty.

But with the vultures that were currently circling us, I had other concerns. "We need to get out of here."

"We can't show back up to the condo after being MIA all night." Jinx watched me as I got to my feet. "Chances are high that Zane will be waiting for us, especially since he had the car bugged."

I winced as it hit me that we might have an even bigger issue. "Yeah, about that… that bug might have been active until I was able to shut down the car's ECU."

She was quiet for a moment. The beeping monitors began to pick up speed as a look of alarm came into her face. "Shit, that means he heard the entire thing." She grabbed her blanket and threw it off her legs, making as if to get up. "If he shows up here—"

"Whoa, slow down." I shifted until I was in front of her, pressing my hands to the mattress on either side of her hips and caging her in place. "Take a breath."

She locked her hands on my forearms, her fingers digging in deep enough to leave an imprint as she did as I asked. I suppressed a hiss of pain as her hold pressed against the bruises running along my arms. I must have given myself away some other way, because she quickly let go. "Sorry." The color swept into her cheeks.

"I'm okay, sugar. Take another one," I said.

She did as I asked, and the beeps slowed while the agitated blush slowly faded.

"Better?"

She gave me a jerky nod, her eyes not quite meeting mine. "This isn't good, Rabbit."

"I know." I softly brushed the unbruised side of her face. I didn't want to add to the bad news, but she needed to know exactly what we were facing. "He hasn't shown up in the five-plus hours we've been here, so that has to count for something." I waited for her reluctant nod before continuing. "Besides, it's not the accident itself I'm worried about."

Her gaze jerked to mine. "Then what?"

"We both used our names—our real names." Only because our faces were so close did I catch the wash of trepidation behind her eyes. I knew she was remembering using both of my names.

She swallowed, her throat working. "Do you know if it was transmitting or not?"

"It was active when we got in, but I can't confirm if it was still live when I realized what was happening." I went back through the events, but some of it blurred together, making it difficult to pin down. "I know I fried it when I went after the hacker, but before that?" I shrugged. "Things are still fuzzy." I straightened and went to step back.

She caught my wrist, bringing me to a stop. "That's normal, isn't it? The fuzziness? When it comes to carbon monoxide poisoning?"

"According to the doctor, yeah. It does funny things to your memory." I rubbed the back of my neck, trying to ease the dull pain.

She tugged on my hand until she had my attention. "Maybe we got lucky and dodged a bullet."

It was a slim possibility. "Maybe. When I fried that damn bug, I wasn't subtle about it. There's a good chance it managed to corrupt the recording, but I can't guarantee it." That left us with two choices—scrap the mission and pray we got another opportunity to infiltrate Falcon soon or ride it out. I knew what I wanted to do, but it wasn't just my ass on the line. I needed her to pull this off. "I'm willing to stay, but it's your call."

Jinx didn't respond immediately. She kept her expression closed, making it hard to see which way she was leaning. "And if I say no?"

"I'll deal." It hurt to say, but I meant it because there was no room for ego in this job. No matter how much I wanted to pull her out of the deepening shit this mission seemed to be sinking into, it wasn't an option unless we both believed continuing was too risky. Only then could we walk away. Shoving my pain-in-the-ass protective instinct down, because it wouldn't be appreciated, I pushed off the bed, giving her space to think.

She didn't let me get far. "I say we stay."

Her quiet comment held me in place as I fought back my warring emotions. Of course she'd want to stay. Jinx never backed down from anyone or anything—an admirable trait but also a massive pain in the ass. Although if I was being honest, I wasn't ready to let Zane or Elena's mysterious partner get away either. That meant Jinx wasn't the only stubborn one in this partnership. "Then we stay, but it's time Elena and Mercer move to alternate accommodations."

The statement earned me an amused look. "I'm down

with that, but we can't afford to leave our stuff at the condo."

Yeah, those specialized suitcases hold way too many damning secrets to leave behind. "As soon as we show, you know he'll come or send someone after us." She scooted off the bed.

I stayed close just in case, but she found her balance quickly. She had a valid point, but I had a plan. "Not if he doesn't know we're there." I grabbed the set of scrubs from my bed and handed them to Jinx. "You up for getting changed?"

She nodded, taking the scrubs as she eyed the cords and tubes. "How about you use your superpower and convince Pauline we're ready to leave?"

I began shifting the IV pole around so she could drag it along to the bathroom. "And which superpower is that?" The wheels of the pole squeaked as I pulled it close so Jinx could grab it.

"You know exactly what I'm talking about." She wrapped her hand just below mine on the pole, giving it a tug. I refused to let go and waited until she looked up at me. Her eyes met mine, and her nose wrinkled. "That Cajun voodoo that you do."

Unable to resist, I dropped a butterfly kiss on her adorably wrinkled nose. Making sure to let my accent reign free, I drawled, "There's that green again, *cher.*"

She snorted, and this time, when she tugged, I let it go. "Go, Rabbit." She began making her way to the bathroom. "I want to get out of here."

"As you wish."

I wondered if I should tell her that her tantalizing ass was playing peekaboo with her gown. Before I could decide, she reached back and closed it. After a couple more steps, she was in the bathroom. She turned to close the door and caught me before I could look away. "And stop staring."

She closed the door, leaving me alone, a stupid smile on my face.

It took us just over an hour to escape the hospital. Despite our reassurances that we weren't going to collapse the minute we left, the doctor wasn't keen on us going. However, with no real reason to have us stay, he was reduced to glaring at us while we signed out. Thanks to Ricochet and Nurse Pauline, we managed to slip by Zane's right-hand man without detection. Still, I didn't take an easy breath until Ricochet pulled away from the hospital's entrance.

"Looks like luck is on your side," Ricochet said from the driver's seat of yet another rental sedan.

Jinx twisted around to scan the hospital parking lot, but I saw right away what had caught Ricochet's attention. An unmarked police vehicle was parking in one of the spaces by the door. It seemed the detective was back. "We'll have to deal with him eventually. I'd just rather it be after we're out of Zane's reach."

"Guess he'll be waiting a while, then," muttered Jinx. Since she might be right, there was nothing for me to say to that.

Ricochet got us back on point, his gaze flicking to the rearview mirror. "What's your plan here?"

I shifted, trying to ease the stiffness in my left side as the nifty painkillers the hospital had given me began to wear off. "We need to get our things out of the condo and check into a hotel." I felt a twinge in my shoulder and grimaced, rubbing the heel of my hand against the ache.

"I'm assuming it's not going to be the Holiday Inn?"

"Can't be," Jinx said. "Elena wouldn't be caught dead somewhere so mundane. We'll have to get a room at one of the high-end places."

I dug out my phone and handed it to her. "Why don't you take care of getting us booked."

She began digging through the plastic bag of our stuff that the hospital had given us. "The colonel gave me a card under Elena's name. We can use that to get settled."

"You sure that's wise?" Ricochet asked. "It wouldn't take much for Zane to sniff out where you're at."

"We don't need to hide from him," I explained. "We just need to be out from under his surveillance."

Rico flicked on a turn signal and moved over. "How much is this going to screw with the mission?"

"I'm not sure." That was the only answer I could give, because no matter how I played it, this move might be enough to set Zane off.

"You know, we may be able to make this work for us." Jinx looked up from the phone, her expression thoughtful as she absent-mindedly tapped the corner of the credit card against the open wallet on her lap. "If we play this right, we'll not only get out from under his electronic eyes, but we also might be able to get in front of Elena's mysterious partner."

I wasn't sure what she was seeing that I was missing. "How do you figure?"

"You know how we made the threat when we found the bugs that first night?"

I thought back, remembering her words during the call

to Zane after we fried the bugs in the bedroom. "Where we threatened to stay somewhere else?"

She tipped the card in my direction. "That's the one." She set it and the phone on her lap. "We know Zane's going to track us down, and when he does, we can use the accident to justify our leaving."

"It shouldn't be long. If his man hasn't already informed him you two were released, he will soon," Ricochet said.

"Right." Jinx turned to me. "They'll probably hit us while we're at the condo. I'm assuming you plan on taking the cameras offline, right?"

"First, there's no *us*. You're staying in the car with Ricochet." I kept going even as her mouth opened to argue and she glared at me. "I can move faster on my own, and I don't want you sitting here unprotected, especially since we've got more than one player in this mess." Her mouth snapped closed, but her glare didn't lessen. "Second, yes, I plan on taking out the cameras. It's a hell of a lot easier than trying to loop the feed from a distance."

She barely managed to keep her voice level. "The minute they go offline, Zane will know we're here, so you'd better watch your ass, Rabbit."

I teased, "I always do, *cher*."

"Okay, you two, enough flirting," Ricochet grumbled. "I hate when you two get like that."

Tough shit. I wasn't about to stop. Teasing Jinx was one of life's small pleasures. "You need yourself a woman, my friend."

He flipped me a one-finger response without taking his attention from the road. "We're almost there, so can we please let Jinx finish telling us how this is going to work?"

"Thank you," Jinx said, sounding a little snippy. She continued in a more serious tone. "When Zane finally confronts us, we give him just enough truth to justify our moving out."

Cautiously following her line of logic, I asked, "What exactly? We admit we were targeted by an unknown hacker and almost killed?"

She nodded. "Except instead of admitting that the hacker may be Elena's pissed-off partner, which Zane wouldn't buy since he thinks that partner is Mercer, we go on the offense." Her expression took on Elena's familiar haughty scowl, and her voice went sharp. "Why didn't you share that we weren't your first choice? Who else did you make this offer to before us?" Elena disappeared, and it was just Jinx again. "Things like that."

Her plan made a twisted sort of sense, enough that it might work.

She leaned forward. "By turning the tables, we put Zane on the defensive, which should keep him busy trying to cover his ass instead of digging at our cover."

"That's actually pretty damn devious." There was a note of admiration in Ricochet's voice.

"Devious enough that it might actually work," I agreed.

"The real question, then, is can you two pull it off?" Ricochet turned into the road leading to the condo. "Because if you can't—"

"We're fucked," I finished as I shared a long look with Jinx. "You up for this?"

She started to shrug, only to wince and cut it short. "I have to be, don't I?" She held my gaze. "We're too far in to back out, Rabbit. We have to make it work."

I hated that she was right. "Then we make it work."

With nothing left to say, I took a few precautions before we arrived. Ricochet handed over an earbud so he and I could stay in contact. He also handed over a compact Glock

19 and clip-on holster. I cleared it then secured it at my back, leaving my T-shirt untucked. A few minutes later, Ricochet pulled into the condo's parking lot. I had him go around the side and toward the back, since I wasn't planning on using the front door. He backed into a spot between two larger vehicles.

I had my door open and a leg out when Jinx called my name. I turned, unprepared, and she caught my face in her hands and gave me a hard, quick kiss. My hand tightened on the door handle as she drew back without breaking eye contact. "For luck."

With savage satisfaction, I recaptured her lips for my own hard, fast kiss. When I pulled back, she gave me a long blink. I grinned. "Can't have too much luck."

Then I left. I walked through the parking lot, my attention appearing to be on the phone in my hand when in actuality, I was noting the cars in the lot, on guard for any movement. My goal was the side entrance guarded by an electronic keypad.

As I closed in, I stretched out my psychic touch, tracing the electronic signatures emanating from the building. With the ease of practice, I separated out the lines connected to the door lock and the sturdier ones that daisy-chained the internal and external video cameras. First up were the cameras. With a mental flick, I sent a psychic surge through the video system, effectively shorting out the cameras. The vibrating electronic signature flared and went dark.

Head still bent over the phone, I covered the last few feet to the door as I mentally traced the well-worn signal patterns of the lock's code. At the door, I followed the pattern and punched in the code. A soft buzz sounded as the lock released, and I pulled the door open and slipped inside.

With the cameras down, the elevators would be the quickest way up. *Down* would be another story, considering I was probably racing the clock. I called the elevator and was grateful when the doors opened and nothing but empty space greeted me. Once inside, I hit the button for our floor and informed Ricochet, "Cameras down, heading up."

"Copy."

The doors closed, and the elevator began to rise. I pulled the Glock out and kept it down at my side. A soft ding sounded as the elevator came to a smooth stop. I moved to the side of the opening doors and waited. After ensuring that the hall was clear of unexpected visitors, I headed toward our door. A check of the electronic lock came up clean of any interference, but I still paused, doing a psychic sweep. The bugs lit up against my mind. With a flex of psychic muscles, I snuffed them out and started my mental countdown to Zane's possible appearance.

I entered the condo and cleared it with cautious efficiency. Nothing seemed out of place, but even more reassuring was the sense of emptiness permeating the air. Some of the tension in my spine eased.

Reholstering the gun, I hit the office first and gathered up our papers and the laptop. Next stop was the bedroom. After dumping everything on the bed, I dragged the two suitcases out. The electronics and weapons went in one, clothes in the second. I didn't care if they were folded or not —they just had to fit. Fortunately, we hadn't brought much. I didn't bother with the stuff in the bathroom—that could be replaced—but we needed the clothes.

"Security's on the move." Ricochet's warning filled my ear.

"Copy." I zipped up the second bag then grabbed both and headed for the door. Juggling two bags was a pain the ass, but I'd make it work. If worse came to worst, I'd ditch the clothes.

A check of the hall confirmed it was still empty, but the soft ding of the elevator warned me that it wouldn't stay that way. I turned away from the elevator, aiming for the emergency stairwell, the steady ding of the approaching elevator nipping at my heels. The final ding sounded as I hit the stairwell door. I slipped inside and hauled ass down the six flights of stairs, doing my best to keep my movements quiet, which was not easy when juggling two cases.

I made it to the bottom. Before stepping into the hall, I warned Ricochet, "Coming out."

"Copy."

I inched the door open and found the hall empty even though voices echoed somewhere out of sight. I made the dash to the exit, hit the door, and burst into the parking lot just as Ricochet pulled up. The back door opened, and I tossed in the cases and slammed it closed.

I yanked open the passenger door and jumped into the front seat even as the car began rolling forward. "Go."

As I pulled the door closed behind me, Ricochet picked up speed—not enough to draw undue attention but fast enough to get us the hell out of dodge. From the back seat, a phone rang.

Jinx answered. "Hello." Nothing in her voice revealed our current situation.

I twisted in my seat to see her looking at me. When she had my attention she mouthed, "Zane."

Ricochet turned out of the lot, but through the window behind Jinx, I caught condo security coming around the corner. We were far enough away that I couldn't see their faces, but it was clear they were watching us drive away.

"No, Zane." Jinx's voice was sharp, her gaze locked on

me. "I don't." She raised a brow at his response as I motioned for her to put it on speaker. She dropped the phone and hit the screen.

Zane's coldly furious voice filled the car. "Agreement was clear—"

"Yes, it was," Jinx cut him off, her tone sharp. "Considering I spent my night in the hospital, I think it's you who owe me an explanation."

"I had nothing to do with your accident." The denial was swift.

"Didn't you?"

A heartbeat passed, then Zane asked with silky menace, "What are you insinuating?"

Unfazed, Jinx maintained her queen-to-peon voice. "Who did you approach besides me?"

Silence filled the line, tension spinning throughout the car, as we waited him out. "What are you talking about, Elena?"

"The car was hacked, Zane, by someone who knew what they were doing."

"How does that connect to me?" True puzzlement was woven through his anger.

"I don't have anyone gunning for me. You, on the other hand, I'm not so sure. Especially considering our previous conversations. It leads me to believe that if I'm the one being targeted, it's because of my involvement with you. So let me ask again. Who did you approach about this job before you reached out to me?"

A low growl came over the phone. "You know how things work. There is no name."

She raised a brow in my direction.

I gave her a nod because Zane was right. The dark web didn't do names. Silently, I mouthed, "Handle."

Giving me a grim nod, she smoothly demanded, "But you will have a handle and a way to contact them." She paused, but when he remained silent, she nudged him along. "Mercer and I will be finding alternate accommodations so I can work on your request in peace. I can't afford to waste time looking over my shoulder for whoever's determined to prove you wrong."

"If that's really what's happening." The snide comment indicated that Zane's patience was worn paper-thin. While in other circumstances, that could be dangerous, in this case, it meant our plan to keep him off-balance was working. We needed him reacting, not thinking.

The car slowed, made a left, and soon stopped. I turned to see Ricochet watching Jinx through the rearview mirror. A quick check out the windows verified that we were on the far edge of a shopping-center parking lot.

Fierce satisfaction filled Jinx's face as Zane stepped neatly into her web. "Do you have a better theory? Because I'm all ears."

I wanted to curse. It wouldn't take much for Zane's anger to focus on an easier target—Amalia. As if Jinx had realized the same thing, a pained grimace replaced her expression of satisfaction.

Zane homed in on her comment and went exactly where I didn't want him to go. "You're the one who cleared Amalia. Perhaps you missed something."

"Don't." Jinx made the one word sharp enough to draw blood. "Unlike your people, I didn't miss anything in regard to Ms. Black. Nothing I found on her indicates she would be involved in this. Your involvement, however, is questionable." Every word dripped with Elena's typical arrogance.

"This partnership is purely business," Zane all but snarled. "Killing you would be bad for business."

She was getting under his skin in a big way. It made me worry she might go too far. Completely undaunted, she came back with a cool swipe. "And that's supposed to reassure me?"

A minute ticked by, then another. The only sound was Zane's breathing on the other end. Finally, he must have managed to corral his temper, because a faint derisive snort came through the phone. "My job isn't to reassure you. My job is to provide my employer with the requested program."

"That may be. But if that's truly what you want, then perhaps you may want to ensure that your disgruntled hacker gets the same memo, because I can guarantee you, the longer I spend discouraging him, the longer your project will be delayed."

"Unacceptable, Elena." Zane made no effort to hide the threat. "You have three days to make good on your commitment."

Jinx's shoulders stiffened, but her voice remained unaffected. "Last night, you never mentioned a deadline. Why the change?"

"After your disappearance last night, my employers became concerned about your commitment to the project. I'm sure I don't need to remind you that disappointing my employers is not in your best interests."

Her gaze went to mine and held it as she took a hell of a gamble. "And I'm sure you don't need the reminder that crossing me would not end well for you or your employers." Silence hummed over the line. "Now, if you're done threatening me—"

"Be very careful, Elena. Arrogance can be blinding." Menace crawled through Zane's silky tones. "And this is not the time to be fumbling in the dark. You never know who or what is lying in wait."

Jinx's eyes narrowed as she glared at the phone. "Is this where I volley back some witty reply so you can continue playing your game, or would you like to make your employers happy? Because honestly, I'll be more than happy to take care of this problem myself so I can work in peace, but I don't want any whining if it interferes with your precious timeline."

"You work on my program. I'll take care of ensuring your privacy."

Before she could respond, the dial tone filled the car. She swiped her thumb over the screen. "Well, that was fun."

Relief, frustration, and worry slammed together, and I fisted my hands so I wouldn't reach back and shake her. *Damn infuriating woman. She took too many chances.*

She eyed me a bit warily. "You want to take a breath before you explode, Cajun man?"

I didn't dare unclench my jaw. Instead, I shifted in my seat until I faced forward. Then I snapped my seat belt in place. Only then did I talk. "What hotel are we going to?"

A second ticked by before she said, "Juniper Plaza."

As she gave the directions to Ricochet, I stared out the window, worrying about whether she'd managed to dodge a bullet or paint a brighter target on her back.

Chapter Eighteen

JINX

Sitting tailor style on the king-size bed in the luxurious hotel suite, I hit Send on one last encrypted email. Then I set my laptop aside, lifted my arms, and twisted my spine as I worked out the kinks and stiffness. Surrounded by empty soda cans and coffee cups, Rabbit was hunched over the desk, his fingers flying over the keyboard, muttering in a charming mix of English and Cajun French, his hair sticking up every which way, the picture of the mad hacker. I secretly adored that look.

Unfolding my legs, I put my hands behind me, setting them against the bed as I leaned back. Then I wiggled my toes and rotated my ankles to help restore my circulation. As expected, after being bounced around to hell and back in the car the night before, my body was nothing but stiff muscles and dull aches. My stomach rumbled, a reminder that I needed something more than caffeine and aspirin to keep going.

I tipped my head back enough to see the digital clock on

the nightstand behind me. It was closing in on ten. "Rabbit."

Not surprisingly, he didn't respond. Once he locked on to something, it took a hell of a distraction to regain his attention. Not in a hurry to move, I continued to watch as he worked, amazed at his focus. From the first, I'd been intrigued by the apparent dichotomy in his personality—the lazy Cajun charmer and the über-focused tech geek—but it worked for me in a big way, probably because part of me longed to be the object of that kind of focus.

Unfortunately, not long into our partnership, I realized it worked for other women just as much. At first, his flirtation with those women was simply irritating, something I could laugh off while teasing him relentlessly just to watch him squirm. But somewhere after the first year of working together, it got harder to smile and joke. Not that I stopped with the teasing. Nope. If I'd done that, not only would Rabbit know something was up but so would the rest of our team. All of them—Kayden, Tag, Cyn, Risia, Ricochet, Wolf, Doc, and even the colonel—got a kick out of watching the two of us do our flirtation dance. Any change in my reactions would be a dead giveaway that my frustration with the role of friend was growing by leaps and bounds. It was a hell of my own creation. I knew that, but it still sucked.

When he cornered me in Elena's apartment and kissed me that first time, he blew through my emotional protections with destructive accuracy because it was hard for me to fight myself and him simultaneously. Logically, I knew it wasn't smart to start anything with him, but now that I had his taste in my mouth and his touch branded into my skin, I wanted more. The urge to take Rabbit up on his offer and explore what lay between us stretched its roots deep, but fear of losing him kept me trapped within the familiar. The fact that I felt torn was an easy truth to admit but a harder one to handle. Call it curiosity or call it lust. Whatever it was, I wanted to say, "The hell with it" and sink into the sensual indulgence he offered, no matter how dangerous the consequences. If I took that step and changed our relationship, the impact wouldn't be limited to the two of us. The team was our family, and changing the family dynamics would guarantee a dangerous ripple effect. Or dangerous to me, in any case. Unlike Rabbit, I had no family ties outside of the team—a choice I'd consciously made, mainly for my own sanity. I had no idea where my father was, nor was I interested in finding out. The last I knew, he'd finally finished serving his time somewhere in Las Vegas and returned to running simple street cons on the Strip. He'd tried to be a dad, back when my mom was still alive, but his good intentions never lasted long. It got worse after Mom died. Whatever tied us as father and daughter had disintegrated into an embarrassing memory, especially when he found another use for me—the cute child sidekick who distracted his marks.

In essence, the team was my only family, so if what burned between Rabbit and me flickered out, I would be the one who would lose. And it would be a big loss—no Rabbit, no family, just me and my stupid broken heart. There would be no way I could stay with the team and watch him go back to chasing the pretty shinies without wanting to carve his damn heart out, mainly because no matter how good I was at recognizing what was and wasn't real, when it came to Rabbit, the need for it to be real was a soul-deep ache.

Having one person to call mine, who called me his, was a

dream that I'd tucked away when I realized people didn't work that way, but I'd never abandoned it. Rabbit, with his unswerving loyalty and that seductive lure of single-minded focus on what he cared about, made me cautiously consider taking a chance that he would buck the curve. The day before, walking into the bedroom, wrapped only in a towel, I'd been completely unprepared for what lay in wait. If we hadn't had to leave, I had no doubt that we'd have ended up tangled together on that bed, regardless of Zane's damn bugs.

But no one's watching now.

I silently groaned at the voice coming from the little devil perched on my shoulder, who eyed the possibility of Rabbit like a mouth-watering steak as she provided visual encouragement. Not that I needed the extra nudge—my imagination had played hell with my dreams since this damn mission started. Actually, way before, if I was being honest.

She leaned in and whispered, *It would be fun.*

He'd break my damn heart. Nothing fun about that.

My horny little sidekick all but purred, not at all discouraged by my practical argument. *He can't break it if you don't give it to him.*

She had a point. The problem was, I couldn't promise I wouldn't offer it to him.

You almost lost him. That unexpected support came from the angel on the other shoulder. *Rabbit had a point. This could easily go sideways. If it does, will you be happy just having fantasies to hold on to, or would you rather have memories?*

I'd rather have him. My response was immediate and uncensored and way too revealing.

Then go get him, girl, encouraged the devil while the angel nodded in agreement.

Trepidation warred with cautious anticipation. *Am I really going to risk it all? For what? A quick fuck?*

Oh, he won't be quick, said the damn little devil.

And it'll be more than a fuck. Like all angels, this one uttered the absolute truth.

I winced, knowing I was going to lay it all on the line just for a chance. Before I could chicken out, I slid off the bed and came up behind Rabbit, who was still bent over the desk, his nape peeking through his hair. Taking my heart into my hands, I curled my fingers over the chair's back and bent in, placing my lips a breath away from his ear. I whispered his name.

His concentration broke with a nearly audible snap. He stilled as anticipatory awareness curled between us. I took advantage of his momentary stillness and feathered a kiss along the top edge of his ear.

A shudder rippled down his spine. "Jinx, *cher...*"

The sound of my name in a husky combination of a groan and growl triggered a definite reaction on my part. Heat coiled low, leaving me damp and wanting before spiraling out and up, creating a sensual echo that trailed down toward my center. Keeping my hands locked on his chair, I left his ear to sprinkle kisses along his jaw. My move pressed my aching breasts against his back. The rasp of his five o'clock shadow against my lips left them tingling. He angled his head in silent demand for more. Since I was going all in, I gave him more, tracing the line of his neck with my tongue.

His head pressed back into my chest, and he raised his arm and cupped the back of my head, his fingers tangling in my hair as I played along the cord of his neck. "*Mouche à mielle,* don' be teasin', yeah?" His other hand made a fist on the desk.

I lifted my head and drew back just enough to watch him. Color rode deep and high on his cheeks, his eyes almost pure gold with lust and hunger. That look found its twin in me as desire rose hot and fast, turned any lingering reservations into ash. "No games, Rabbit."

His eyes locked on to mine. I held my breath as I braced myself.

He tangled his fingers in my hair, holding me close. "Not that I'm tryin' to talk you out of this, but why the change of heart?"

Held in place, his face inches away, there was no way to escape him. I licked my lips, tasting the lingering salt from his skin, and put my cards on the table. "I almost lost you." It hurt saying it out loud, as if giving weight to the possibility.

His eyes flared, and his face softened. "I'm right here. Safe and sound."

"I know, but…" I dropped my forehead against his and closed my eyes, unable to finish.

His soft kiss made me lift my eyelids. Heat and want stared back from the golden depths. "You done bein' smart, Evangeline Thorne?"

The sound of my given name in his sexy-as-sin drawl wrapped around me like a silken ribbon. Holding that devastating gaze, I let go. "Someone once told me smart is overrated."

His lips curved. "Clever man."

Mesmerized by his grin, I murmured, "Mm-hmm." When his full lips quirked again, I lifted my gaze to find that my slumbering need had morphed into a fierce flame. My voice came out with a breathless edge. "You going to share some more wisdom, Mr. Tessier?"

He pulled me down a little closer, rubbing his nose against mine. "That's Wyatt to you, *cher*."

The playful move made me smile, and heeding his not-so-subtle demand, I whispered, "Wyatt."

He twisted in his chair and, with a move I couldn't follow, had me tumbling into his lap. Before I could catch my breath, he took my mouth in a kiss that set my world on fire. With destructive intent, our tongues tangled, teeth nipped, and hands played. His taste was an intoxicating mix of coffee, sweetness, and something spicy that was uniquely Rabbit. It went straight to my head and left me craving more. My fingers dug into his shoulders as I lost myself in his kiss. The passionate exchange turned from demanding to coaxing to teasing, only to do it all over again. I didn't fail to miss the rising evidence of his arousal against my ass as I squirmed in his lap, trying to get closer.

His fingers tunneled through my hair and gripped it, holding me in place so his mouth could continue to ravage mine. Not happy about my limited ability to move, I nipped his bottom lip then soothed the small sting with a swipe of my tongue.

His fingers tightened against my scalp as he drew back. "Not nice, *mon ange*."

My fingers kneaded his shoulders as I tried to get him back on track and kiss me. "Never claimed to be nice, Cajun man."

His slow smile was all kinds of wicked. "*C'est bon.*" He pushed back from the desk and, with an unexpected ease, stood, keeping me tight in his arms. "Then let's be bad."

Curling my arms around his shoulders, I couldn't help but laugh as he stalked to the bed. When I felt his muscles coil, I realized his intent. I barely managed to warn, "Watch the laptop!" before I was bouncing on the bed.

He crawled up from the end of the bed until he was poised above me on hands and knees. He reached over, snagged my forgotten laptop, and by stretching managed to set it on the nightstand before resuming his previous position. "Now, where were we?"

Using his arms, he lowered his torso till he was so close I could feel his heat, but he kept the slightest inch between our bodies as only our lips touched. This time, his kiss was a slow seduction—soft, lush kisses, warm, gentle brushes along sensitive spots, careful nibbles meant to entice. The slow mating dance heightened my restless aching desire. Needing to feel his skin against mine, I stroked down his chest until I could burrow my hands under his T-shirt. The feel of his skin under my hands—warm, hot, and hard— was heaven. I used my fingers to trace the lines of muscle that his position created. When that wasn't enough to satisfy my touch hunger, I grabbed the edge of his T-shirt and pulled it up.

He lifted his head, shifted his weight to one arm, and reached backward to grab his T-shirt. He pulled it off and tossed it to the side. With his shirt gone, I was free to play. And that was just what I did. I ran my fingers over his chest, playing with the light line of hair that stretched between his nipples and trailed down the center of his surprisingly muscular abdomen, as he continued to use his mouth with devastating accuracy. It didn't take him long to find a particularly sensitive spot where my neck met my shoulder. His mouth worked it as my body bowed in unabashed need, my legs moving restlessly.

"Oh God," I gasped, arching my neck for more.

He didn't make me wait. "No God here, *cher*. Just me," he whispered against my sensitive skin as he continued to nibble and kiss. He stroked my breast, tracing the slope until he could cradle it in his hand. He dipped his head and sucked the nipple, shirt and all, into his mouth.

"More," I demanded.

He let my breast go, and with stunning speed, my shirt and bra were gone and his mouth was back, hot, wet, and wicked against my incredibly sensitive skin. The sensation seared through me, making my spine arch as I fought for more. Hunger wound through me, etching the craving deeper.

I tangled my fingers in his hair, determined to hold him close. "Wyatt!" His name came out on a half wail, half moan.

His tongue traced the tip and surrounding curves as he palmed the other side, his fingers mimicking the destructive play of his mouth. His weight shifted, dropping lower and pressing into me. "Open for me, sugar."

Instinct had me shifting my legs. One fell to the side as I curled the other over his hip, my heel digging into his ass as I ground the damp, aching center of me against the hard length of him. This time, we both groaned. He lifted his head, his face flushed, eyes bright, and lips damp as he ground his cock against me with slow deliberateness. My neck arched, my eyes fluttering closed as I let the feeling slide through me.

"Beautiful." His murmur had me lifting my eyes, and then he was kissing me. This time, it was hard, rough, and exactly what I wanted. When he let me up for air, his hands were at my waist, pushing down my yoga pants until I was left in nothing but lace and ribbon. He sat back on his heels, chest bare, the top two buttons of his jeans undone, the outline of his cock straining the material as he used a finger to trace the ribbon of silk that curved over my hip. Unable to help myself, I rolled my hips, trying to chase that delicate touch.

He flattened his palm against my stomach, his fingers brushing over the lace covering me. "Stay still, *mon ange*. Let me look."

Fisting my hands at my sides, I complained, "I want to touch too."

"In a minute." He cupped my hips and then dipped his head to press an open-mouthed kiss against the damp lace.

A soft sob escaped me as my hips bucked in his hands, but he didn't stop there. *Oh, hell no.* His wicked tongue played with me through the lace, every lash whipping the fire higher, every suck a searing strike of lightning. Just when I thought I'd explode, he pulled back, laying a line of kisses along my trembling thighs. Then his weight was gone.

I fought my way back from the edge to find him standing at the bed's end, pushing his jeans over his hips and freeing what I wanted most. I scrambled to my knees and crawled forward, eyes on the prize. My breasts ached, and the emptiness between my legs spurred me on. As he leaned over to kick the jeans off, my hands went to his deep-blue boxer briefs. They soon followed his jeans, leaving Wyatt in all his stunning glory.

It was my turn to murmur, "Beautiful."

I wrapped my fingers around his stiff length and slowly began to pump, enjoying the silky slide against my palm. My thumb brushed over the leaking tip, smearing his need over the heated core of him. Then I leaned in and used my mouth and tongue to trace teasing lines along his stomach.

His hands went to my hair, holding but not stopping me. "Evangeline, *mon ange*."

Oh, I have no intention of being anyone's angel. Switching directions, I tongued a path to his cock and then took him deep, sucking hungrily. His groan sank through me, his fingers flexing against my scalp, his hips pumping as I licked and laved and sucked.

"Enough." He tugged my head back, keeping me from my play.

I continued to glide my hand over him even as I pouted. "I wasn't done."

His thumb swept over my bottom lip. "That's not how I want to finish."

Still holding my hair, he forced my head back as he bent and took my mouth in an insatiable kiss that tore through me until I was nothing but sensation. I lost my concentration. Somehow, I found myself on my back, underwear gone, while Wyatt stretched over the edge of the bed, leaning over me. Since the position gave me unfettered access, I let my hands roam and my mouth follow, his firm muscles flexing under my hands and mouth.

Then he twisted and sank onto his heels as he tore open a condom wrapper. As he started to roll it on, I came up halfway and took over. Taking my time to tease as I ensured our protection. He didn't let me play long. Once it was in place, he leaned forward, forcing me to lie back. Then his hands and mouth swept over me, need and longing taking me deep.

When all that mattered was assuaging the burn that left me restless and hollow, he stopped teasing and got serious. His mouth tempted me as his hands slowed, taking us from frenzied hunger to an almost painful anticipation as he slid himself through my heated center. He shifted his weight, not leaving me but adding just enough space so he could watch us. His hips rolled as he teased me, pushing the want higher. "Ah, *cher*, such temptation you are."

We were pressed so close I could feel his deep groan

against my chest. My heels dug into his ass as I helped the delicious friction by rolling my hips so that I rode along his length.

"Stop teasing, Wyatt." I followed my demand with a series of punishing nips along his neck and chest. "You promised no games."

His head came up, his eyes glittering with an intensity that held me still, waiting. For what I wasn't sure, but there was nothing playful in his heated gaze. He cupped my face and dropped his head. "This is not a game, Evangeline." He was so close that his lips brushed mine as he spoke. "Last warning. You let me in now, I'm not leaving."

I knew my next decision would make or break us. Under the desire, fear lay in wait. Swallowing hard, I drew my hands up from his waist in a gentle glide and mimicked his hold, cradling his face between my palms. Searching his eyes, I found what I needed to take that last step into the frightening unknown. "If you ever try, I'll hunt you down and make you regret it."

His body stilled, and since he was covering me, I felt how deep my words had hit. Male satisfaction joined the hunger in his face, his eyes taking on a fierce, proprietary light. "No huntin' needed, *mon ange*. I'm well and truly caught."

Then he took my mouth as he sank inside me. The crumbling remains of my emotional walls drifted into dust as our groans were muffled by our kiss. As he moved, he filled every hollow, including the ones deep in my heart. It was a sensual dance designed to fan the flames into incendiary heights. My world became nothing but his taste, his touch, and the sensation of him riding me with a rough tenderness that spoke to something much deeper than lust.

As the fire threatened to implode, our movements lost

their grace, becoming more frantic until we were poised on the beautiful edge. When he found the perfect spot, I tore my mouth from his and arched my neck, nails digging into his shoulders, body ready to fly. "Wyatt!"

"Now, love!"

Following his guttural command, I let go and flew, hearing and feeling him follow me. It burned through both of us, tearing away the remaining barriers. Caught in the bright, explosive beauty we created, I didn't fight it but let it burn through me instead, trusting that when I drifted back down to reality, he'd be right where he promised—at my side.

Chapter Nineteen

It was hard to leave Jinx sleeping. She was the picture of feminine temptation, wrapped in sheets that played peekaboo, offering tantalizing glimpses of the luscious skin. Our night together had taken the edge off my hunger but had also created a deeper addiction—to her taste, her touch, her heart. I tore my gaze away, hoping to dodge the urge to get back in bed and wake her in a totally different way.

Coffee would be required when she woke. I dressed as quietly as I could, letting her sleep. I nabbed my laptop, since there were some tweaks I had to make in the program, not to mention that I needed to get information to Ricochet and the team. Slipping my keycard and phone into a back pocket of my jeans, I couldn't resist bending down and brushing my lips over the tangle of Jinx's hair. I pulled back to find her lashes lifting, revealing her sleepy gaze minus her normal guardedness.

She gave me a smile filled with beauty that hit me like a

shot to the heart. I never thought I'd see that look from her. It was a gift, especially after the night before.

"Hey," I said. It came out husky.

"Hey."

"I'm heading down for coffee."

Her gaze went to the laptop. "You expecting a long line?"

I grinned. "Got a few things I need to get to. Might as well multitask."

"Mmm." Her lashes drifted back down. "What time is it?"

"Almost seven. Go back to sleep. I'll wake you when I get back."

"Okay." She snuggled deeper into her pillow.

It sucked, but I left her there because that damn clock was still ticking. Zane's patience wouldn't last long. Before it ran out, I wanted the players in place to make sure we took him and his boss down once and for all.

I made sure the door locked behind me and headed down. I'd done a quick internet search and found her preferred coffee supplier a couple of blocks away. Now that we were out from under Zane's baleful eye, leaving Jinx behind so she could rest was a hell of a lot easier and less risky than taking her. Still, I kept a mental eye on my surroundings as I made my way to the coffee shop.

Images from the night before kept diverting my attention. Not that I minded—in fact, I had to work hard not to flash a smile and tip an imaginary hat at every person I passed. It was corny as hell, but it was the truth.

As much as I fantasized about Jinx and me, the reality left my flimsy imagination in the dust. Her surrender had left me stunned and humbled. I thought for sure I would have a hell of a battle on my hands. Never had I expected her to take the first step toward making us something more than partners and friends.

But I wasn't complaining—hell no. I wasn't about to question my luck when it came to her. I wasn't stupid. I knew a serious conversation loomed in our future, probably after we got out of this mess. Until then, I was going to do my damnedest to convince her that she'd made the right decision.

This morning, however, I was going to make sure she got some uninterrupted sleep after our rather busy night. We'd called up room service after the first time and enjoyed our dinner in bed. It was an eye-opening experience. Jinx was cautiously playful, and it took a bit of coaxing, but I managed to soothe that wary edge she carried until I got honest-to-God giggles from her.

I also managed to take my time during the second round, driven to gentleness by an awareness that we'd just walked out of a hospital hours before. Sore muscles didn't stop her from taking over a third and final time, when she all but stole my heart with her teasing touches and slow, drugging kisses. We finally fell into an exhausted sleep in the wee hours.

I woke early, as was my habit, and lay in bed, enjoying the fact I finally had her where I wanted her—in bed, curled in my arms. The connection we shared as friends hadn't been marred by the sex. In fact, our physical intimacy added a depth that I'd never found with another woman. Maybe I was getting jaded, but I was bored by the predictability that came with my previous hookups. With Jinx, nothing was predictable, and that filled me with a deep sense of satisfaction. Sex with Jinx wasn't about feeding my horny curiosity. I could scratch that kind of itch easily enough and had done so in the past.

I knew things had changed for me when months after meeting Jinx, those encounters with other women became fewer and fewer and further and further apart. I hadn't actually advertised my growing boredom, since there was no sense in giving the team—including her—fuel for their teasing or speculation. It took me a while to figure out that I wanted more from her. I wanted something real and lasting. What I didn't want was my teammates' opinions. I knew how they viewed me—player, flirt, charmer—but those labels weren't accurate when it came to Jinx. If I'd shared my feelings, their input would have set me so far back in Jinx's opinion that I'd never live long enough to even take a chance with her. So I kept my growing feelings quiet.

I found the coffee shop and held the door for a guy who was juggling two trays filled with various drinks. Despite the early hour, I was in line for ten minutes before I made it to the counter. I put in my order and claimed a recently deserted table set toward the back against the window. I was going to take an hour and get some work done, which would give Jinx time to rest.

First up, I tried my hand at accessing the police report on the car accident. I didn't get far because the test results on the ECU weren't back yet. Since we were hours out of the accident, it was a long shot, but not having a face for Elena's partner was like a mosquito bite. I couldn't stop scratching at it.

With effort, I turned my attention to the more immediate concerns of Zane's program and ensuring that the information remained contained. Before long, I was splitting my attention between communicating with the team as we set up the details on a possible sting and tweaking the program I was creating. The Rosetta Stone type of program Zane wanted had its own set of challenges, but it was doable. What was making me twitchy was trying to rework it so it became a virtual double agent, sending the same information Zane wanted to the good guys without giving away the game to the bad guys.

Normally, creating a complex program like this would require days of coding, test runs, and deliberate breaks, but we didn't have days. Hopefully, what we were able to hand over would hold together long enough to satisfy Zane and his employers before the cavalry swept in.

I continued to work on the program, pausing once to read a report from one of my contacts who was working Elena over. It made for interesting reading. It seemed that Elena's fall from hacker grace was precipitated by a devil's bargain between her now-identified partner—Keith Alders —and the FBI. Despite Alders's skills at hacking, he was also the one who'd tripped the alarm on the electronic safe in the dark web. There was one more key piece of information that hadn't been widely shared—that electronic safe had been nearly empty when Alders hit it. He took what little remained, but my contact was scratching his head as to why Alders would try for a nearly broke account. I had my own opinions about that, but I wasn't ready to share. For the moment, Alders's whereabouts was the agency's main focus. I planned on making a call to help those searchers out when I got back to Jinx, but for the moment, I stayed on task.

In between the coding and texts, I edited the list of potential targets, trying to narrow it down as much as possible. By the time my allotted time came around, I'd downed two cups of coffee and demolished a muffin. After sending one last update and directing the program to run another fail-safe check, I put in Jinx's order and went back to pack up.

I backed up my work on an encrypted flash drive then

gathered my stuff before going back to get Jinx's drink. I wove through the group of waiting customers and had my hand on the cup when someone stumbled into me hard enough that the drink wobbled then tipped, the coffee spilling out, landing stinging drops on my hands. I hissed.

"I'm so sorry!" a woman said, anxious and embarrassed.

Shaking my hand, I turned to find a red-faced brunette either on her way to or coming from a workout, trying to steady the cup in her hand as she stared in mortification at the mess on the counter. Behind her, some guy continued to rudely shove his way through the small crowd around the counter.

As the baristas began cleaning up the mess, I gave the redhead a small grin to help ease the sting of the stumble. "It's good."

She snatched up some napkins and began dabbing at her hand. "You sure you're okay?" She didn't wait for my answer but continued blithely on, her gaze behind us. "I wish they had a little more room here." She tossed the napkins into the nearby trash, shaking her head. "Seems like every day it gets a little more crowded and people get a little more impatient. Let me buy you a replacement coffee."

"No worries, ma'am," the young barista said as she wiped away the last of the coffee. "We'll get you a new one." She flashed me a grin and turned away.

"Oh, okay." The redhead seemed flustered.

I muttered, "No harm done, darlin'."

She gave me another smile, this one brighter than her initial one, and her embarrassment was replaced by feminine interest. "Well, I'd be happy to make amends."

"None needed, thanks." My mama hadn't raised me to be rude, but as much as I appreciated the intent behind her offer, I had something much better waiting back at the hotel. "Got someone waiting for her caffeine fix."

Her smile dimmed with disappointment, but she was quick to shrug it off. I turned to wait for Jinx's new coffee just as the woman was saying, "Lucky her."

She said goodbye and left. I waited patiently at the counter and, once I had Jinx's coffee in hand, headed back to the hotel. Fortunately, the return trip was incident-free. I snagged an elevator as a mixed group exited. I hit the key for our floor, my nose wrinkling at the overly floral scent that lingered like a cloud from the recent occupants. The doors slid shut, and by the time they reopened, that unforgiving scent had left its mark as a dull ache in my temples. Out in the hallway, I sucked in deep breaths, trying to dispel the scent's hold. A few doors down, I passed a maid's cart that had stopped near an opened room. Hopefully, they hadn't woken Jinx.

With my thoughts occupied, it took a second for me to recognize that our door wasn't latched completely. My good mood winked out in an instant, replaced by a primed vigilance. Scenarios ran through my mind, not all of them innocent.

Not about to walk into an unknown situation with my hands full, I didn't miss a beat as I passed the door and went a few more doors down. I stopped and set the coffee on the floor. Then keeping my approach as quiet as possible, I retraced my steps.

I did a visual sweep of the hall. Other than the cart, nothing was out of place. The seeming normalcy didn't ease my rising tension. I'd left my weapon behind, figuring that going on a coffee run wouldn't require firepower. I was regretting that decision.

Angling so the door was at my back but keeping enough

distance so the laptop bag wouldn't touch the wall, I used my palm to push the door open enough to slide inside. It swung wide, and cool air and quiet were the only things to greet me. The curtains were still drawn, shrouding the room in a false dark. Light cut a path from the bathroom to the desk. When no one lunged at me, I slipped inside, keeping a hand on the door as it began to shut. I stopped it before it could close completely.

Even as my instincts blared, there was a sense of emptiness to the room. The room was called a suite, but everything was in one large space. The flat-screen TV hung on the wall opposite the bed, and a couch stretched between, delineating the space. Opposite the door was a window with a panoramic view. It wound around the corner housing the desk but was currently covered by blackout drapes. The bathroom was on the far side of the bed, the closet on the other side. The open layout meant it didn't take much to scan the room. It also meant there was no sense in calling Jinx's name, because she definitely wasn't there.

I hit the switch on the nearby wall, and light washed away the shadows. First, I noted the rumpled bed, sheets, and blankets in disarray. A towel was tossed across the foot of the empty bed. Moving closer, I put hand on it. *Damp.* The next thing I noticed left me biting off a variety of creative curses. The chair I swore I'd left tucked into the desk was shoved up against the corner window, and one of the drawers was half-open.

I rounded the end of the bed and pulled up short when I realized the blankets weren't just messed up—they were half-pulled from the mattress. Dread hit me like a Taser shot. I tried not to think about the implications as I continued my inspection.

Taking care not to step on the bedding pooled along the

side of the bed, I went into the bathroom and found more evidence that Jinx had grabbed a shower—wet shower stall, plugged-in hair dryer, brush beside it, and toothbrush and toothpaste resting on the side of the sink. Every disquieting sign took my dread higher as I tried to ignore the images flashing through my mind.

I left the bathroom, my gaze on the floor, looking for anything that would tell me what had happened while I was out getting her damn coffee. I made my way around the bed. Between the closet and the bed, the device that was both alarm clock and Bluetooth speaker lay on the floor.

At the partially open closet, I tried to open the door, but something held it closed. I pulled out my phone, hit the flashlight, and leaned in. The suitcase stand was on its side, and Jinx's suitcase was on the floor, her clothes spilling out. Even knowing it might get me nowhere, I turned my phone around and dialed her number. A faint buzzing sounded. Homing in, I found her phone half-hidden between the bed and the nightstand on the same side as the alarm clock. I reached in and pulled it out, checking it for any clues as to what in the hell had gone down.

Nothing. No text, no half-finished messages, no missed calls, no dialed numbers. My hand tightened on the phone. "God dammit, Jinx, where are you?" Even as I fought my way through teeth-grinding worry, I grimly hung on to the knowledge that Jinx knew how to handle herself.

I pocketed her phone as I thumbed a number on mine. It rang once before it was picked up. I didn't wait for a greeting. "Get to the room. Jinx is MIA." I hit Disconnect, knowing Ricochet would haul ass and appear in minutes.

While I waited, I pulled my laptop bag over my head and set it on the dresser. Then I went over every inch of the room. By the time a sharp rap sounded, I not only had an idea of who might have gone after Jinx, but I also knew she hadn't made it easy on that person.

I found the biggest clue under the bed and set it on the nightstand, frustration and anger sharing equal headspace. *A fuckin' pressure syringe.*

I went to the door and opened it, letting Ricochet in, then moved to the end of the bed. I turned to find that he'd stopped in the undisturbed area by the couch. Wolf's big body was behind him, his gaze taking in the room.

"What happened?" Ricochet asked calmly.

"Left her sleeping to grab her coffee an hour and"—I checked my phone—"twenty-three minutes ago. Came back to this."

His gaze went to the single rumpled bed with its obvious story and then came back to me. "Notice anything on the way in or out?"

I shook my head. "No tails, no sense of being followed. We were clear."

"Is this Zane's handiwork?" Wolf asked.

"Considerin' they drugged her"—I indicated the syringe —"I'm fairly sure it's Elena's silent partner."

"Proof?" Ricochet asked.

"Give me two minutes, and I'll have it." I didn't wait but walked by both men toward the door and its electronic lock. Ricochet and Wolf played silent audience as I reached out with my ability and took control of the lock. A quick psychic scan showed that the lock had been electronically wiped. "Whoever it was hacked the lock."

Wolf's light-green eyes went hard, his face even harder. "They had to be watching you."

"Watching and waiting," I muttered, running a hand through my hair. My gaze went back to the nightstand and what sat on top.

Ricochet followed my attention. "They waited until they were sure Jinx was alone."

"They took her by surprise," I said as he picked up the pressure syringe. "She managed to get a few hits in."

Ricochet brought the needle up to his nose. "Chloroform."

"Yeah." I didn't like the thought of her unconscious and at the mercy of the asshole who'd taken her, but if he'd drugged her, that meant he wasn't planning on killing her. I wasn't sure if that made it better or worse.

"She's going to have a hell of a headache when she wakes," Wolf murmured.

I hoped that would be the worst she'd endure. "Can you reach her?"

Wolf's brow lowered. "Not if she's drugged. Can't connect with an unconscious mind."

I turned to Ricochet because as a dream-walker, he was all about the unconscious mind. Before I could ask, he was shaking his head. "Can't, brother. We need to move fast, and there's nothing fast about dream-walking. And not to be mean, but our girl has a hard head. I only got in before because I had time in the waiting room to create a path. Not to mention, she was worried about you."

Normally, my curiosity about all things Jinx meant I'd jump all over his comment, but this time, there were other things on my mind.

"What about the tag?" Ricochet asked.

The obviousness of his question left me cursing. I was so rattled that I hadn't even thought about the damn tag. It had limited range, but maybe we'd get lucky.

I went to the dresser, pulled the laptop out of its bag, and brought up the tracking app while anticipation curled through me. "They haven't been gone long, which means they may not be out of range yet."

The second it took for the program to come online seemed to stretch forever. I didn't realize I was holding my breath until the first signal pinged. When it came again, my air escaped in a harsh exhalation. "Got her."

"Where?" Ricochet and Wolf asked, crowding close, trying to see the screen.

I got the location, orienting myself, and rattled off an address. Ricochet stepped back and pulled it up on his phone. We crowded around the satellite map, which showed an L-shaped single-story building a few miles out from the airport. The geotag was The Sleepy Oak.

"Looks like a no-tell motel," Wolf noted.

I really didn't give a damn what it was just so long as we got Jinx back. "How far out?"

"Thirty minutes," Ricochet answered.

Not about to repeat being caught empty-handed or unprepared, I left our huddle and dragged my suitcase out of the closet. "Rico, you drive." I threw out more orders as I got my gun and holster out of the hidden compartment. "I'll monitor the tag. Wolf—"

"I'll do what I can to reach her, but, Rabbit…"

Hooking the holster into place, I looked up to find him watching me.

"No promises."

Jerking my chin up in silent acknowledgement, I rounded the bed and grabbed the laptop. "It would be helpful if you could reach her, but if you can't…" I left the rest unsaid because it was understood. One way or another, we would be getting Jinx back. I pocketed the encrypted flash drive then shoved the laptop in its bag and slung it over my shoulder.

"Head check," Ricochet said.

"Clear and straight," I shot back, holding his gaze. It wasn't a lie. My emotions were in turmoil, but they were locked down tight, leaving my mind crystal clear. "We ready?"

Ricochet spent a few more seconds studying me before he jerked his chin up. Only then did Wolf say, "Right, then. Plan en route. Let's roll."

Chapter Twenty

JINX

My throat was burning, and nausea clutched my gut. I couldn't figure out what was worse—the pain of swallowing or my need to hurl. Unfortunately, to make sure I didn't vomit, I had to swallow rapidly. It was a very uncomfortable catch-22.

So was the fact I was being held hostage. I didn't even have to open my eyes to remember that lovely tidbit, as it was a situation that left me equal parts embarrassed and angry. A plane passed overhead fairly close. As its rumble faded, faint sounds of traffic reached my ears. That was a good sign, considering that if I managed to get out of here, help wouldn't be too far out of reach. But that was a worry for later. At the moment, I needed to know what I was up against. I kept up my pretense of being unconscious, not sure if anyone was nearby, as I tried to piece together how I'd gotten here.

A few minutes after Rabbit left, I went back to bed in an effort to reclaim sleep. When that didn't work, I got up and showered. After pulling on a T-shirt and yoga pants, I was in the midst of toweling my hair dry when a knock came. The unexpected sound made my hands stop moving on the towel over my head. My instincts flared as I turned to the door. That reaction should have been my first clue, but curiosity shoved it aside. Pushing the towel to my shoulders, I eyed the door, thinking there was no way it was Rabbit, since he had a key and it was too soon for him to be back.

When the knock came again, it was followed by "Housekeeping."

Slightly embarrassed by my paranoid thoughts, I shook off my unease and set the towel aside then went to answer the door. Looking back, I knew that had been the wrong damn move. I opened the door to find a pile of towels partially screening the housekeeper's profile. Before I could even try to get a glimpse, the towels and the body behind it rushed me. The unexpected attack had me releasing the door and stumbling back. As a distraction, it was beautifully simple. My kidnapper shoved the pile of towels into my face and followed that with slamming me hard in the chest. The hit knocked my air out of my lungs for the second it took to force me to back farther into the room. Even as I fell back, years of training came to my rescue. I struck out, getting lucky and connecting. But my luck didn't hold, and after that, things kind of blurred together.

My memory served up a montage of snippets—evading a fist, managing to sneak a hit in, exchanging strikes as we stumbled through the room. There was a flash of my attacker lurching back to the bed before rolling out of reach and off the side. Unfortunately, when I came around the end of the bed, I was met with a needle to my calf.

As dire as the situation was, the kidnapping wasn't my only problem. Reminders of the car accident were superseded by new aches, such as the uncomfortable position of my arms and the dull throb in my head. There was a stiff-ness in my knuckles that indicated I'd managed to land some serious hits on my attacker, which was nice to know. The downside was, I had no idea where the hell I was, which meant neither did Rabbit. When my thoughts veered toward what his reaction would be when he walked in and found me gone, I yanked them back.

First up, figure out where I'm being held. Whatever I was lying on was hard and cool under my cheek and had a slightly bumpy surface. A floor, then, most likely tile or linoleum. I shifted a little bit to ease the pain in my shoulders, since my hands were duct taped behind me. It didn't help. My fingers felt twice their normal size, so whoever taped me had done it too tightly. *Asshole.*

The faint scent of mold and something nasty tickled my nose. I had a sense that the room was somewhat enclosed. Taking a risk, I cracked my eyes open. A checkered pattern of white and blue filled my vision.

Hmmm. Without turning my head, I took in my surroundings. The floor was definitely linoleum, aged and pitted with wear. Some of the color was hidden under stains. In fact, in a few spots, the linoleum no longer existed and gray cement was all that remained.

A little farther away, exposed rusted pipes curled inside a dilapidated frame of wood. It took a second for me to realize that the frame used to be a cabinet. My neat-freak gene began to whine in dread, and I couldn't blame it.

With a little shifting of my head, the rusted bottom of a toilet became my view. Fortunately, it was far enough away that I could pretend that whatever foreign life form existed near it was nowhere near me. A glance down toward my feet revealed more duct tape around my ankles and a warped door pulled against the doorjamb. It wasn't completely closed, because the water-damaged wood made that impossible.

Listening closely, I couldn't hear any movement outside that door. Not keen on lying on the floor of a hazmat scene that had once been a bathroom, I used my feet and shoulders to sit up until I was leaning against a graffiti-covered wall. While I was happy not to have my face on the disgusting ground, I wasn't sure my new position was that big an improvement.

Bright light came through a narrow half-boarded-up window above a rust-stained tub-shower combo. With no hint of which direction it was coming from and no way to tell how long I'd been out, I hoped it was still morning. No matter how long I'd been gone, Rabbit would be out looking for me. I studied the window before crossing that off my exit list. No way could I squeeze my ass out that opening, even if I could get the wood off without clueing my kidnapper into what I was doing.

The shredded remains of a shower curtain hung from an aluminum rod that looked as if a touch would turn it to dust. It was also the source of the moldy smell. Using the rod as a weapon was a no-go. I turned to where the mirror should have been to find a yellowed, pitted empty space. *Right, so no sharp weapons.* The urge to thump my head against the wall was strong. I refrained and went back to my survey. I hadn't gotten far when noise on the other side of the door warned me that my alone time was up.

The warped door shuddered then scraped across the floor. As it swung open, I managed to draw my legs close to avoid getting caught between the door and the wall. A fairly unremarkable man stepped inside—brown hair, brown eyes, light skin, and what looked like a compact .22 held with obvious familiarity at his side. His gaze was aimed at the spot where he'd initially dropped me. He tensed, his hand and weapon coming up as he turned and found me off to the side. His reaction caused an equal amount of tension to streak through me.

Our gazes locked as his hand lowered. Then he reached out and shoved the door back farther until he had a clear view of me. "You're awake."

I didn't say anything. It wasn't a question, and he was stating the obvious. Undeterred by my silence, he held my gaze as he shifted into a crouch in front of me. He braced his arms against his knees, the gun dangling between them. Even if I hadn't been trussed up in duct tape, there was no way I would try for his gun, because that was exactly what he wanted. The proof was in his watchful gaze and the way he let the weapon sway back and forth.

Not keen on getting shot, I remained still, waiting and watching. His gaze roamed over me, impersonal and calculating. That look caused a spurt of relief because there was nothing sexual in it, which moved one possible scenario to the back burner. Those eyes came back to me, and I tried not to flinch at the fury radiating within them.

"Got to give you credit." Unlike his gaze, his voice gave nothing away. The incongruent reactions were unsettling. "You're good."

That was nice to know, but with no idea of why I was getting this compliment, I felt it wise to continue holding my tongue.

He reached out and, with two fingers, pinched my chin, forcing my head one way then the other. "Yeah, you're good, but you missed a few things, *Elena*." He sneered the name as he jerked my chin straight until we were face-to-face. He leaned in, the fury adding a manic light to his eyes. "So, tell me, who the fuck are you?"

Shit shit shit! With that one icy question, my situation went from dire to well and truly fucked. I stared into the cold eyes of the man I was pretty sure was Elena's partner. I licked my dry lips and said, "Hello, Gatekeeper."

The fingers on my chin tightened, pinching deep enough to bruise. A snarl of disgust twisted his lips before he finally let me go to push to his feet. He glared at me, the seconds stretching into one another as I tried not to notice how he tapped his gun against his thigh. His nervous movement was making me twitchy.

Then it stopped. "Where is she?" His question snapped through the tense silence.

Futile though it was, I played dumb. "Who?"

Without changing expression, he whipped his hand across my face. I had no way to block his strike, and my head hit the wall as pain bloomed over my cheek. The impact wrenched my neck and split my lip.

"Where is she?"

Working my jaw, I licked at the blood welling on my lip. "Don't know."

"And if you did, you wouldn't tell me, would you?"

Since there was only one possible answer, and I wasn't keen on getting slapped again, I kept quiet.

His lips curled in disgust. "Bet you think keeping your mouth shut will save you, eh?" He bent down, grabbed my arm with cruel fingers, and all but dragged me up to my feet. "It won't."

Upright, I wobbled, trying to find my balance, not that he gave me much of a chance. He dragged me out of the disgusting bathroom and into a space maybe a quarter of a step above it. It had yellowing walls with peeling paint, a popcorn ceiling with water damage, and a bare light bulb still hanging on for dear life in the center. A cockeyed dresser with no drawers sat across from a bed with a dip so deep a person would need a ladder to get out of it. The threadbare mattress was decorated in Pollock-like stains. The smashed remains of an old TV lay on the floor, keeping company with a plethora of trash from residents who liked their booze and drugs.

Yeah, we were definitely in some old hotel, one that from the looks of it hadn't had a paying customer in decades. Being barefoot with my ankles hobbled by the damn duct tape, I was forced to concentrate on hopping my way carefully across the floor so I wouldn't step on one of the discarded needles or broken glass and find myself becoming patient zero for some plague.

My kidnapper didn't share my concerns as he yanked me forward and around and shoved me toward the bed. I twisted as I fell, trying to land on anything but my face. It didn't work. Trying not to inhale or gag, I rolled to my side. It didn't help when he kicked at my feet as he passed. The petty move had me narrowing my eyes as I fought the urge to slam my feet into his ass and see how much he'd like landing face-first on the disgusting floor. Since I was still trussed up like a DIY project, that retaliation was out of the question.

Grinding my teeth together, I clumsily managed to push and squirm into a sitting position. By the time I got there, he was facing me, straddling the only solid piece of furniture, a ladder-back chair, his arms folded across the back. "Let's try this again, shall we?"

Behind my back, I forced my swollen fingers into a fist, fighting to maintain circulation despite the tight tape. It hurt, but I kept my face blank as I faced Elena's partner.

His empty gaze held mine. "We'll go with something easy. Which agency are you working for?"

Apprehension walked in and set up shop, but I masked it by raising a brow and keeping my voice cool. "What makes you think I work for an agency?"

He reached out with his gun, put the barrel under my chin, and forced my head to tilt back. "Because whatever it cost to get you to look like Elena didn't come cheap."

He was close enough that I could see his finger twitch against the trigger, and ice formed in my veins. That did not bode well since the barrel was against my throat. Self-preservation had me jerking my head away.

He gave me a weird smile and kept up his questions. "DOD? Homeland? The Feds? Spooks?"

As he ran through the alphabet list, I refused to react.

Undaunted, he kept poking. "Not that it really matters."

"Then why ask?"

"I like to know who I'm up against." There was a hardness behind his words. "Considering how deep you and your buddy are buried, I'm leaning toward NSA."

Well, he'd managed to nail one of the groups holding Elena, but there was no way he would figure out I was with PSY-IV since they weren't officially sanctioned. The only positive thing about his continued questions was that they revealed that he had doubts about which enemy held Elena. That gave me something to work with.

"Sucks to be you," I murmured.

His amusement disappeared. "Actually, sucks to be you."

Our eyes locked, and I refused to look away. My mind spun, and the option it landed on was risky as hell, but it wasn't like I had much to work with. I dug deep into my role and channeled Elena's ice-princess persona, allowing a hint of disdainful amusement to peek through. "Maybe, but I'm not the bargaining chip you are, am I?"

Sure enough, that sliver of doubt gained me a little

more ground. Anger crept in, burying his worry. "I'm no one's bargaining chip."

I made a soft hum, neither agreeing nor disagreeing with his statement.

"Fuck you, bitch." He shoved out the chair to loom over me, his knuckles going white as they tightened on the gun. "Don't try to play me. I know the only reason you had access to Elena's shit was because she's locked down in some black site somewhere."

Despite my bound hands, I leaned forward and hardened my voice. "You sure about that?"

Red rode through his face as he sneered, "There's no other reason she'd let you waltz in here, pretending to be her. She's been dodging the federal alphabet for years. If it hadn't been for that fuckup of a general, you and I wouldn't even be having this conversation."

"Oh, I don't know." I kept chipping at his uncertainty, wondering if this was why Elena had chosen him as a partner. He not only had hacking skills but was also easy to manipulate. His emotions rode close to the surface, right alongside his fragile ego, bucking any kind of self-control. "You and I both know Elena's intelligence is off the charts. You really believe she'd let herself be caught and caged?"

His pride took the implied hit, and when temper overshadowed his logic, I knew my gamble had paid off. He began to pace in front of me. "Don't try to mind fuck me, bitch. Elena has only one partner, and it sure as hell isn't you."

"Because Elena shares everything with you, right?"

I could all but hear Rabbit in my head, telling me to cool it, but I couldn't back down now. Like most relationships based on a shared con, secrets slithered underneath the smiling surface of this man and Elena's, causing damaging waves. With a few more nudges, whatever held him to Elena would break. Then I might have a shot of getting out of this.

"You think I could pull any of this off without her help?" I asked.

He came to a stop in front of me, and I tried not to notice that the gun was once again tapping against his leg. "No way is Elena working with you." He dropped to a crouch, putting us at face level. "You know what I think? I think that you're fucking with the wrong people, and I'm not just talking about me. It also makes me wonder what exactly is in this for you, eh?"

He knew something, and I had a bad feeling I knew what it was. Instead of breathing life into that worry, I managed to keep it from my voice. "Why would I fuck with the wrong people?"

His uncertain temper took another step back, and cunning intelligence stepped forward. "For the same reason Elena considered it—money. That Hawes asshole was as dirty as they come, and his fingers were in some deep shit. The ones he was in bed with, they're even dirtier. Which is where you come in." From his position, he studied me with a disconcerting intensity. "Know what I think?"

I was dying—no pun intended—to hear it, but I didn't have to say a word because he was eager to share.

"I think your agency picked up Elena and gave you an assignment to get dirt on her clients."

My mind stuttered, and it was all I could do to keep my face blank and my breathing even. It helped that he wasn't done laying it out.

He came out of his crouch and stood over me. "I think you did your due diligence, and—smart cookie that you are

—when you realized the depth of Elena's gold mine, you decided to play both sides."

"That's a dangerous accusation." I was proud of how bland my voice sounded.

He shrugged as he moved back to his previous position in the chair. "It's a dangerous game you're playing."

"If I'm even playing."

"You're playing, and you're playing for keeps. Want to know how I know?" He didn't wait for my answer. He was too excited to share his twisted insight. "Government pay is shit, and whatever deal you have in the works will fix that right up. I've been watching you."

Yeah, that's a given, considering my current predicament.

But he wasn't done. "And I've seen how well you take to Elena's lifestyle, schmoozing her clients, spending her money like you've been dying to swim in it."

Something in his voice indicated that he had his own green-eyed monster lurking under the darkness. I poked at it, widening that sliver to a full-fledged crack. "And you haven't? Isn't that why you hooked up with Elena in the first place?"

Some emotion flickered in the back of his eyes. "What does it matter to you?"

I managed to shrug even though the move hurt. "It doesn't, but I am wondering, what's your next step? Take me out, and take over what she built?" A muscle jumped in his jaw, but he stayed silent, so I kept going, twisting the knife of doubt a little deeper. "You know it won't work, right? She was the one with the contacts, the one who knew how to handle people. You're just the hacker."

"Yeah, I'm the fucking hacker," he all but snarled as the crack began to snake through his certainty. "I'm the hacker who ensured that her services are in high demand. The same damn services you're profiting from, so who's the greedy bitch now, eh?"

Part of me wanted to giggle hysterically at the fact that he'd basically called himself a bitch, but I couldn't afford to lose ground. Instead, I layered my voice with scorn. "So what's your play here? What do you expect to gain from kidnapping me?"

He smiled as he sat up and tucked his gun behind his back. "Oh, you're going to replace my retirement fund."

"What? You need investment advice?"

"You've got a smart mouth considering your situation." He got up from the chair and closed in. "See, I went in to retrieve the money I helped Elena earn and discovered someone got there first."

Rabbit's comment about the electronic safe hit me, and my stomach dropped. *If this jackass didn't clean it out, who did?* Two possibilities hit my brain—Elena or the agency that held her.

"I'm not keen on being played, and I'm damn sure your current client isn't either."

I braced myself because there was something sly and mean in his face. His hand shot out and grabbed my hair at the back of my skull. With a painful yank that made my eyes water, he pulled my head back far enough to pull me off-balance. The ache at my skull went from *ow* to *triple ow* as he all but held my torso up by my hair.

He leaned in, his hold forcing me to look at him. "I've been at this a hell of a lot longer than you—long enough to recognize when someone's playing both sides. The question I have for you is, which side is paying you?"

Swallowing down all the things I wanted to say that would only end badly, I forced out, "Who says I'm working for anyone?"

"What? You're doing this for you?" He jerked his hand, which was still in my hair, yanking my head back and forth. "Why?"

My only response was a sharp hiss at the stinging pain. With a disgusted snort, he tore his hand free, and what felt like a good chunk of my hair followed. Unfortunately, since I couldn't use my hands, I ended up sprawled on the disgusting mattress.

"No answer, eh?" He stood there as I rolled to my side and awkwardly pushed up. Before I could do more than that, he stepped back, out of kicking range, and folded his arms as a sneer curled his lips. "That's even more evidence you're just a fraud."

"And you aren't?" I used my shoulder to brush the tangled strands of hair out of my face. "I don't see you rushing to Elena's rescue. In fact, you're dicking around with me, which makes me think your partnership is a bunch of bullshit."

"Nope, it's practical. When Elena found out how well alternate business transactions paid, she also realized there was another revenue stream to be mined. You know what people hate losing more than money? Their anonymity. They'd pay whatever she asked just so she wouldn't air their dirty laundry."

And the man in front of me wanted that power like an addict wanted his next fix. *How long did he stand by Elena, nursing his green-eyed demon?* Jealousy that ran that deep didn't happen overnight. I wondered how much longer the Gatekeeper partnership would have lasted if Elena hadn't been picked up. It wouldn't have surprised me if the reason Elena was caught was standing right in front of me.

"Does Elena know what a coldhearted bastard you are?"

"Yeah, which is why we work." I saw no sign of guilt or

remorse, only a chilling ruthlessness. He cocked his head as he studied me.

That look worried me. There was something working in his mind, something I couldn't pinpoint.

"I'm sure you know what that's like, right? You and your partner seem to have a similar arrangement."

Even knowing I shouldn't answer, I did, because hearing him compare Rabbit and me to his twisted relationship was vile. "We're nothing like you."

He gave a low chuckle. "I don't know about that. I think you two might be just like us." He dropped his arms and propped his hands on his hips. "Got to give him his due—he's a worthy opponent. I almost had him in that damn car."

Since I couldn't take him down physically, I struck low and mean, nailing his ego hard. "But you didn't because he's better than you."

Thunderclouds moved over his face, leaving it dark. "You believe what you need to. Just know he's not that good. In fact, I've got a few questions for him."

"Good luck asking. I'm fairly sure he won't be all that keen on answering."

The anger drifted away, and what replaced it left me jonesing for a hot shower. "I'm going to disagree, considering the mess of the bed in that room back there. I'm sure he'll be poking his nose around soon. Too bad he won't find you."

Since I knew differently, I was determined to give Rabbit as much time as I could to close in. If it wasn't for the damn duct tape, I could have handled this on my own, but the silver stuff was living up to its reputation. Left with nothing else, I went back to chipping at my kidnapper's arrogance. "You sure about that? If he can keep you from taking over the car, what makes you think that finding me will be any more of a challenge?"

"Because you won't be here."

Okay, I do not like the sound of that. At. All.

He moved around the bed and went back to his chair. "In fact, since you've managed to screw me out of what Elena and I built, you're going to repay me."

I watched him, trying to figure out where this was going. "Is this where I ask how you expect that to happen?"

He shifted to a hip and pulled a phone out of his pocket. Then, watching me, he hit the screen. I could hear it ringing through as his smile went sharp, his eyes sharper. He hit the speaker button and lowered the phone between us. I sent up a useless plea, knowing it would go unheard.

Sure enough, when it was picked up on the other end, I heard Zane's voice. "Hello?"

"Mr. Seward, how much would you pay to learn who's betraying you?"

Chapter Twenty-One

RABBIT

Ricochet wove through traffic as we headed toward Jinx's signal. In the passenger seat, Wolf used the GPS to make the necessary course corrections. I sat in the back, my mind locked on possible extraction scenarios as I alternated between monitoring Jinx's signal and trolling through what public records I could on the property.

"Left here," Wolf said, pulling my attention to where we were. "Then slow. Should be on our right in about three hundred feet." He cranked his head around. "Approach?"

"Direct. There's no viable rear entry."

The single-story motel sat just off the main road, the bottom half of the L-shaped building running parallel to the street. Behind it sat an industrial warehouse surrounded by a block fence. The narrow alley between the two buildings might have worked, but a check of what I could find of pictures and old building plans showed no entry points on the back side. A series of narrow rectangular openings near the roofline indicated that the rooms' baths were located at the back. That meant our only option was approaching from the front.

"There it is," Ricochet said.

Wolf and I turned and checked out the building as we drove by at a leisurely pace, just another car in the passing moderate traffic. I tried very hard not to think of Jinx as I took in the state of the property. The parking lot was a mix of potholes and trash. The chain-link fence gamely holding on in front sagged in places and did shit-all to keep anyone out. Signs from the city were posted along the fence, warning that the property was off-limits. Based on the scorched remains of what used to be the front office and the layer of street tags running all along the exterior, neither the fence nor the signage was much of a deterrent. I noted that some of the rooms no longer had doors and most of the long-gone windows were boarded up.

Now that we were here, I put my phone in my pocket. "Plans on file with the city indicate thirty units plus office."

I opened the small pass-through in the back seat and slid the laptop bag into the trunk. Ricochet kept up his steady pace and made a right. He pulled into a warehouse parking lot next to the abandoned motel.

"Best guess, she's in one of the secured units," Wolf said.

"Agreed," I said. The asshole who had Jinx would need privacy, which meant a workable door and boarded-up window. These units were crap for soundproofing, but there were other ways to ensure that no unwanted attention came their way. I cut my thoughts short, unable to go any deeper and remain steady. "It takes our options down by at least half."

"We'll need a spot out of sight so I can work," Wolf warned as Ricochet pulled the rental into a space and parked. "I should be able to get us down to one or two options."

The geotag couldn't get specific enough to target a room, so instead of trying to clear the entire building, Wolf was going to do a telepathic scan for Jinx. If she was awake, we'd have the advantage of an inside person. If not, well, we'd deal.

"If we come in from the alley, we can keep our approach quiet," I advised the group. All three of us did a weapons check before we exited the car. A familiar quiet anticipation swept through me, but an underlying icy rage threatened to burn through my control.

Knowing just how dangerous that emotion was, I caught Ricochet's gaze as we stood by the car. "You take lead."

Understanding flashed in his eyes, and some of my edgy tension eased when he nodded. We started our approach. The trick to not drawing attention was keeping movements casual but purposeful, so with a deceptively casual gait, we quickly moved away from the parking lot and over into the alley. The stench of decay hit my nose first, and I breathed through my mouth until I could adjust. We took positions at the west end of the building, the farthest point from the burnt-out shell of the office. That choice was driven by the fact that it was the section with the most intact doors. It was just after midmorning, and the sun was still making its way to its zenith, which meant our position had the added advantage of morning shadows to help mask our movements. Standing under the overhang, our backs to the motel, we waited, weapons out, while Wolf did his thing. Rico was crouched in first position, I had the middle, and Wolf was bringing up the rear.

A familiar buzz of energy raised the hair along my skin. It was a sensation only I seemed to have whenever a team worked with his or her ability. Doc, the healer on our team, theorized I had this sensitivity because my ability was centered on energy. Whatever caused the reaction, it came in handy. Ricochet and I kept our eyes open and braced ourselves for anything while Wolf worked. I felt the energy ebb and flow.

A minute passed and turned into two, then three before Wolf finally said, "Got her."

My eyes closed for the briefest moment as relief coursed through me. "She okay?" I didn't care what my question gave away. I needed an answer.

"Banged up, but she's good." Wolf's voice sounded distant.

"Target?" Ricochet asked.

"Male, thirties, twitchy, armed with a twenty-two. He's on a call with Seward."

Fuck! That meant not only was our cover likely blown, but so was our op.

Wolf touched my shoulder, and I turned to look at him. His normally light-green eyes were an eerie crystal green. "Jinx wants you to take out his phone."

"I need thirty seconds, maybe less."

Wolf paused then nodded. "She says make it quick, or we're fucked."

I didn't need any further encouragement. I dropped my normal mental shields and swept out with my ability. I found the faint hums of the devices closest to me then widened my net until I located a strong, steady signal coming from back and behind me.

Narrowing my focus, I leaned out and stared down the back wall, counting windows. "Six units in. Get in position before I do this."

In front of me, Ricochet nodded. It was vital that we

move fast once I killed the signal—we didn't want to give the asshole time to react. Ricochet led the way as I curled my psychic hand around the cellular signal. We followed in formation as we closed in on our target.

I moved to the far side of the door, weapon up and at the ready, then stayed below the boarded window. Wolf stayed to the other side, back to the wall, weapon drawn. We studied the door.

A solid kick or two should do it. The door was warped as fuck, but time and weather had left the wood dry and brittle. I looked at Rico and used the hand signals we were all familiar with to share my assessment. He agreed then gave me a countdown. I nodded as Ricochet moved silently into place, facing the door. He dropped his chin, starting the count. On two, I tightened my psychic grip then made a sharp hand motion indicating that the phone was dead. Ricochet reared back and slammed his foot just above the doorknob.

The door shuddered and cracked then swung open. Rico stepped back, and I took his place, weapon up, sweeping for threats. I moved in, Wolf following, Rico bringing up my six. For a couple of seconds, my eyes adjusted from the bright outside to the dim interior. Then I heard a pained grunt followed by the loud report of a gun being fired. A figure stumbled in front of me, regained balance, and managed to shift that movement into a blurring kick. The hit slammed into my forearm, nailing the deep bruise from the accident. The impact made me loosen my grip, and my gun tumbled to the floor.

Without slowing, I rushed forward, closing the distance between my man-shaped target and me. I blocked the incoming arm and the weapon trained on me. Landing a brutal palm strike to his chest, I forced him back a step.

Then I was jerking my face out of the way to escape getting a fist to my jaw. I trapped his wrist and weapon in my grip. Yanking on his arm, I pulled him off-balance without letting go. His retaliatory strike sank painfully just above my kidney. I tightened my hold and pivoted, viciously twisting his wrist. Bones broke with an audible sound quickly followed by a pained howl that left my ears ringing.

The .22 fell from his nerveless fingers, and he staggered back, jerking his arm from my punishing grip. Unfortunately, I caught sight of Jinx, her lip bloodied and her bruised face pale and drawn in lines of pain. I lost my shit. Fury painted my vision red. I shifted my attention to the bastard cradling his arm. Between one blink and the next, I sank a fist into his gut, making him double over. I followed up with a brutal uppercut that sent him stumbling back into the wall, my rage a living, breathing presence scouring away all but the need to hurt.

The asshole pushed off the wall, feral fury twisting his face as blood dripped from his nose and mouth. "Motherfucker!"

I shook out my stinging knuckles and bared my teeth in a vicious grin. "Bring it, asshat."

He charged. I dodged the first wild swing and targeted his ribs. With a quick one-two combo, the bone snapped. Despite the hit, he managed to nail me with a brutal punch just below the back of my neck. I wobbled, shaking my head clear just in time to block the next clumsy hit. I shifted my balance and barely avoided the fist coming for my head. Unfortunately, I also missed the shoulder that took me just under my sternum, driving the air from my lungs as he rode me to the floor. I got an arm at his neck and used it to pull him off me enough so I could grab his broken wrist and yank.

He shifted his weight to the side in an attempt to roll away. He didn't get far. I switched our positions until I could straddle his torso. From my dominant position, I sank two wickedly brutal punches to his face before a big arm wrapped around my chest and a hard hand caught my arm. I bucked against the restraining hold but could feel my body being lifted.

"Okay, wild man—we need him conscious." Wolf's raspy voice cut through my rage and brought my brain back online.

I let him pull me back as Ricochet crouched next to the groaning asshole lying on the floor. Ricochet picked up the forgotten .22 and tucked it behind his back.

Still laid out on the floor, face painted red with his blood, the kidnapping fucker glared at me. "Asshole broke my wrist."

"You're lucky that's all he broke." Jinx was down on one elbow on the bed, struggling to get back into a sitting position.

I shrugged off Wolf's hold and went to her, shoving down my anger as I took in the signs of her extremely rough morning. Gently, I helped her upright, fighting the urge to go back and hit the still-moaning asswipe a few more times. Noting the awkward angle of her arms and the duct tape hobbling her ankles, I asked Wolf, "Got a blade?"

Ricochet handed over a lethally sharp switchblade. "Use this."

Taking it, I crouched in front of her and sliced through the tape at her ankles, carefully tearing it free. Her feet were dirty and scratched. I looked up and met her gold-flecked brown eyes. "You okay?"

She gave me a shaky smile and swallowed, her voice

suspiciously husky. "I've been better, but I think I bruised a heel when I kicked his ass."

That explained her awkward position and his stumbled approach when we burst in. "I appreciate the assist," I said.

Her smile lost the trembling edge, and she blew out a soft breath. "He didn't give me much to work with."

"It worked, didn't it?" I waited for her tiny nod.

Unable to resist, I reached up and cupped her face, careful of the bruises. As much as I wanted to pick her up and get her out of this pit so I could baby her, I knew better. I dropped my hand, stood up, and put a knee on the bed, biting back a curse when I saw how swollen her hands were. This was going to hurt.

Pulling back, I studied her. "I'm going to do your hands. You ready?"

Her jaw firmed, and she gave a half-suppressed wince. "Make it quick."

Yeah, she knows what's coming. With extreme care, I got Rico's blade under the tape.

She hissed as the tape tore along the sharp edge. "Ow, ow, ow, ow." The complaint came out under her breath, but it pierced through me.

I closed the blade and stopped her from pulling her arms forward. "Slowly." I began a soft massage before slowly bringing her arm forward. "Flex your fingers for me."

Wincing, she bit her lip but followed my directions. I continued to work on her arms while Ricochet took care of the idiot on the floor. From the other side of the room came the sound of ripping duct tape.

"Here, found this," Wolf said.

I turned to see Wolf handing Ricochet strips of duct tape, which Rico put to use on the man on the floor.

There was a flurry of activity as they got him restrained. Meanwhile, I kept working on Jinx. We'd shifted positions so that I was behind her, and she leaned against me as I continued to work on restoring blood flow to her hands and arms.

As much as I wanted to enjoy having her back, safe, we had more important things to address. Besides, I'd promised not to let my emotions get in the way of our assignment. "I'm guessing that's Elena's partner?" When her soft assent came back, I managed to dip my chin in a short nod. "How bad did he screw us?"

She shifted so she could turn her face to me, her head pressing against my chest. "Zane now has confirmation that someone's betraying him."

"Does he know who?"

She shook her head. "No, but..." She stopped and looked down at the man glaring at us from his position on the floor. "Even without giving our names, that dick did serious damage."

"Fuck you, bitch."

At his venomous snarl, I stared down at the asshole I now knew was Keith Alders and let everything I wanted to do to him show in my eyes. "If you want to keep your teeth, Alders, I suggest you shut it." I felt Jinx stiffen as I used the asshole's name, but I didn't take my gaze off the man.

His face paled as his mouth settled into mutinous lines. "What're you going to do? Kill me?"

"That would be the easiest solution." That brutally casual assessment came from Wolf, who stood off to the side, his arms folded, his focus on our prisoner.

The trussed-up jackass sneered as he took us all in. "Like that's an option."

Wolf raised a brow. "What, you don't think we'd do it?"

"Of course you won't." He turned back to Jinx. "Because your superiors won't allow it, will they?"

"Superiors? Who do you think we are? Government?" Ricochet's questions were silky with menace.

"He's convinced I'm working both sides," Jinx said. "According to him, not only am I working for the government, but you and I have also decided to take over Elena's business for ourselves." She continued to rub her hands together as I worked her upper arms.

"And Seward's role in this?" Wolf asked.

Jinx stared at the hacker, her voice hard. "Dumbass over there decided to recoup his money by offering me to Zane for—what was it? Ten million in Bitcoin? Wasn't that where you two were at before your call was cut short?"

For once, Alders kept his mouth shut, but if looks could tear a person apart, Jinx would have resembled a gory puzzle. Undeterred, she held his furious gaze. "I did warn you he was better than you." Her voice was laced with cold venom.

When his gaze shifted to me and his anger deepened, I knew Zane wasn't the "he" Jinx was referring to. Seeing Alders's rage and the damaged ego fueling it, something vicious and lethal bared its teeth, hungry to return what he'd given to Jinx. Instead of feeding it blood and pain, I decided to satisfy its craving a different way. This was the asshole who'd broken into our rooms, bugged my laptop, and almost turned Jinx and me into roadkill. But thanks to this morning's report on who we were dealing with, I knew exactly how to rip his world apart.

I gently set Jinx aside and went to crouch in front of him. "Pissed you off, didn't it, when Elena took all the credit for your programs?"

A muscle jumped in his jaw.

"Even worse when you realized how much you could make without her in the picture—so much so that you made a deal with the devil, or in this case, the FBI's cybercrime division. You gave them Elena. Then, while they were sifting through the multiple layers of her shit, you tried to siphon her money into your accounts. You figured by the time they uncovered all her accounts, you and the money would be long gone. But it didn't quite work out that way, did it?"

Alders's gaze slipped away from mine even as his lip curled, but he was smart enough to keep his mouth shut.

"Because when you went in for the cash, the accounts were empty. Want to know why? I'm happy to explain it," I said. His gaze came back to me, and I held it as I made sure he knew exactly what his future held. "Elena may have partnered with you because of your skills, but she had skills of her own. Once she figured out that you were up to something, she created a program of her own—one that moved the majority of her cash and contacts to a secured server you couldn't reach if she didn't check in at the allotted time."

"Damn paranoid bitch," he muttered.

"That paranoid bitch took it one step further." I waited until I'd regained his full attention before I brought his world crashing down around his ears. "She kept meticulous records. Every transaction, every client, every program, every payment—she documented it all, including who she brought in when demand required more than she could handle on her own. So, Keith Alders, I suggest you enjoy the fresh air as my friend here hauls your ass in, because it's going to be the last time you breathe it for the foreseeable future."

His face paled before he jerked forward, trying to reach me, but Ricochet was there to hold him back.

My mouth stretched into a cruel smile, and not quite done taunting him, I finished with, "And when they've got you locked in the box next to Elena, give her our regards. We'll be sure to take real good care of her clients and money." I pushed to my feet and went back to Jinx.

Behind me, a string of curses erupted. They grew in strength as Ricochet hauled Alders to his feet and dragged him out of the room. Wolf followed, and the door swung shut behind them, leaving Jinx and me alone in the hovel.

I moved to her, and she grabbed my hand. "He set up a meet with Zane."

"I thought we interrupted their call."

Her thumb absent-mindedly stroked the back of my hand, her voice terse. "They were finalizing the payment amount, but they'd already agreed to meet someplace called Arbor Gardens in two hours."

I squeezed her hand as I sat on the edge of the bed next to her. "You think he'll still show?"

Her gaze went distant. "Yeah, I do, if for no other reason than curiosity. Even if Zane isn't convinced of what Alders was telling him, his curiosity will make him keep that meet." She bumped my shoulder with hers. "We need to get in front of this."

I knew that "this" was the mess Alders's call to Zane had created. "You're worried about Amalia."

She nodded. "We can't leave her with him."

"If she's with him." I understood Jinx's concern. With Alders's call, Zane would be actively looking for the one betraying him. His current choices were limited to Elena and Amalia. If Amalia was close, he'd go for her first.

"We can figure that out easily enough. Do you have my phone?" she asked.

I shifted to a hip, pulled it out, and handed it to her.

She thumbed the screen and turned it to me. "Track this number."

I sighed but did as she asked. While I waited for the program to work, Ricochet came back in. I looked up. "They on their way?"

Ricochet crouched in front of Jinx, carefully turning her face one way then the other as he studied the damage. "Yeah. Wolf's holding him at the car until we can hand him off to the local FBI agent." He held her chin. "You okay?"

She gave him a tiny smile. "I'm good."

A small sound indicated that the program had finished its search. I checked the screen. "Well, shit," I muttered, recognizing the familiar address. "This is going to be a bitch."

Jinx grabbed my hand and turned the screen toward her. "Isn't that Zane's address?"

"Yeah." Seeing that Amalia was there did not sit well with me.

"What are we looking at?" Ricochet asked.

"Amalia Black," I answered, my voice tight.

"Delacourt's mole?" Something flashed through Ricochet's eyes too fast to read.

"Yeah. She's at Zane's place," Jinx said.

"That doesn't bode well," he murmured before going straight to the heart of our newest problem. "We getting her out?"

"I think the better question is, how do we get her out?" I said. That house of Zane's was a fucking monstrosity, which meant Amalia could be anywhere.

Jinx said, "We'll need to go in while Zane's at the meet."

"What meet?" Ricochet asked, so Jinx quickly filled him in. When she was done, he stood and took a few steps away, not answering immediately. When he turned, he asked me, "We have—what? Three hours tops?"

I gave him a grim nod.

"Is that enough time for you to come up with an exfil plan?"

"It'll be tricky as shit, but yeah, I think we can come up with something." I wasn't sure the end result would be ideal, but I couldn't justify leaving Amalia hanging when everything was about to implode.

Ricochet checked his watch. "The Feds should be here in fifteen. We can set them on Zane at Arbor Gardens. That will keep him busy and give us space to go after Amalia."

"Rico…" I waited until I got his attention before I stated the obvious. One of us had to play devil's advocate, and unfortunately, it was my turn. "If we do this, and it goes bad, we blow the whole mission." *And Falcon slips away once again.* The Feds would probably do their part and follow through, but Zane had proven more than once that he was far from a sure thing.

Ricochet held my gaze. "We can't be in two places at once, and we aren't leaving Amalia out in the cold. We bring her home."

I dipped my chin. "We bring her home." Hell, we all knew she should have been pulled out a while ago, but whether it was Delacourt's choice or Amalia's to cut the operation short, that call hadn't been made.

Rico nodded sharply. "Right. I'll go make sure our guest isn't driving Wolf to commit a felony."

"We'll be right behind you," I said. Jinx and I watched him leave. When he was gone, I turned to her. "You good?" I hadn't wanted to ask that question in front of the others.

She sat there, bruised and battered, and smiled at me. "I'm good."

I ran a hand through my hair. "I shouldn't have left—"

"Stop." She caught my other hand and squeezed, waiting until I looked at her. "Just stop. We both know how often shit happens." She leaned in, tugging me closer. "I'm okay, Cajun man."

I used my free hand to cup her chin, taking her in as my thumb brushed, featherlight, over her bottom lip, careful to avoid the raw cut. Finally, I asked, "You ready to get out of here?"

She nodded. "Just tell me I don't have to share a seat with him."

I shook my head. "No worries. He's traveling with the Feds."

"Good." She went to get to her feet.

I stopped her with "Sugar, you're barefoot. No way in hell I'm letting you walk out of here."

"I'll be fine."

"Yes, you will." Without any more discussion, I wrapped an arm around her back and one under her knees. "Hold tight."

Her arm curled around my neck as I lifted her and left the disgusting dump behind. I was carrying her toward the car when she asked, "Rabbit?"

"Mmm?"

"Thanks for coming." The words came out soft but hit hard.

I stopped, looked down, and found her watching me. I dipped my neck and took her mouth in a gentle kiss, mindful of her cut lip. When I was done, I lifted my head and said, "I'll always come for you, Jinx."

Her eyes were suspiciously bright, but she brushed her thumb over my lower lip. "I know." Then she resettled her head against my shoulder, and we got back to work.

Chapter Twenty-Two

JINX

Since our window of opportunity was tight, once Wolf handed Alders over to the Feds, we were on our way. A quick side trip to a nearby box store netted me a cheap pair of shoes and basic necessities so I wouldn't look like the walking wounded. Getting back into Zane's neighborhood was easy. Trying to find a way into his house without giving the game away was an altogether different challenge.

Rabbit worked his phone, digging up floor plans, security permits, and anything that could help us piece together what we faced in getting Amalia away from Zane. Although Rabbit's tracking program put her in Zane's house, it still left us with some serious square footage to hunt through.

Like hunting a mole in a mansion. I choked back a snort of hysterical amusement. *Okay, maybe I'm still a little on edge.*

Rabbit looked up from his screen and shot me a quizzical look. "You okay?"

Not about to unlock my lips in case my hyena imitation broke free, I waved a hand between us and nodded. Since I was no longer worried about escaping a pissed-off egomaniac, my coursing adrenaline left me a little shaky. *Get your shit together, girl, and focus.*

Rabbit held my gaze, worry moving through his eyes. With a couple of deep breaths, I managed to curb my crazy. "I'm good."

It took a few beats for him to believe me and resume his search. We were closing in on the neighborhood when Rabbit said, "Looks like we might have a small break."

In the front passenger seat, Wolf turned so he could see us. "How small?"

Rabbit continued to work on his phone. "There's this neighborhood app where people share all sorts of shit—sales, suspicious activity, complaints about barking dogs. Looks like there's a house a couple doors down from Zane's that's been recently reacquired by the bank, thanks to a nasty divorce. It's got some of the neighbors worried it'll be picked up by investors looking to flip the property."

"Let me guess," I said. "They're worried about the flip dropping property values."

"Sure sounds like it," Rabbit answered.

I caught Ricochet's grimace as he slowed to turn right. "No price tag is worth nosy neighbors."

"Based on the property lines in the city's planning office, it backs onto Zane's property." Rabbit kept working, the screen flickering so fast I didn't even bother to try to follow along. "It's a damn good in if we don't want to invite unwanted attention." He looked at me. "What do you think? Can you get us in?"

Since using the code Zane had given us to get through the neighborhood gate was out, I knew he meant something more devious. "You want me to convince the guard at the gate we're just a bunch of interested investors?"

He nodded. "Looks like the property is set to go to

auction next week, which gives weight to potential bidders doing drive-bys."

I thought it through. Working with four faces and the car would be tricky, but limiting the illusion to a single individual, especially one who was bored with the monotony of the job, might work in our favor. Crafting the illusion wouldn't be hard. The challenge would be finding the initial thread to weave the illusion into the guard's perception so that he believed it.

"I can do it, but whether or not the guard buys it…" I shrugged. "If he's hypervigilant, it'll make getting past his natural wariness tricky."

"What if we work together?" That unexpected question came from Wolf.

I shifted so I could see his face, not surprised to find there wasn't much to read. As a telepath, Wolf had some serious personal lines about using his ability to manipulate others. His lines were harder and closer than mine, but the fact that he'd asked meant he, too, felt the urgency of the situation.

"You sure you're up for that?" I asked.

He regarded me with his sea-green eyes. "Do we have any other option that doesn't have us storming the gates?"

We both turned to Rabbit, who shook his head. "If we had more time, maybe, but with the limited information and window of opportunity, this is our best bet."

Wolf ran a hand over the back of his neck then looked back at me. "Then yeah, I'm sure. If you run into pushback, I can step in."

I didn't miss the reluctance in his voice and decided that if I could pull this off without him, I would. I got the whole anything-for-the-mission mentality, but I wasn't keen on hurting my family. Asking this of Wolf would be doing just that. "How about I'll signal if I think it's not working?"

"Maybe we'll get lucky and the guard will be on lunch," Ricochet said.

I wished I shared his optimism, but considering how things were going, that was difficult. "How far out are we?"

Ricochet glanced at the phone on the dash. "ETA is three minutes, thirty."

"You do the talking," I told Ricochet because I wanted to make sure the illusion didn't waver.

Building the image wasn't hard. Working with Ricochet, Wolf, and Rabbit to turn them into the expected casual businessmen and contractors was easy. I, on the other hand, required a little more work, thanks to my ragged appearance, but by the time the car turned into the neighborhood, I had the image set.

Using my ability created a buzz in my head that only I could hear. If I had to try to describe it, I would say it was like being a virtual filmmaker, but instead of actual film, I used ribbons of images. The funny thing about the human brain was that it wasn't a fan of inconsistencies. Once I threaded one of my ribbons through someone's mind and created the illusion's basic framework, the person's memories and perceptions would rush in to fill in the details. Luckily for me, the brain provided the finer details, stitching each illusionary ribbon into a cohesive fabric, adding depth and believability until it resembled a true memory. The only way I knew an illusion had taken root was the sudden disappearance of the buzzing sound.

Ricochet slowed as we approached the gate. The guard stepped out of his shack, and we came to a stop next to him. I sat in the back seat, keeping my face averted as I carefully unfurled the first illusionary ribbon. I wound it around the guard, letting it settle over him like a blanket, soft and barely there. I found my psychic way in when the guard studied the car, slowly shifting his perception of our vehicle from an average dusty rental to a dark-colored luxury sedan with tinted windows.

The guard stepped closer, and Ricochet's window went down. "Morning," Ricochet said casually.

"Morning, sir." The guard kept his distance, but his attention moved to the car's occupants.

I spun another ribbon as the guard nodded at Wolf and Ricochet, completely ignoring Rabbit and me in the back seat. I kept up the psychic pressure until the guard saw Ricochet as a lean Hispanic man in a collared shirt and Wolf as a beefy contractor. As the weave settled, I could feel the instinctive click as the illusion caught and became the guard's reality.

I lifted my lashes and made a short negative motion with my head, letting Wolf know his help wasn't necessary. The guard wasn't expecting trouble, and when Ricochet explained that they were there to check out the house going up for auction, the man bought it. He stepped back into his shack and began to make notes on his clipboard. As we drove through, I held the illusion in place, subtly keeping his attention on his paperwork and not on the car passing through.

Only after Ricochet went around the curve and out of the guard's sight did I release my hold on the illusion. I took a couple of deep breaths as the low level of tension eased from my head. A touch on my fist brought me back. I found myself staring into Rabbit's eyes.

"Jinx?"

I licked my lip, wincing when my tongue hit the sore cut from Alders's fist. "I'm good."

He squeezed my hand then gave Ricochet directions to the empty house. There was another locked gate barring the driveway, but Rabbit bypassed the lock in a handful of seconds. Once through, we headed up a drive that ended in a four-car garage. Rabbit slipped out and did his magic, and we drove into the large, well-lit bay.

The door rolled down as Rabbit walked toward us. We exited the car and followed Rabbit to the side door. In less than a minute, the alarm system was disabled, and we were inside. Because the house was set back from the road and the windows were veiled with custom blinds and shutters, we had free range of the interior.

We didn't go far. We stopped at the oversized island in the kitchen and got to work. First up was figuring out how to find Amalia without clueing Zane or his security in to the fact that we were there. Wolf offered his ability as a solution, volunteering to scan Zane's house for mental signatures.

"You sure it's not too far?" Ricochet asked.

"It's a stretch but should be doable." Wolf went to the expanse of windows at the back of the house, which looked out on a yard that stretched into a mock forest that blocked any view of Zane's house. Without turning around, he asked, "You have any idea what kind of staff he has on hand?"

"My impression was it was just Zane and his buddy, John." I looked to Rabbit for his take.

"Same," he agreed.

"Right, then. So if I pick up a female, chances are it's her." Wolf didn't wait for a response but settled on the tile floor, legs folded Indian style, as he closed his eyes and did his thing.

Ricochet, Rabbit, and I kept our voices low and continued to plan as Wolf worked his angle. Zane's security system was complex and challenging, even for Rabbit. Rabbit confirmed that what was listed on file did not match what he could sense.

"Any way to hack our way into his security feed?" I asked. We needed eyes on the interior, but the security was a closed system, which meant Rabbit would have to get up close and personal with it on-site.

"Not until we're inside." Rabbit pulled up another screen, a frown creasing his forehead. "Paranoid bastard doesn't even do remote backups."

"Can you override it?" Ricochet asked.

"Yeah," Rabbit muttered. "But again, I'd have to be inside, and I've got a feeling it's trickier than it appears."

"Got her." Wolf's raspy voice cut through our discussion.

We all turned to see him still sitting on the floor. His head was cocked as if he was listening to something. We waited, knowing there would be more.

"She's on the south side of the house. I think Zane's got her locked down." His jaw tightened, and his hand on his thigh curled into a fist. "I keep losing her."

There were reasons a telepath wouldn't be able to connect. One of those was because the person he was trying to reach wasn't conscious. I tried not to think about what that might mean.

I shared a look with Ricochet and Rabbit. "I guess Zane decided not to trust Amalia."

Rabbit's face darkened, and he went back to his phone, flipping through screens until he found what he wanted. He set the phone between us. Floor plans stretched across the screen. "South side of the house." He turned to Wolf. "Upstairs or down?"

Wolf was silent, but the muscles along his neck were visibly tight. "No windows. She thinks basement level."

Rabbit shifted the image on the phone. "Basement's showing a theater room, nothing else."

I used my phone to pull up the initial floor plans Rabbit had found, trying to compare them to whatever set he was looking at. I set my phone next to his. We all bent over the two phones.

It was Ricochet who saw the discrepancies first. "Measurements don't match here." He shifted Rabbit's phone, pointing out the differences between the theater room and what was labeled as workspace. "I take it these"—he tapped Rabbit's phone—"are from a recent renovation."

Rabbit nodded as he studied the layouts. "Safe room?"

"Most likely," I agreed. "Especially since they'd make sure not to note that on the plans."

"It would make the perfect spot to hold someone without raising suspicions," Ricochet added.

Maybe, but it would require specific materials, and those would have to leave a trail of some sort. "That kind of specialized construction is hard to keep off the record," I said.

Wolf cut into the conversation. "Amalia says the door's thick, probably metal, and heavy." Lines of strain were spreading across his face.

My hand fisted on the counter. Based on Wolf's strained expression, we were about to lose our inside connection to Amalia. I turned and met Rabbit's gaze, seeing the same realization in his expression. The clocking was ticking.

Rabbit rubbed a hand over his neck. "We don' have time to run down the details."

"And it's not the only possibility we have." I went back to the property map. "Amalia said no windows, and I'm counting at least two more possibilities here." I zoomed in on one of the two exterior structures behind the house. "Looks like a pool house and maybe a guest house? Either way, she might be in one of those."

"We'll have to split up," Wolf said, joining us at the island.

I gave him a questioning look, which he answered with a short headshake. My gut tightened. He'd lost his connection with Amalia. Maybe it was the distance, or maybe it was her losing consciousness. Either way, it sucked.

"Two teams of two," Ricochet said. "Rabbit and Jinx, you've been inside before—you take the house. Start at the basement and make your way up. We'll join you as soon as we clear the other structures."

After a round of nods, we did a weapons and ammunition check. The results weren't pretty, but it was better than nothing. When we were all ready, Ricochet stood with his hand on the knob, looked over his shoulder, and said, "Quiet and quick."

With that, we slipped out the back door and made our way across the expansive backyard. It didn't take us long to cross onto Zane's property. Despite the terrain's wild appearance, we made our way through it quickly. Rabbit held up his hand, signaling us to hold, his focus on the house.

We stopped just inside the shaded area of the tree line, taking in the immaculate landscaping that left Zane's backyard fairly exposed. Green grass rolled between clusters of flowering shrubs and majestic trees. Hefty but elegant deck furniture sat around the pool that stretched between the two structures that Ricochet and Wolf would have to clear. What was left was an obstacle course of planters and greenery for Rabbit and me to navigate before getting into the house.

We waited for Rabbit's assessment. A minute ticked by. Then he had us move back into the coverage of the trees. We huddled together, and Rabbit shared a quick recap of the security. Cameras were strategically placed around the exterior, and even more electronic signals echoed from the interior. It was a decent setup, but the cameras were nowhere near as prevalent as expected, which left me uneasy.

Something in my expression must have revealed my worry, because Rabbit asked me, "What?"

I managed an uncomfortable shrug. "Considering what happens inside those walls, that kind of setup seems a little simplistic."

He grimaced. "Sometimes simple is better. The more complex a system is, the easier it is to exploit."

That idea didn't offer much by way of reassurance, but then again, nothing in this situation would. If we hadn't needed to get Amalia free and clear of Zane, none of us would have even considered taking this risk.

We spent a few more minutes finalizing our strategy before splitting apart to start the search. Rabbit and I waited until Wolf and Ricochet disappeared behind the building on the left before making our approach to the house. I followed Rabbit around the back and along the side of the house. Our goal was a little-used access door hidden behind a thick climbing shrub. With Rabbit keeping a psychic finger on the exterior cameras, we made our approach in short bursts of movement to coincide with the brief blind spots he was able to create.

In the protective screen of the hedge, I crouched by the door, a pick set in hand, while Rabbit stood guard and interfered with the camera feed. At his signal, I got to work mentally counting down the twenty seconds we had to get inside. My lock-picking skills were a little rusty, but I heard the last snick of a tumbler falling into place at the sixteen-second mark.

I tucked Ricochet's pick set back into the lone zippered pocket of my yoga pants and reached up to grasp the door-knob. I touched Rabbit's leg, got his nod, then twisted the handle and inched the door open. When there was enough space, I rose and slipped inside with Rabbit on my ass. He carefully closed the door, locking us inside, out of camera range. My nose twitched at the overpowering scents of laundry soap and softener. I pinched the bridge of my nose and successfully fought back the urge to sneeze. It didn't keep my eyes from watering, though.

Rabbit moved around me, taking the lead. After wiping my eyes clear, I followed at his six, ears trained, eyes constantly scanning for threats. As we made our way through the quiet house, a thread of unease wove through me, leaving me on edge. The interior hush wasn't an easy quiet. A tension rode the air—one that might be more in my mind than in reality, but I couldn't shake the feeling of being watched. I tried to take comfort in the fact that if we were being watched, Rabbit would know. Since he kept moving forward, it had to just be me.

We made it to a set of stairs hidden on the back side of the kitchen without incident. Rabbit slowly opened the door, and I sent up a prayer that it wouldn't squeak and give away our presence. It swung open without a peep, and we slipped inside to huddle at the top landing as Rabbit carefully pulled the door closed behind us. The landing wasn't dark but dim. Natural light from below drifted up.

Staring down the stairs, unease riding my spine, I tapped Rabbit's shoulder, getting his attention. When he turned to me, I mouthed, "Eyes?"

He frowned and shook his head. Normally his reassurance would be enough to settle me, but not this time. He closed what little distance existed between us, his body brushing against mine, triggering a reaction so inappropriate to our situation that I shivered with a mix of adrenaline and apprehension.

He put his lips next to my ear. "What's wrong?"

His breath fell down my neck as I turned, feeling my temple brush his jaw, and kept my voice equally quiet. "Not sure. Got an itch."

He drew back, his eyes searching mine, worried. Yeah, he would know that if I felt the need to share, something might be up. "Stay alert."

I gave him a nod. He led the way down the stairs and paused at the foot. He raised a hand and cocked his head. Standing so close to him, I couldn't miss the hair-raising wave of energy seeping from him as he began manipulating the interior security, looping its signal and blinding any possible cameras to our movements.

Finally, he moved into the basement, and I followed. Sunlight came through the basement window wells situated in an open area just in front of the theater. They provided the weird dusk-like lighting effect. A pool table and comfortable chairs filled the space. *Obviously, the preshow waiting area.*

Just beyond that was the theater room guarded by heavy curtains, an old-fashioned popcorn stand and a decorative unlit marquee. The stale odor of butter and corn rode the cool air. *I guess the popcorn stand is more than decorative.*

To our left, a hall stretched away from the entertainment area. Since that was where the floor-plan discrepancies lay, we crept down the hall, our footsteps muffled by the thick carpet. Along the left side were little niches filled with a variety of artwork ranging from paintings to statues, illuminated by individual lights. The hall wall to the right was broken by a couple more niches and two widely spaced closed doors.

We hit the first door, Rabbit in front, me at his back, a hand at his shoulder. He brought his gun up, reached up, and twisted the knob. The door swung open on a rush of cool air and silence. I dropped my hand so Rabbit could slip inside and clear the room. It didn't take long before he was back. A quick shake of his head indicated that it was empty. So did the fact he pulled the door closed behind him. We repeated the approach on door number two with the same results.

With that side clear, we began working our way down the mini art gallery. Even though time was of the essence, we worked methodically, checking for anything that didn't belong or didn't fit. It made sense that if there was an entrance, it would be at this end of the hall. I cleared the first two niches as Rabbit worked the third and fourth. When nothing stood out, I wondered if we would need to move into the theater room itself. Maybe the entrance was hidden there.

Rabbit touched my arm, bringing my attention back. He tilted his head toward a beautiful marble statue of what I thought was supposed to be one of the three Fates. It sat in the fourth niche, taking up most of the space. In fact, it was almost too large for the space. The mismatched sizing made me wonder if it was a last-minute addition.

Next to me, Rabbit dropped into a crouch, tugging my hand so I would follow. Once down, he indicated the frayed edge of the carpet where it met the baseboard. The wear was just enough to make me reassess the niche. I rose and ran my hands over the cool marble, running my fingertips over the lines and dips of the surface, feeling for anything that didn't belong—a bump, a depression, something. Below me, along the wall, Rabbit did the same. He got a soft click before I did.

We shared a look and stepped back. A dark crack appeared, running down a cleverly concealed bend in the niche's wall. When nothing more happened, Rabbit pressed his palm against the wall and pushed gently. It gave, but instead of swinging open, it slid aside like a recessed pocket door.

I gave the architect props because that was a brilliant use of space. So was the little alcove that came into view as muted lights flickered on when the door opened. As the light chased the shadows back, it illuminated a narrow space, about four feet by six feet, defined by soft gray walls.

We peered inside, but there was nothing to indicate what this space was—no cameras, no doors, nothing but three walls and us. With nothing for it, I stepped inside, and with a hard look, Rabbit followed. The space was narrow enough that our shoulders brushed, but as soon as we were in, the sliding door retraced its path and closed us inside.

I tensed as the seconds ticked by and nothing happened except that we were now trapped inside a coffin-like room. Rabbit shifted, but in the tight confines, I couldn't see what he was doing. Whatever it was resulted in a shift and a soft hum of mechanics, then the floor was slowly dropping. I grabbed his free hand and squeezed. We brought our weapons up as our unexpected ride stopped. The space opened to reveal a narrow entryway blocked by a heavy door complete with a computerized lock.

I guess we found Zane's safe room.

Rabbit lifted his arm, holding it in front of me and keeping me in place. He studied the space. The electrifying energy seeped over my skin as he scanned for threats.

Finally, he dropped his arm and moved forward to the door. While he went to work on the lock, I stood between him and the hidden elevator just in case we ended up with unexpected company. There wasn't much down here but that door and us, but I still couldn't shake the damn itch crawling along my neck. It left me jumpy.

The minutes stretched as Rabbit worked, each one winding the tension higher. I could feel the same edginess in Rabbit's body as he worked the complex lock. Then there was a soft click.

He rose, bringing his weapon out and up in one hand while using the other to push the thick door open. As it swung inward, harsh light spilled out, along with a stomach-churning scent that did not bode well. Rabbit turned to me with a grim look. I tightened my grip on my gun, brought it up, and gave him a nod. He returned it then pushed the door wide and stepped inside.

Chapter Twenty-Three

RABBIT

I adjusted my grip on my gun and shoved the door of the safe room open. It swung back, and the overly bright light spilled out, leaving me blinking rapidly to clear my vision. Recycled air hit my nose, carrying the scent of blood, sweat, and pain. I'd never associated pain with a particular smell until I spent too damn long in places no one admitted to being in, doing things no one admitted to doing. The fact that it filled my nostrils with its stench now meant things were worse than we'd imagined. I was three steps in when I saw what waited inside.

Fuck.

In the middle of the room was a chair bolted to the floor. In the chair was the unmoving body of the woman we knew as Amalia Black.

Dammit, are we too late?

Thanks to the garish lights, I caught the rise and fall of her chest. Relief hit, but it was short-lived. In the bright room, it was easy to see the grim details of Amalia's situation. Her head hung forward, blood matting the sable hair, creating macabre streaks. Her arms were pulled behind her, her blouse ripped at one shoulder, revealing torn skin. There were other signs that she hadn't come willingly in the scraped, bruised skin of her legs under her torn skirt. Her ankles were locked to the chair legs, and her feet were bare.

The bright light was directly above her, giving her no escape from its harsh illumination. Against the side wall was a metal table like something in a hospital operating room. Various instruments were neatly laid along its top. The walls were sectioned, pieced precisely together, most likely to ensure that they were soundproofed. I could feel the shift of air against my skin and realized it was being filtered through the paneled seams. There were no windows and no other exits but the door we'd come through.

Jinx moved from behind me, reholstering her weapon as she went to Amalia. She pressed her fingers to Amalia's neck. Amalia didn't move, and the tension in Jinx's jaw eased just a bit. "I've got a pulse."

"Good." I moved farther inside, scanning the room, this time psychically.

As I was doing that, Jinx crouched down behind Amalia. I could hear the faint clicks as she worked on whatever held Amalia's hands behind her back. "This is going to take a minute or two." Jinx's voice carried in the heavy quiet.

When my psychic scan didn't return any electronic signatures, I shrugged off my apprehension and moved in to help Jinx. I was steps away when the flare of energy rushed through the room like a lightning storm. I pivoted as the heavy door swung shut as if shoved by an invisible hand. I darted to it and had my hand on the interior handle when the ominous sound of the lock engaging filled the heavy quiet.

"Shit!"

"Rabbit?" Jinx's voice was tight with worry.

I locked my teeth around the string of profanity that wanted to escape as I reached for the lock—physically and psychically—only to jerk back at the painful shock that ran through my hand and brain simultaneously. It was like being kicked in the chest and head by a three-ton horse. I doubled over, catching myself on my hands and knees before I could hit the floor.

"Rabbit!" Jinx called my name again as I fought back the mind-numbing pain.

When I felt her hand on my back, I turned my head, still blinking to get my vision to steady. "I'm good." Her worried frown didn't disappear, probably because my words were slurred. I swallowed and tried again. "I'm good, *cher.*"

This time, it worked. She bit her lip, wincing when she hit the raw cut. I pushed back until my butt rested on my heels and my hands were fisted against my thighs. After a couple more deep breaths, I could think and move again.

Jinx looked at the door then turned back to me. "What the hell just happened?"

"I think we tripped Zane's security."

"Dammit."

Yeah, that's putting it mildly. "How long to get Amalia free?" I braced a hand against the floor, preparing to get back on my feet.

She grabbed my arm and provided support as I stood up. "A minute, maybe two."

I gently pulled my arm out of her hold. "Go work on that. I'll work on this." I nudged her back to Amalia.

When she was working on the restraints, I turned my attention back to the door and whatever twisted security Zane had set. This time, instead of coming at it head-on, I let my ability slowly unfurl, allowing it to taste the energy working through the room. Like a snake flicking its tongue, I tested the undulating waves only I could sense. A couple of minor shocks later, I pinpointed which energy was directing the painful shocks.

It was like watching radio waves battling a magnetic pull. Every time my ability got close, the wave would morph to snap at it, sending electricity along my nerve endings. A few trial-and-error runs later, I realized I had to slip under it and over the other waves that indicated the more mundane security.

Witnessing the sophistication of this system that worked on both the psychic and physical planes made me wonder why Zane had needed us in the first place. I looked at the cycling energy, thinking that he might have no idea of the psychic implication—it could just be an unexpected by-product of the physical security system. Studying it, I realized there was another layer to this security, something I was missing.

"Done." Jinx's voice cut into my thoughts, and I turned to see her crouched in front of Amalia, her hands cupping the unconscious woman's face. "Amalia, open your eyes."

There was an unmistakable note of command in Jinx's voice. When nothing happened, she repeated the order. She waited then did it a third time, adding a light tap to Amalia's pale cheek. A frown formed on Amalia's forehead, and her eyelids fluttered.

As she fought to get her eyes open, I moved closer and crouched next to Jinx. "That's it, Amalia. Wake up, yeah?"

Awareness seeped back into her eyes, but there was pain in the white lines fanning from her eyes and mouth. Her mouth worked, her tongue coming out to her bruised lips. She winced and lifted a hand to a purpling bruise at her hairline, only to let out a soft pained hiss. "What happened?"

"Based on where you're at, I think it's safe to assume Zane decided to call your bluff." Jinx's tone was matter-of-fact.

Amalia studied Jinx then me before proving that her training was more than intact. "I don't know what you're talking about."

"Since we don't have time to waste," Jinx said, "let's cut through the bullshit." It was the only warning she gave before her features began to shift, the changes settling into place between one blink and the next until Amalia was staring into her twin's face.

As verification that Jinx was a friend, not a foe, it worked. Frustrated anger replaced Amalia's pale coloring as she leaned in toward Jinx. "Illusionist." It wasn't a question.

Jinx nodded.

Amalia continued on a low whip of sound. "What the hell happened that fucked two years of work?"

"A self-absorbed hacker," Jinx answered. "More explanations later. We need to head out before Zane gets back." She moved in, wrapped an arm around Amalia's waist, and helped her get to her feet.

Amalia winced and leaned heavily into Jinx but didn't give any other sign that she was hurting.

Jinx looked at me. "Can you get us out of here, or do we need to reach out to Wolf?"

I wasn't sure we could get to Wolf from where we were trapped. "Try to reach him. I'm going to need a few minutes."

"Let's get—" She cut off as a low hiss sounded. She craned her neck, searching for the newest threat. "What the hell?"

The hiss remained steady, but there was nothing else—no odor, no faint clouds, nothing to indicate what we were facing. I shifted my focus back to the security system, seeing the undulating energy spike. My pulse quickened. "Drop to the floor!"

The security system was flooding the room with an unknown gas. I was damn sure it wasn't something fun and amusing but agonizing and lethal. "Keep you heads down and breathe shallow. It's a gas of some sort."

Both women dropped as I began working with the elements only I could see. There was no time for caution or finesse. I worked brutally fast, going deep and hard with no thought but to get our asses out of this box of death. It was a dangerous move, but the alternative was worse. I dove into the swelling waves of fluctuating power, capturing the energy then manipulating it into a possible weapon. I could feel my sense of self stretching along the psychic fibers, reaching and infiltrating the various systems linked to create the convoluted security system. My awareness narrowed to the battle only I could witness. Without a physical body to use, I was left to rely on my mental strength. I tightened my psychic hold on the battling energy until there was nothing but the struggle to regain control of the power grid.

I managed to block a series of cloaked strikes, redirecting them to help take down those signals directing the flow of gas. Somewhere in the back of my mind, I could hear Jinx and Amalia coughing, and there was a faint pressure against my face. I didn't pay it much mind. I was too busy fending off the next attack while searching for the trigger that would release the door.

I took a couple of hard hits, feeling the energy scrape over my nerve endings, the pain sharp on my nonexistent skin, leaving me raw and aching. Gritting my teeth, I tunneled deeper, getting to the core of the security system. As I swept through, I began to pick up a particular pattern indicating that this system was being actively monitored.

Son of bitch. Zane is fucking watching us. Fury roared through me, and with one last brutal shove, I shattered the protective programming and found my target. Everything went quiet, options flashing through my mind with a strange clarity.

"Jinx?" I asked faintly.

"Right here." Her voice sounded hollow and was followed by another cough.

"Being watched." It was the only warning I could give before the program closed around me, sucking me down into a world of unforgiving energy. "Do cleanup."

Despite the blinding pain building around me, I gathered everything I could reach, forced it into a blunt instrument, and slammed it as hard as I could at the security system's heart. It impacted with a blinding detonation that sent me spiraling into nothing.

Chapter Twenty-Four

JINX

With breathing becoming more and more difficult, I almost missed Rabbit's warning and his strange request for cleanup. When it sank in, I realized I didn't have long to get my shit together. He was crouched by the door as Amalia and I lay prone, all of us staying low in search of breathable air. Knowing Rabbit, he'd take down whatever surveillance was aimed at us, which meant we needed to be invisible when he got the damn door unlocked. And he would get it unlocked. I refused to think otherwise.

Pulling off an illusion complex enough to get us out of this mess required more than just me. Fortunately, I might just have the help I needed. I turned to Amalia and opened my mouth. Before I could say anything, her expression changed. Her eyes widened in alarm, and her hand rose to signal behind me as she choked on another series of coughs.

I twisted back to Rabbit and barely got my hands under him as he dropped face-first to the floor, unconscious. His weight hit my hands, pinning them between his face and the floor, bruising my knuckles in the process.

It was awkward, but I managed to get my hands free. Then Amalia was there, helping me turn Rabbit over. She moved away, but I was staring at Rabbit's pale, blood-streaked face. Worry fought with my sense of urgency as I spotted the crimson streaks seeping from his nose, ears, and eyes.

Shit shit shit.

Seeing the disturbing evidence of how much energy Rabbit had expended added even more weight to my chest. I fought through my rising panic, knowing that the only way out of this mess was to keep my shit tight. If I failed, it wouldn't just be me paying the price.

"Jinx!"

It took a second to realize Amalia had called my name twice. I twisted to see her standing next to the door. She had her shirt pulled up, covering her nose and mouth, her hand on the knob. She twisted it. "It's open!" The words came out muffled.

I wrapped my hand around her ankle. "Stop!" Another cough cut me off, and when it passed, my voice was hoarse. "They're watching."

She let go of the door and crouched down next to me. "Plan?"

"Rabbit probably took out the cameras, so we don't have much time. We need to make Zane believe we're passed out in here." I got up on my knees and pulled Rabbit's arm over my shoulder as I started pulling us up.

Amalia got on Rabbit's other side and did the same with his other arm. "Can you do that?"

"Yeah," I huffed as we lugged Rabbit upright, both of us straining under his limp weight. "It'll take me a minute, though."

"Better hurry."

She was right. The headache from earlier was back, stronger than ever, but there would be time later to bitch and moan about it. *Hopefully.*

As we shuffled to the door, I began crafting the illusion I wanted Zane to see—Rabbit sprawled facedown by the door, unconscious, and Amalia and I in the positions where we'd initially dropped. My skull felt two sizes too small, but I shoved the discomfort aside, ignoring the warm drip from my nose and what it meant.

I tightened my hold on Rabbit as we stopped in front of the door. Amalia grabbed the door and looked at me, waiting for my signal. When I was sure the illusion was set, I gave her a tight nod.

She pulled it open, and fresh air hit us, making me light-headed. I kept my breaths shallow, not wanting to trigger a coughing fit, as we managed to drag Rabbit out into the small entryway. I locked my knees as Amalia let go of Rabbit to shut the door behind us. When she reclaimed her spot on his other side, I finally sucked in the clean air. Sure enough, the change in oxygen left me coughing.

I could hear Amalia doing the same as we shuffled toward the narrow elevator. It sucked, but we had no other option for getting out. *Here's hoping the system stays down until we reach the top.*

The narrow space was extremely tight with all three of us in it. I was all but plastered against Rabbit as I backed him up to the rear wall. The return ride seemed agonizingly slower than the descent. As the hidden elevator came to a soft stop, I felt Rabbit's breathing change and his body tense as he regained consciousness. I tilted my head back to see him blinking down at me.

"Hey."

"Hey." His voice was rough. His hands tightened on my

waist as his gaze shifted to take in where we were. "How long was I out?"

"Three minutes max."

Amalia's elbow landed in the small of my back. "Damn," she muttered. "How do we get this door open?"

"Hang on." Rabbit nudged me to the side. "Stay inside until I make sure the system is still offline."

I squeezed over as far as I could so he could maneuver around me. "Won't it reboot?"

"Yeah, but we should still have a minute or so to get clear." He didn't sound particularly convinced, but considering that things were going sideways quickly, I wasn't surprised. "Jinx, get a heads-up to Wolf."

"Copy."

On his other side, Amalia pushed back, and we tried to give Rabbit what little room we could so he could work the door. I didn't see what he did, but the door slid aside. He held his position, and taking our lead from him, we did the same until he gave the all clear.

As soon as we were out of the narrow space, I pulled my gun free and reached for Wolf. Silence answered. We made it to the base of the stairs, and Rabbit led us up, gun in hand.

He stopped at the landing and turned, his brow raised in silent question as he mouthed, "Wolf?"

I held up my free hand, signaling for him to wait, and reached out again. *Wolf, do you copy?*

A heartbeat passed, then Wolf's familiar mental voice replied, *Copy. Status?*

Inside stairs at the back of the kitchen. Retrieved package but picked up eyes. Rabbit blinded him, but it won't last.

Understood. We're heading your way. Rendezvous at entry point.

Copy.

I shared with Rabbit and didn't miss Amalia's fierce scowl. She'd barely waited until I finished before she hissed, "We bail, and that bastard will crawl back under his rock. I didn't give up two years of my life so that asshole can walk away."

As much as I understood her frustration, I wasn't keen on holding a meeting in the dimly lit stairwell, which made my response short and this side of bitchy. "Unless you've got some brilliant master plan, this is not the best place for a strategy discussion."

She shot me a dark look, but Rabbit gave a sharp warning hiss, cutting off further discussion. When we both zipped our lips, he turned back, lifted his gun, and inched the door open. Once he'd cleared it, we moved out and made our way through the kitchen, but when Rabbit went to head back toward the utility room, Amalia broke and headed in the opposite direction.

Stifling my urge to tackle her and drag her out by her hair, I changed direction and followed, as did Rabbit. I had no idea where Amalia was going, but she sure as hell did. We passed the English-style study I recognized from our initial meet with Zane, but she didn't slow. Instead, she headed for the curving stairs that led to the open hall of the second level. Through the upper railing, I could see an open space and a set of closed double doors to the right.

I took a position at the base of the stairs, my weapon trained on the upper level. Rabbit followed Amalia, weapon out, doing the same. She was halfway up when our luck broke.

A door opened upstairs, and voices drifted out. "Started the wipe."

"Good."

Above me, Amalia tripped, a quiet pip of sound escaping. Distracted, I was slow to react.

I heard a harsh "What the fuck?" and whipped my head around to see John and Zane staring at us.

Time stretched impossibly long, even though what happened next only took seconds. John shoved Zane hard, pushing him out of range, before he reached behind his back and brought out a gun and turned it toward Amalia. I brought my weapon up, sighting on both men even as Zane ducked back out of sight. Rabbit lunged for Amalia, who lurched forward, hands out, knees hitting the stairs, in a vain attempt to get out of target range.

John fired, and so did I, our shots sounding on top of each other. He jerked back as a pained cry came from Amalia. John turned toward me, gun still raised, and I pulled the trigger again. This time, he fell back and dropped.

I kept my gun up as I rushed the steps to where Rabbit was crouched over Amalia. From my new position, I could see the bottoms of John's shoes. He wasn't moving, but I didn't dare lower my weapon. Somewhere up there was Zane.

I could hear Rabbit muttering curses under his breath. That did not bode well. "Rabbit?"

"Amalia's been hit," he said grimly.

A rush of feet had me swinging my weapon around toward the base of the stairs. I jerked the barrel to the ceiling when Wolf and Ricochet appeared. They barely paused before Wolf's gun was out and up, his gaze scanning the upper level as he and Ricochet joined us.

"Status?" Ricochet bit out, taking over from Rabbit, his hands pressing tight against the stain spreading across Amalia's chest.

Rabbit shifted back, wiping his hands down his pants. "Entry is upper-right side."

"Through and through?" Rico demanded.

"No, it's still in there."

"Dammit, I need—" Ricochet looked around, his face grim.

"Hang on." Rabbit stood, and I stepped back, giving him room to move. He tore his shirt off, revealing a thin white T-shirt underneath. He folded his shirt into a makeshift compress and handed it to Ricochet, who took it with a muttered thanks. Rabbit watched Ricochet work. "I think she hit her head on the way down."

Ricochet craned his neck and looked down to where Wolf was still keeping vigil. "Wolf?"

Wolf caught my eye, and I went back to watching our surroundings so he could divide his attention. It wasn't long before he was shaking his head. "She's out cold."

"You need to get her out of here." With each passing moment, the urge to rush the stairs and chase Zane's ass down grew, leaving me antsy, but I knew better and held my position. "Get her out now. Shooter's down, second floor, eleven o'clock. But Zane ghosted."

Ricochet lifted his head, his gaze hitting Rabbit and me. His chin jerked. "Go. We'll get her help."

Rabbit and I didn't wait. Together, we rushed up the stairs, determined to get one positive thing out of this entire FUBAR situation.

Chapter Twenty-Five

Amalia's blood left my skin tacky against my gun's grip, but I had one goal—bringing Zane's ass in. Cold focus buried the residual pain from grappling with Zane's security and heightened my awareness as Jinx and I moved steadily toward the open door.

The body of Zane's right-hand man was sprawled across the hall. I kicked his weapon farther away from his outstretched fingers and stepped over him, pausing while Jinx checked his pulse.

"Dead," she said in soft confirmation and tapped my shoulder, indicating that we were clear to move forward.

Approaching the double doors, I slowed my steps and stayed close to the wall, weapon up, finger hovering over the trigger. There were no sounds and no shifting shadows to indicate movement inside, but there was no way I would risk getting my head blown off. So I dropped down and let Jinx cover high. Together, we moved in.

A glance confirmed we were in an office. Half-opened shutters covered the windows, the afternoon sun drifting over the thick area rugs and dusting the built-in shelves heavy with books and other items. A massive desk crouched to our left, the leather chair pushed back.

Jinx tapped my arm and pointed to a monitor that was angled on the far side of the desk. I inched out the psychic part of me I'd curled into a tight ball after it had been brutalized, and I did a sweep. As soon as it touched the computer, I was moving, my pulse racing. Proving one of the many, many reasons she was my perfect partner, Jinx barely blinked at my reaction and instead stayed on target, taking my six.

I rushed around the desk, shoving the leather chair back, and set my gun down. I yanked out the keyboard tucked underneath and let my fingers fly. When the screen came up, I bit off a curse. *Fuckin' Zane was trying to wipe the hard drive.*

Instinct kept me working on both the psychic level and at the keyboard. I raced the program, trying to slow down the programmed orders as I rewrote the code to reverse the objective. If Zane didn't want us getting the information on this machine, then we damn well needed the information.

My sense of time slipped as I worked the machine and the code. I hit a particularly vicious line of code and buckled down. I hit the final keystroke, and prayed as I stared at the cursor, waiting. One second, then two passed. As the third second ticked down, code began scrolling over the screen. Vicious satisfaction filled me as I muttered, "*Piké twa*, Seward, you bastard!"

"You done?"

I turned to Jinx as I dug into my pocket for the flash drive I'd put there before dashing off to Jinx's rescue. "Almost, sugar." I plugged the drive in, hit a command, and watched while the program loaded.

"What are you doing?" Jinx stood on the other side of the desk, watching me, her gun back to wherever she holstered it.

"I didn't get a chance to tell you, but I finished that program we were going to give Zane."

"The Rosetta program?"

"Callin' it Janus program now." Reading her raised brow, I explained, "Janus, Roman god of duality. I figured he'd be good to call on, considerin' this program's doing double duty for us."

Despite the tense situation, her lips twitched. "Right, so your Janus program?"

"It's our backup plan. It's going to burrow into Zane's system and spread its love far and wide. When it's done, we'll have an inside track into what he, and whoever he's hooked up with, are up to."

"Right." She shifted back and headed toward the wall of bookcases. "When you're done, come help me figure out how Zane disappeared."

I checked the screen and confirmed that my creation was well and truly off on its adventure. Then I reclaimed my drive and joined Jinx on the other side of the desk, starting my search of the shelves on the opposite end. "You thinking he has another one of his hidden rooms up here?"

"More like an escape route." She dumped another set of books onto the floor with a wince. She stared at the haphazard pile of books. "I hate doing that."

I dumped my own pile. "We don't have time to keep it neat."

"True." She went back to her search.

Together, we cleared the ends of the bookcases and met at the middle. She was running her hands along the shelf's interior when she turned to me, eyes bright. "Got it!"

She did something with her hands, and the edge of the case popped out a couple of inches. She stepped back, her hand going to her back and coming out with her gun as she moved around me to take her position.

I wrapped my fingers around the exposed edge of the shelf and waited for her nod. When it came, I pulled the camouflaged door open, exposing a hidden passageway. *Points to Jinx on that one.*

She held her position while I brought my weapon up and took lead. I moved into an enclosed hallway illuminated by evenly spaced lights set along the top. Smooth walls ran into concrete floor. The air wasn't stale, so the passageway likely led outside the house.

I strained my ears but didn't hear any indication that anyone was in here with us. I looked back at Jinx. "Ready?"

Her earlier amusement was gone, replaced by a familiar focus. "Let's do this."

In we went, moving quickly through the hall. As we headed deeper inside, the lights flicked off behind us, leaving us chasing pools of light. At first, it messed with my vision, but by the time we came up to the first bend, I was fine.

I stopped at the blind corner, my back to the wall as I carefully peered around it. Even though my mind screamed that caution was pointless since the motion-sensing light would give away our presence to anyone watching, I stuck to my training. More than once, it had saved my life.

My quick scan left me uneasy, but I wasn't sure why. Catching my frown, Jinx cocked her head in silent question. I shook mine, indicating my uncertainty. A muffled sound reached us, echoing dully.

Jinx got close and put her mouth to my ear. "What was that?"

I turned just enough to respond in kind. "Don't know. Hold tight." With that, I crept around the corner and started moving down the hall. Another muffled sound rolled out, this time followed by a distinctive scent and a wave of heat.

Heart pounding, I spun on my heel. "Shit, Jinx, run!"

I caught a glimpse of wide eyes as she followed my orders. I stayed on her ass, using one hand on her back to urge her faster. Behind us, the dull sound grew into a bowel-loosening roar. Heat and the nose-curling odor of scorched materials washed over us, sucking the air from our lungs.

Zane, the motherfucker, had lit the place on fire. Since his ability didn't follow natural law, the fire burned way faster and hotter than a natural one would. The leading wave of heat scoured our skin, sucking away any moisture. Somewhere farther behind us, another concussion of sound hit, this time not muffled. My mind spun, counting the seconds from that explosion to the resulting battering wave of heat and smoke. Both of them came way too fast for comfort.

I pulled the edge of my T-shirt over the lower half of my face as we kept racing the inferno behind us. Coughs racked Jinx, and I could feel her back shudder with each one, but she didn't slow. Instead, she reached back and grabbed my hand, her grip painfully tight. The heat was oppressive, and smoke began to fill the hall around us.

"Drop!" I followed my hoarse order with a tug on her hand, pulling her down. Past her, I saw the faint outline of the open door. With the end in sight, I dug deep, and we all but spilled into the office on our hands and knees.

Jinx was on all fours, head down, coughing. My chest hurt like a bitch, but I managed to get to my feet, stumble over to the bookcase door, and slam it shut. Pitiful deterrent though it was, we needed every minute we could get.

"Come on!" I reached for Jinx as she struggled to her feet, face pale, eyes dark and wide.

We were halfway across the office when the bookcase door blew open and an explosion rocked the floor under our feet. We fell into the upper-floor hall outside the office as a wicked lash of fire belched from the exposed passageway. The flames found fuel, devouring the fallen books and eating at the rugs and other furniture.

We didn't stick around but ran through the hall and rushed down the stairs. I didn't let go of Jinx's hand as we skipped steps with dangerous recklessness. We hit the bottom, and I turned toward our exit, only to pull up short.

"God dammit!"

Flames were creeping their way toward us, cutting off our escape route.

"This way!" Jinx tugged on my hand, dragging me back.

I stayed on her heels, my eyes watering at the abrasive haze. We hit a familiar dining room and Jinx's exit strategy.

She stopped, coughing hard as she drew her weapon and aimed it at the bay window. She fired. The sound of her shots was drowned out by another explosion somewhere at the back of the house. We both turned our heads as something heaving crashed outside the dining room. Flames roared, painting the interior in writhing shadows. We were running out of time.

I turned back and noted that the glass now sported five round holes with spiderweb cracks, but it was still intact. Jinx lunged for a tall vase on the table and dumped its contents to the floor before pitching it at the shot-up pane of glass.

Realizing what she was doing, I grabbed one of the

chairs and swung it like a baseball bat. It took two hits before the glass finally gave. Together, we cleared out enough to get free.

The deafening crackle of the fire taunted us as I boosted Jinx through the opening and dove after her. The broken glass bit at my skin, but that was better than being burned. We tumbled into the bushes surrounding the window.

Next to me, Jinx was cursing as she struggled free of the greenery and rose to her feet. I grabbed her hand, and then we were dashing across the lawn. I caught sight of an ambulance parked some distance from the house and two figures who looked like Ricochet and Wolf running toward us, waving their arms. Jinx stumbled, and I'd half turned to see why when the fire found the gas mains.

The explosion ripped through the house, and the resulting wave slammed into us, lifting us off our feet with a cruel fist and shoving us up and back. It tore Jinx from my grip, but there was no time to worry because it slammed me to the ground with a brutality that barely registered before my world went dark.

Chapter Twenty-Six

JINX

Two Days later

My body felt like I'd been worked over in a boxing ring. The glimpse I dared in the bathroom mirror was even worse. Small cuts dotted my face, a purpling bruise went from temple to chin, and my lips were swollen where my teeth had cut into the inside when my face hit the ground. And that was just my face.

I shuffled down the hospital corridor like an old woman, vainly trying to keep the lame paper gown from flashing everyone. Everything was stiff and sore, and it would only get worse because even I knew that two days out was not long enough for my body to voice its protest at being thrown across Zane's front yard.

Not that I remembered much of it. When I woke up in the ER next to an unconscious Rabbit, Wolf filled me in on the details. I didn't pay all that much attention to him, since I was freaking out about Rabbit. I watched the hospital team rush around him, hearing and feeling the urgent tension in their actions. Seeing him there, pale and unmoving, sent terrifying fissures through my heart.

Despite Wolf's reassurances that Rabbit would be okay, I couldn't stop my freak-out. Maybe it was because I'd been knocked on my ass one too many times, or maybe it was the aftermath of almost being cooked alive. Whatever the reason, I lost my shit, demanding that the staff stop fussing over me and fix Rabbit. It got so bad that they ended up tranquilizing me.

Any other time, I'd have been mortified by my actions, but not this time. Nope, the reason I was sneaking out of my room despite the eagle-eyed nurses was because when things had gone sideways in a blink and I was flying through the air and waving at death, one thing was crystal clear—if this was the end, I was damn glad I'd taken my one shining moment with Wyatt Tessier. My only regret was that I wished I had done it sooner.

Since I was still in the land of the living, I intended to make that wish come true. So no matter how scared I was of what the future held, the one thing I knew for sure was that I wanted to take that ride with Rabbit. I just needed him to wake the hell up so I could tell him he was right—smart was definitely overrated.

I made it to Rabbit's room, three doors down from mine, without being caught. Sweat ran down my spine, and I really, really wanted to lie down. Gritting my teeth, I shuffled inside, dragging my IV stand with me.

The lights were dim, but I could see the familiar form of Kayden Shaw, our team's unofficial leader, sprawled out in a chair. He watched me cross the floor and shook his head. "Weren't you supposed to stay in bed?"

I didn't waste time or energy responding but just shot him a grumpy look and finished my trek to Rabbit's bed.

Kayden sighed, dropped his feet, and leaned in to lower the railing so I could perch on the edge. I settled carefully and traced the back of Rabbit's hand, noting that his collection of scrapes and cuts was similar to mine. The window and bush had left their marks on both of us.

I slipped my fingers under his. "How is he?"

"He's fine, *cher*." Rabbit's voice was rough as his fingers curled around mine.

I swallowed hard against the wash of relief and emotions that pressed for release.

His eyes opened, softening when they focused on me. "How are you?"

"Better now." The words came out husky.

I felt Kayden put a hand on my shoulder. "I need to call Cyn. I'll be back in a few."

Rabbit's gaze flicked over my shoulder to Kayden. "No need to rush, man."

I didn't see Kayden's reaction since I was busy staring at Rabbit. His lips twitched, and a mischievous light hit his eyes. In an effort to regain some semblance of my normal control, I closed my eyes and tried to breathe away the last few days of worry. Maybe it was the painkillers they had me on, but that control kept slipping through my fingers.

A tug on my hand had me opening my eyes to find Rabbit watching me with an indescribably tender expression. "Come here, *mon ange*."

The damn tears were back, and I was losing my fight to keep them in check, so I let Rabbit tug me down. Together, we managed to carefully shift positions until I was curled at his side, staying clear of his bruised ribs, my head on his shoulder.

I dragged his scent into my lungs as the band around my chest loosened. Under the rhythmic strokes of Rabbit's hand, the anxiety and tension I'd carried since I woke in the ER slowly faded away. I turned my face into his chest, and the first tear escaped. The others rushed the breach. Held in Rabbit's arms, I gave up the struggle to hold them in check and let them run free.

Rabbit continued his careful petting, interspersing it with soft, reassuring murmurs, and when the storm passed, he tucked a finger under my chin and tilted my head back. His warm gaze drifted over my face as he brushed away the lingering traces of tears. "What was that?"

"Adrenaline crash?" I tried to tease, but it fell flat. Wincing, I closed my eyes and regrouped because there was no wimping out allowed. I sucked in a shaky breath, lifted my eyes, and carefully shifted position so I could cup his face. I brushed my thumb over a bruise peeking through the stubble along his jaw. "Things went sideways." I wasn't sure he'd catch my reference to our eye-opening conversation in Elena's condo. "But we both walked away."

Understanding flashed in his eyes, and a wary hope lit in their depths as his hand settled against my back.

Holding tight to my courage, I leaned in and confessed against his lips, "I'm glad you didn't back off, Mr. Tessier."

His lips curved under mine, his eyes dancing. "Are you, now?"

I nodded, never losing eye contract.

"*C'est bon, cher*, because I'm not letting you go."

Meeting his gaze, I let all the feelings that filled my heart show. I knew he understood when his face went soft then hungry. "That's a good thing since I'm well and truly caught."

Then I kissed the dream I never thought I'd have, my best friend and lover, knowing that whatever the future held, we'd do it together.

If you're not quite ready to leave the covert world of Jami's PSY-IV teams you can sign up for her newsletter at: **https://www.sub scribepage.com/jami-gray-psy** *to feed your need for more with these alternate scenes.*

Or, if you're willing to step into a future where the world's gone to hell and it's hard to tell the good guys from the bad, pick up Jami's **LYING IN RUINS**, *the first in her evocative and steamy post-apocalyptic romantic suspense series, Fate's Vultures.*
Now available at your favorite bookseller.

The world as we know it is long gone and in its place is the ravaged, post-apocalyptic landscape known as The Collapse. From the ashes rises a new breed of mercenary warriors called Fate's Vultures, four enigmatic protectors who hold to their code even as loyalties shift with the winds of this chaotic reality, testing their bonds to each other and their found families. Get ready for a wild ride because these evocative couples will stop at nothing to claim their future.

LYING IN RUINS

Charity & Ruin

On a shared mission of vengeance, what will destroy them first—their suspicions or their enemies?

BEG FOR MERCY

Havoc & Mercy

Will an assassin and a mercenary find their balance on the thin line of loyalty, or will it snap under the weight of their wary hearts?

CAUGHT IN THE AFTERMATH

Vex & Math

Caught between a looming conflict and the fallout of a brutal betrayal, will they survive vengeance's aftermath?

FEAR THE REAPER

Reaper & Lilith

Two adversaries must navigate a minefield of past betrayals and broken promises to defeat a common enemy before it all turns to hell.

About the Author

"This story is an emotional roller coaster, from betrayal, anger, fear, love…" —InD'tale Magazine

 Jami Gray is the coffee addicted, music junkie, Queen Nerd of her personal Geek Squad, Alpha Mom of the Fur Minxes, who writes to soothe the voices crammed in her head. Her series combine high-stakes urban fantasy and edgy paranormal romantic suspense into books you don't want to put down. Buckle up and get ready for a wild ride through the fascinating worlds of the Arcane, the Kyn, the PSY-IV Teams, and the Collapse.

Come visit Jami's website at **https://www.jamigray.com** and stay up to date on what kind of trouble she's getting into and when you can expect to join in.

amazon.com/author/jamigray

instagram.com/jamigrayauthor

facebook.com/JamiGrayWriter

threads.com/@jamigrayauthor

goodreads.com/JamiGray

bookbub.com/authors/jami-gray

www.ingramcontent.com/pod-product-compliance
Lightning Source LLC
Chambersburg PA
CBHW070830190726
48292CB00006B/2180